Deadliest Rhymes

Book 3 in the Deadly Rhymes Trilogy

Deadliest Rhymes

Some sacrifices are greater than others

Cory Blystone

Kwirk Publishing
Vancouver

A Kwirk Publishing Original

Published by
Kwirk Publishing
Vancouver, WA

Kwirk Publishing Print Edition ISBN: 978-0-9966948-9-6

Kwirk Publishing Kindle eBook Edition ISBN: 978-0-9966948-6-5
Kwirk Publishing EPUB eBook Edition ISBN: 978-0-9966948-8-9

Cover art by Cory Blystone

Published in the United States of America

First Printing December 2016

Why are you reading this? There is nothing of importance here! Nothing at all! Unless, of course, you want to be one of those people who literally read a book from cover to cover, then, I suppose, you are forgiven.

This is a book. Duh.

For all of my parents, Jess, Patti, Ruth, and Dan. Your sacrifices
have not gone unnoticed.

Deadliest Rhymes

Chapter 1
Aftershock

Banging on the door, crying for help, Sheree wondered if the rest of her life was also going to be filled with darkness.

Alone.

Trapped.

Scared.

"The itsy bitsy spider went up the water spout..."

Suddenly she wasn't alone any longer, but trapped and scared were still around, preying on her fragile emotional state and eating it like candy. Even though the chamber was pitch black, she swore she could see a faint glow coming from where the voice—the eerily familiar gravelly voice—sang.

"Down came the rain and washed the spider out..."

A teal silhouette pushed itself out of the shadows at a snail's pace, creeping closer and closer to Sheree. Her feet were stuck in concrete. Her body stiff as a corpse.

"Up rose your sister quietly from the grave…"

Closer.

Closer.

So close she could feel the coldness of the monster's breath on her face, freezing her eyes, nostrils, and lips until her lungs stopped.

"And soon my power will be restored again!"

Sheree Hollins woke up screaming as the image of a large spider slowly vanished from her mind's eye; sweat pouring down her matted golden hair, onto her cheeks, nose, and chin. Her younger brother, Brendon, dashed into her room with such force the doorknob dented the plaster wall as it struck, chipping away to reveal a bit of lath. His dogs followed, ever at his side.

"What? What happened? Another nightmare? I thought those would all be over now!" he said, failing to hold her due to their size difference. She was tall and sixteen—about to turn seventeen—and he was short and barely ten.

"Just tell me that Kayla really did not come back from the dead and that Sky is still alive!" she yelled, clutching a round purple pillow, fearful her evil twin sister was actually brought back to life, and one of her very good friends actually killed herself.

Fear is sometimes justified.

There was so much panic and pain and pleading in her wildly questioning eyes, begging to be lied to. Brendon bowed his head to avoid seeing it. "I can't. Sky really did commit suicide, and Kayla…"

"Is right here," Kayla said, walking into the room, sitting on her bed beside her.

Sheree started bawling. Then her bawling turned to anger as she thrashed her arms, punching the air, and shouted, "NO! No no no no no no no!" over and over again.

"Bren…" Kayla started, but was interrupted.

"No, I'm not leaving her right now," Brendon said, tears threatening their escape from the orb prisons holding them in.

Kayla smiled. "I don't want you to leave her, I want you to help me."

"Help you what?" Brendon asked.

"Help me let Sheree know that I'm not evil anymore," Kayla said. "I have a bad feeling I may have semi-permanently damaged her psyche after I hijacked it the last few months." She made it sound like an everyday occurrence, like car bombings in the Middle East or commercial airline attacks on skyscrapers in New York. Oh wait, that last one won't be for another year.

"Makes sense. Give me your hand," Brendon said to both of them, giving his fidgety dogs a look that made them lay down and barely look at him back with sad-yet-obedient ASPCA eyes that, had he bothered to turn his gaze in their direction, would have filled him with a pool of guilt.

"And here I thought I was going to have to teach you to be a witch." Kayla beamed with pride, trying to disguise the sadness underneath.

"You did. Then the rest just started coming naturally," Brendon said, squeezing both their hands until Sheree's hysterics subsided.

Sheree, Brendon thought and Sheree heard in her head. *I need you to focus on looking into Kayla's soul.*

How can you ask me that? Sheree thought back, especially after everything Kayla had put her through for the last eight months; murdering friends and loved ones; trying to kill her; taking over her mind and body; destroying any chance of becoming a cheerleader at Ravenwood High School. Seriously, that last one made the list of Top 10 Reasons for Hating Kayla.

Because you trust me, and you can trust Kayla now, but you won't until you see it for yourself.

I'm not ready.

You are.

But...

Focus.

As Sheree focused, her expression softened as she knew, really knew, that the monster that had been trying to destroy her was truly gone. That the person claiming to be her sister—her identical twin sister—really was back. Tears flooded her face as she pulled Kayla in for a hug.

Too bad it was all a lie.

The Monday after Easter was beyond hectic to deal with as Sheree managed to pull herself together once the anger and resentment and fear subsided thanks to magicky witchy poo shit. Still, how was the day going to go? Since Friday, the school had lost three of its own to suicide: two seniors and a sophomore. Sheree couldn't bring herself to say Sky's name out loud. Another senior was in jail on suspicion that those suicides were possible homicides, though word on the street was that it would be more of the involuntary manslaughter variety. Designer drugs made by entrepreneurial high school students may have been all the rage in the year 2000, but a little slip in the chemistry and *POOF!* there goes the clientele! Ah, life in the small town of Ravenwood, Washington.

Then Sheree spotted her best friend, Jennifer Hoang, looking about as depressed as she'd ever looked as she opened her locker after pulling her straight black hair behind her ears. Apprehension ran through her body like a golden shower when you least expect it and your mouth is open. "Shit," Sheree said quietly. *Jen doesn't know about Kayla being back. Shit shit shit shit shit! How am I going to tell her? Maybe I can get away without telling her? She doesn't even have to know, right? I mean, we could just keep Kayla hidden away and nobody would have to be in on the fact that a raging psychotic witch is on the loose, but wait! There's more! She's a real live girl now, too!*

"Sweet Fat Buddha, Sheree! You need to calm your mind before it explodes!" Jennifer said, inches from her face.

Sheree hadn't even noticed Jennifer walk up to her, too engrossed in her own thoughts until her breath assaulted her nostrils with essence of Colgate. "Kayla's back!" *Fuuuuuuuuck.*

Jennifer started visibly shaking, then whispered, "Your sister is back?"

"Sheree! Why you not tell me you gotta sistuh?" Courtney Jones, co-president of the Fashion Committee (Sheree the other half of that duo), cheerleader, over-achieving extracurricular activities bitch slash soon-to-be very close friend said, bobbing her Afro without any movement from her head and defying the laws of physics, gravity, and at least a dozen other scientific theories as she stood there in six-inch sandal-style stilettos gracing her well-manicured toes, hands on her extravagant hips, waiting for the answer to her query.

With a deer-in-headlights look on her face, Jennifer tried to backtrack her words in her brain, but her mouth was having none of it. Instead, she looked like a drunk stutterer someone pressed the mute button on.

"Okay, so, my family doesn't talk about this much, but I have a twin sister. Identical twin sister, actually. She's been, uh, away for a while? But now she's back. For good," Sheree said, hoping Jennifer caught on to the double entendre behind those last two words, and that Courtney wouldn't grill her too much more. A Monday morning migraine was slowly making its way into her mind behind her left eye.

"Don't be fuckin' with me, girl. You got a identical twinsie? Why'd you not say nothin' 'bout her? Why'd Brendie not say nothin' about no other sister? She like a family secret? Oh! She is, ain't she? Dirty little secret you ain't want nobody find out about, but now she back 'cuz she got kicked outta wherever she be and you gotta deal with it now? Oh! The suspense is killin' me, girlfriend! Why ain't you tellin' me?" Courtney said rapid-fire, not allowing the responses she was expecting, though in her mind, Sheree could have answered while she was asking the next question and still would have been able to keep up. That's so Courtney.

"Yeah, she got kicked out? Kind of. More like… they let her leave," Sheree said.

Jennifer was still silent. Scared and silent.

"It be juvie, huh?" Courtney asked, but then continued with, "Damn, girl lookin' like you in juvie? Shit, she be top notch! Big bitch! She'd work that joint. Mmm hmm." She head bobbed with her lips puckered out for that last utterance. Snaps could be heard, but not identified as to the beholder.

"Yes. Yes it was," Sheree lied.

"I knew it! Ha HA! Damn." Courtney looked so proud of herself that Sheree and Jennifer thought she'd break out into song any moment. Or dance. Or song *and* dance. She didn't. Instead, she yelled, "Boloski! Walker! You are not gonna belieeeve this shit!" and ran off towards her two real best friends who were dating each other, even though Courtney secretly wished she was dating one of them instead.

"Goddammit. Lies only beget more lies," Sheree said as she heard Courtney wildly tell Nikki Boloski and Chad Walker the news.

"So Kayla is really back? Like flesh and blood and real and alive?" Jennifer asked. Her shaking had stopped… on the outside at least.

Sheree scrunched up her face before letting it go. "Yes? Sorry I didn't call you yesterday when it happened, but…"

"She frickin' came back to life on Easter? Jesus!" Jennifer's eyes were wide, hands in front of her like they were waiting for presents.

"Not Jesus, just Kayla." Sheree nodded.

"No, I mean, the coincidences are crazy. We should go tell Sky…" then Jennifer stopped, realizing that would be pointless.

Sky Hawkins was probably busy getting embalmed. She wouldn't care.

Sheree pulled Jennifer in for a hug before they fell apart in tears. Again, grieving over the loss of a friend that secretly Jennifer blamed Sheree for not being a better friend to when things started going very, very wrong in her life, even though she also knew that Sheree was dealing with her own demons and had to focus on herself. But now one of those demons was flesh and blood and real and alive and breathing. Little did she know that four of those demons were not. Yet.

When the cry was over and the tardy bell threatened to ring at any second, Sheree told Jennifer, "She's not evil anymore if that helps."

"Let me guess, she told you that?" Jennifer asked with a you-are-so-gullible look that included a smug smile perpetuating her Asian superiority complex and a rolling of the eyes and some head nodding that showed off just how straight her jet-black hair was.

"Yes?" Sheree said. "And Brendon. He used his witch powers to help me understand."

"Brendon's a witch! Fat Buddha, where have I been?!" Jennifer screamed in-sync with the tardy bell announcing they were late for class.

"I guess the better question is where have I been?" Sheree said, shocked her best friend was learning about stuff that happened weeks ago, but so much had happened in the last few weeks that it made sense that she hadn't gotten around to telling her about Brendon's second coming out.

"I'm skipping school. Please for the love of shoes tell me you are, too?" Jennifer asked with the desperation of a menstruating woman in need of chocolate and red wine and sex.

"No. I can't. And you shouldn't either," Sheree said.

"Thanks for the lecture, bitch." Jennifer said.

"That wasn't a lecture."

"Shit, speaking of lectures…"

"Biology," Sheree said as Jennifer said, "History."

Silence.

"Well, why don't we just skip first period then?" Jennifer offered as a compromise.

"Agreed. I don't think I could face Chad interrogating me on Kayla just yet."

"So, what is the plan?"

"Plan?"

"I mean, what's the cover story going to be? It isn't the juvenile detention thing, because that's too hardcore and might get her a following and the last thing Kayla needs is her own gang of minions."

"I told Courtney. Half the school knows by now."

"Shit. You're right."

"Shit. I know. And now I have to tell Kayla that her cover story is blown. I bet she was hoping for some boarding school scandal or pregnancy scare to bring her back into our lives."

"Sky's dead?!" a horrified voice shrieked from the other end of the hall. It was Courtney. Chad and Nikki, expressions similar though not as exaggerated, followed behind her.

"Shit. I thought they would have known by now," Sheree said, about ready to cry again.

"What happened? How?" Courtney cried, letting herself fall apart like a regular human being and not the stone cold bitch she presented on the outside.

Nikki looked like she was carrying Chad, who was struggling just to stay upright and straight as he sobbed into her right shoulder. Jennifer almost felt sorry for him, but decided against such emotions since they broke up. She left him for not noticing her shoes at the Valentine's Dance. High school.

"Depression happened. She killed herself," Jennifer said, the only one not falling apart because she'd already done so a dozen times and now had to stay strong for her friends. The only problem was that she wasn't the strong one. She was weak and scared and angry and wanted answers she'd never get because the only one who could reply was dead.

"Nooo ohoh ohohhhh!" Courtney wailed, falling to the ground and banging the floor with her hands, chipping her perfectly polished fingernails on the mismatched vinyl tiles begging for another coat of wax.

"Why?" Chad cried, falling next to Courtney to hold her and let her hold him.

Sheree had no answers. She knew that she should have caught some of the clues that Sky wasn't right, but felt so helpless to do anything because Sky's mother was so protective and wouldn't even let them see her those last couple weeks. Except the day after Spring Break when she was allowed to come to school, just not actually long enough to even make it to first period before being pushed out like a baby in a stroller. Sky's last words still lingered like San Francisco fog: "This is why you should never be honest with your parents." Given that keeping secret from her parents the fact that her dead twin sister was trying to kill her since they moved into her eviler multi-great-grandmother's house was moot because said parents already knew about everything, which caused a whole whirlwind of sharing that turned into her being incredibly thankful that she felt she could tell her parents anything and vice versa, made her appreciate transparency even more. Well, mostly. She didn't always enjoy learning about their twisted, perverted sex life, but at the same time loved that they felt comfortable enough to tell their children about their mistakes and regrets and joys and triumphs. The sex stuff was raisins in your oatmeal cookies; you deal with it because it's there, but wouldn't miss it if it weren't.

She had little reason to suspect they were still hiding a fairly monumental secret.

"I still don't understand. Why would she kill herself? She had friends!" Chad cried, face blotchy and wet.

Boys most definitely do cry, don't let anyone tell you otherwise.

"Maybe she thought life wasn't worth living anymore," Jennifer offered stoically. "We'll never know."

"I blame drugs," Sheree said bluntly, remembering the conversation she had with her father the day after Sky's death where he told her without saying as much until she guessed it for herself. "Both prescription and whatever the hell Ami and Kori gave her."

"Crap! I didn't even make that connection!" Jennifer said excitedly. "And now Kori's dead and John is dead and Ami's in jail."

John was Ami and Kori's boyfriend. Yes, they all knew. It was a threesome. (Scandal.)

"What the hell happened this weekend and why'd I not know anyuh this?" Courtney cried, still on the floor, wiping away the tears pooled onto her lashes.

Looking around the hallway, Sheree had an uneasy feeling that their conversation wouldn't be private for long, as they were huddled openly while supposed to be in class being productive students learning important things. "We should find somewhere to talk about this without Creepy Charlie finding us."

Creepy Charlie went by many names. He was the high school's Rent-A-Cop-Security-Guard. He also had a rather nasty habit of making the girls in the school feel violated because he would blatantly stare at their boobs and butts, letting his eyes burn through their clothes like one puts out a lit cigarette. Unfortunately none of the kids ever felt like they had the power to say anything. Nobody should ever feel like that. Nobody.

Courtney stood up, picked Chad up off the floor, and said, "I know just the place."

They walked to the empty auditorium, sat on the stage, and talked. And cried. And hugged. And while bonding over the death of a mutual friend, they felt a connection that would last a lifetime, through breakups and hookups and good times and bad.

Unfortunately, there would be more bad.

Chapter 2
Kayla's Reintegration Back into Society

"Don't worry, I've got this," Kayla said Tuesday morning as she ate breakfast with the family.

"I don't think you understand just what high school is going to be like, Kayla," Mr. Hollins told her, putting his fork down. Today they were having pancakes. On a weekday. They never had pancakes on a weekday unless it was someone's birthday. "We had to fake transcripts and background checks, the works."

Brendon smiled. His handiwork. He snuck a halved pancake to each of his dogs who were begging under the table, much to the chagrin of Mrs. Hollins who detected the not-so-sly attempt to break the rules about giving in to Rex and Deschutes's requests for food while the humans were eating, even if their faces were irresistible.

"I'll be fine," Kayla assured, shoving another mouthful of syrupy flapjacks into her mouth and loving every minute of it.

Being dead, she'd forgotten just how much she enjoyed eating. Being alive, she was going to fight the battle between too much and just enough.

"Your father is serious. Maybe we should get you a private tutor or maybe you don't even need to go to school," Mrs. Hollins said with a nervous laugh as the last word struggled to escape. Her pancakes untouched, but her coffee cup on the third round of refills. Rex started licking her toes. Again. She lightly kicked. He stopped.

Sheree decided to intervene. "How do you think you are going to be able to keep up in class? I mean, you've never gone to school before and here you'll be in the ninth grade doing ninth grade educational studies with ninth graders."

"Listen, when I said I will be fine, it's because I know I will be fine!" Kayla said, her smile eerily plastered to her face like a ventriloquist dummy.

The smile unnerved Sheree to no end as she waited for it to become evil and kill them all, partly because she was terrified of ventriloquists and even more terrified of the dummies after they come to life. Thanks, R.L. Stine. But then her brain reminded her that Kayla wasn't evil anymore and that could never happen… again.

"Besides, I'm starting two grades under where I should because somebody"—her gaze was directed towards Sheree— "didn't want to be the dumb twin. Catching up won't be a problem," Kayla assured, almost sounding annoyed.

"We just want to make sure," Mr. Hollins said after taking a drink of black coffee.

Mrs. Hollins squeezed his arm. "I mean, you've only been alive again for a couple days. It wouldn't be a bad thing to take your time to readjust to, you know, living."

The way her mother spoke about her sister's sudden resurrection in a way another might talk about getting over a cold was oddly comforting. Her parents didn't question why their daughter was given a second chance at life; they only wanted to make sure she wasn't rushing getting back into it.

"You know, I think the thing we are all forgetting is that Kayla is a pretty powerful witch," Brendon said while he chewed, displaying various stages of pre-processed pancakes in his oral portal as he spoke. "I mean, if she can figure out how to cheat death, I'm pretty sure Math and English and remembering dates for History are going to be a piece of cake. Mmmm... like this pancake. This delicious, delicious pancake." He shoved another bite into his already-at-full-capacity mouth, syrup trailing from lip to plate like an artificially flavored umbilical cord before his tongue cut it.

"Thank you, Brendon! Finally, someone who gets me!" Kayla said, far more enthusiastically and chipper than a recently deceased person had a right to be. Or maybe they did.

Their parents nodded in agreement. Brendon congratulated himself. Kayla was happy with her victory. Rex and Deschutes barked out excited yaps. Sheree only had one thing to add.

"The Internet is a magical place in case you are clueless," Sheree told Kayla.

"The Internet will be my best friend. Of that I am certain," Kayla told Sheree.

They giggled, sounding like mirror laughs from mirror images.

The twins were back.

"Oh. My. Gawd," Kayla said as they walked into the main entrance of Ravenwood High School before her and Sheree went to the office to get her schedule.

"What? If this is too much, I will drive you back home." Sheree had her keys out, the sharpest firmly between her fore and middle fingers to stab an attacker in the jugular should the need arise, poised to walk back to the car.

"No. Gawd no. I just saw Courtney," Kayla told Sheree, still staring at the black girl with the giant Afro looking like a fashion queen chatting away with her high-gloss candy red lips framing her glistening white teeth.

"Oh shit. You still don't want to kill her, do you?" Sheree asked, remembering the incident just a couple months prior in a clothing store that almost killed the girl in question. She could still hear Courtney's words, "Denim wall came tumblin' down!" echo inside her head followed by hysterical laughter that, in her brain, caused the rest of the store to collapse.

"Worse. I think I want to… date her?" Kayla said as she deflated. "Fuuuuuck. I must be gay."

Sheree rolled her eyes. "Jesus, Kayla. Really?"

"What? You can't believe that I might be a lesbian?" Kayla asked, scrunching her face in a most unattractive way that made

Sheree cringe because she realized that must be what she looks like when she makes that face and was horrified at the thought other people saw her like that at some point in her nearly seventeen year existence on this planet.

"Oh, please, that isn't what shocks me. I just don't think you are her type. She's got a thing for Nikki." Sheree looked Kayla up and down. "You are, like, anti-Nikki."

Sheree's words stung with truth. Kayla was tall, thin, and strawberry blond. Nikki was short, fat, and brunette (and dating a tall, thin, blond boy who was more than likely gay, but that's besides the point... for now.)

Courtney spotted them and immediately left the kids she was talking to and started walking in their direction, leaving the former kids to wonder just what the hell happened. "Sheree! This must be yo' sistuuuuuhhh!" Her smile was incredibly full of life, like the rest of her.

"Kayla," Kayla said, putting out her hand for a shake.

"Courtney Jones, darlin'," Courtney told her, gently taking the hand.

They held the shake far longer than any usual encounter.

Something's wrong. Crap! Sheree thought, her mind making up a thousand different reasons this encounter might make the universe implode. "So, we were just about to..." Sheree started, but Courtney cut her off.

"Girl, I don't know how to 'splain this, but, damn! I gotta vibe 'bout you!" Courtney said.

"Good or bad? Because I've got a vibe about you too," Kayla told her.

Oh shit. Here it is. The cat is out of the bag and Courtney is going to go ballistic and Kayla is going to murder everyone I've ever cared about.

"Do you speak dyke?" Courtney asked bluntly, scrunching up her nose and making herself look kittenish.

"Do I!" Kayla said exuberantly, eyes so wide they almost popped out.

"I ain't never dated a girl before," Courtney admitted.

Their hands would not unlock, chained at the fingers.

"I've never dated *anyone* before," Kayla admitted.

"Cool. Wanna, you know, be with me?" Courtney asked, seductively raising her eyebrows in quick succession to accentuate the offer.

Sheree's worst nightmare was coming true. Courtney was picklocking her way into her family one way or another. If it wasn't trying to pawn off her ten-year-old brother Darryl who probably wasn't even gay onto Brendon who was also ten-years-old and very out and proud, this new opportunity was definitely her key. Only she didn't count on Kayla's response.

"Damn, really? Yes!" Kayla said, not letting go of her hand. She looked at Sheree and said, "See, Sheree? I'm already making friends and dating and I've only been here five minutes. Told you I'd be fine!"

And she was.

Let this day be remembered for all time: April 25th, 2000. The day everything changed.

By lunch, Courtney and Kayla were making out at the cool table, which Sheree and Jennifer were invited to sit at for the first time. It would be the last time they would have to search for a table to sit at, as they would always be welcome at the cool table. By cool, clarification might be in order. It had the word COOL etched into it with a razorblade sometime in the 1980s. Courtney claimed it first day at Ravenwood High. Nobody took anything away from Courtney. Nobody.

By the time school let out, Courtney was over at the Hollins house, still making out with Kayla, only now in front of Brendon and Mrs. Hollins and soon to be Mr. Hollins who would walk into the front door, see lesbians kissing, and immediately sweep Mrs. Hollins up to their room for mutual pleasure time. AKA sex. Then they'd come downstairs after their tryst and Mr. Hollins would be thrilled to have a lesbian daughter along with his gay son and Sheree would feel like she was left out of some exclusive club and resent them both for their homosexuality, even though her biggest turn on was watching two guys fuck.

The Internet is a magical place indeed.

By bedtime, Courtney would have to be dragged out of the house by Sheree, who took her to her home on Baker Street, only much further down than Jennifer, who also lived on Baker Street. Kayla tagged along in the backseat with her for more lovey-dovey time. Sheree thought she just might vomit, not because of the lesbian lip-locked lovers, but because it was her sister and frenemy. Arriving at her house, Courtney abruptly ended their embrace.

"My mom'd send me to Pray the Gay Away camp if she knew. Fuck that shit," Courtney said.

"That's sad. I must be one of the lucky ones," Kayla said, her voice still resonating with dreaminess.

"You sho' is, Lemon Meringue," Courtney said, using her trademark dessert pet name calling to those she loved that would eventually fade away into the ether as she aged out of such things, her mouth forming a genuine smile Sheree hadn't seen since their heart-to-heart a couple weeks ago when she came out and then helped half of Sheree's closet come out too, only to be donated to Goodwill.

"Until morning," Kayla said, her face so soft and glowing. Not the teal glowing thing she'd done before when she was evil, but just regular girl-in-love glowing.

"I can't wait that long, Lemon Meringue. You be in my dreams."

Kayla melted.

It was enough to make Sheree sick.

"See you tomorrow, Courtney," Sheree said as she pulled out of the driveway, leaving Kayla in the backseat by herself.

"Best first day of school ever!" Kayla said as she sunk into the seat, giggly like, uh, a teenage girl?

Sheree rolled her eyes, but something suddenly softened when she caught sight of Kayla in her rearview mirror. She looked so happy. Part of her was happy that her sister was happy. Part of her desperately wanted everything to work out. She smiled.

"Oh, gawd," Kayla cried out in pain, grabbing her stomach. "I think something I ate didn't agree with me."

"Well, you did eat, like, enough for three during dinner!" Sheree said, laughing after.

Kayla rubbed her stomach, feeling it kick and squirm. "You're right," she lied. "It must be that."

So much for honesty.

The next morning, Kayla walked into the school, smiling, bubbly, and acting so out of character from how she behaved back in the day she was an evil ghost witch, that it scared Sheree and Jennifer even more. Then the thought of having to witness the *Courtney and Kayla Show* again infringed upon their psyches and they fell into a puddle of disgust.

Mr. Riley, the janitor, walked by them and said, "Hello, ladies," then dropped dead.

Kayla just stared at the body in front of them. Old. Wrinkly. Worn like a used leather jacket. Sheree and Jennifer were looking at her, trying to figure out what just transpired. "I swear to God, I had nothing to do with that!" then grabbed her stomach in pain, as if something inside wanted out. It left as quickly as it came.

"Oh my gawd!" Mrs. O'Hurley cried when she saw Mr. Riley keeled over. "Call nine-one-one!"

She didn't appear to say this demand to anyone in particular, just declared it for anyone who would listen. Fortunately the front office attendance secretary—who rarely double-checked student attendance and would frequently offer cupcakes and candy to kids while they waited to be disciplined by the principal or assistant principal, effectively negating the fact that they were being punished—heard this request and immediately dialed.

Unfortunately, it was too late.

Mr. Riley was dead.

The sickening *CRACK!* of a rib while Mrs. O'Hurley performed CPR on him and failed to stir movement was more evidence of this fact. Still, she didn't give up until the EMTs arrived and took over. They declared him dead on the scene. His body was wheeled away. Mrs. O'Hurley sat on the floor, her normally kempt hair disheveled, tears streaming down her face, carving canyons into her alabaster cheeks flushed with patches of scarlet.

It was difficult for Sheree to see her favorite teacher distraught, but she also didn't know if it would be appropriate for her to try and hug her. Chad apparently didn't care about protocol. He swooped in, gave her a hug, and let her cry into his shoulder until she was finished. By then, the tardy bell had already rung.

Classes be damned.

The janitor was dead.

Long live the janitor.

Grief counselors had to be brought in as the death toll continued to rise. Regular counselors had to be fetched from neighboring school districts to lighten the load, on top of the two already employed at the small school of about seven hundred. Kids who never even knew Sky Hawkins were decrying her death as an outrage against the pressures of societal norms, the same kids who tormented her relentlessly until Sky proved that she was a force to be reckoned with when she became a cheerleader and sang a power ballad during the talent show. Sometimes people just don't realize how much someone affects their life until it is too late. Other times they milk the excused class absences for all they are worth.

There was less outcry over Kori and John's deaths than Sheree thought there would be, considering they were born-and-raised local celebrities, probably because they were only popular for their threeway relationship that included Ami who was currently sitting in a jail cell on charges of murder. They're grief might come after the trial when all the salacious and gruesome details come forth. Then again, they weren't very well liked, Kori and Ami. Everyone, however, loved John Upcock, who, considering his disposition towards openly dating two girls at the same time, was appropriately named. Hornball. Rest in peace. Forehead, heart, left shoulder, right.

While out of earshot of Kayla and Courtney, who were comforting each other with cuddles and sloppy tear-soaked kisses, Jennifer asked Sheree, "Are we sure she isn't still evil? That was pretty freaky."

"Yes. I think. Maybe?" Sheree responded before a rush of confidence came over her. "No, she couldn't have done it. She's good now. Mr. Riley's like ninety. Old people die."

"Really?" Jennifer said. "I guess you're right. It's just that Mr. Riley has been here since, I mean, since like when the school opened."

"Oh. No wonder his death is sparking such a commotion. He's a fixture," Sheree said nonchalantly as she stared out at the sea of despair.

"Mr. Riley is more than a fixture! He's a human being!" Jennifer yelled, tears starting to run down her ugly cry face.

"I'm sorry, Jen!" Sheree said, grabbing her friend to hug her, partially out of selfish reasons so she wouldn't have to see her ugly cry face, but mostly to comfort her best friend who was obviously in pain.

Creepy Charlie walked up to them and offered his shoulder to cry on. Sheree politely declined, somewhat aghast at his breath's stench of both fresh and stale cigarettes that lingered in her nostrils long after he closed his mouth. He stayed close by just in case. Until another attractive member of the student body looked like she might need a shoulder to cry on, and he walked over to her offering the same.

"That guy is a bag of dicks," Jennifer said, rolling her eyes as the tears subsided.

"That's offensive to bags of dicks everywhere." Sheree still held Jennifer, waiting for her to make the first move to let go.

So far, the days after Easter were turning out to be shitty. At least there were leftover chocolate candies to be devoured to take one's mind off the shittiness! Sheree had at least eight unopened bags in the trunk of her car, one of which would find itself trapped in the dark crevices behind a never-used emergency kit until years later when her parents finally felt they needed to part with the little blue sedan for closure.

After school let out, or more accurately, when the last bell rang since a majority of students and faculty were in no mood to learn or teach. Mr. Riley was apparently loved by everyone, except for Sheree who barely knew the guy but for the three times he said, "Hello, ladies." The last time was, well, his last. Sheree was thankful that Courtney insisted on cheerleading practice, making herself unavailable to be attached to Kayla's lips on their living room sofa. Kayla was tempted to stay for practice, but decided against it. Something about the evil part of her killing two cheerleaders a few months ago made her reluctant to be around them for the time being.

"Maybe this was a mistake," Kayla said while they drove home.

"Maybe, maybe not. People die," Sheree said, not really trying to cheer her up, but also not wanting to tear her down either.

Rick Astley's "Never Gonna Give You Up" played over the radio that was turned down so low they could barely hear it.

"Thanks," Kayla said, turning the volume up. "I love this song! It totally sounds like something from our childhood."

"It would have been, but you died right before it came out," Sheree said bluntly. "Sucks to be you."

Kayla chuckled, then clutched her stomach. "Sonofabitch! I seriously hope I didn't come back from the dead with Irritable Bowel Syndrome!"

"That'd suck. The family will mock you publicly if you did. You know that, right?" Sheree said, straight faced.

"Yes. Yes I do. Gerrrruhh! It's like that one really scary movie we watched when we were really little and that baby alien shot out of that one guy," Kayla said, holding her stomach with both hands as the vagueness of her words were clearly understood by Sheree.

The image of a spider bursting from her own stomach during one of Kayla's tormenting nightmares crashed into Sheree's head as she drove. *No wonder she chose that plot device. Of course, she mixed it with that one Looney Tunes that had the singing and dancing frog for comic relief.* Looking at Kayla, she recognized the look of actual pain. Something was wrong. Or maybe it was just gas. Holding in a fart for vanity's sake can do that, which Sheree was well aware of as she waited until the right time to expel.

Kayla went to her room as soon as they got home.

Sheree let Rex and Deschutes outside, allowing her fart to rip through the air before she closed the door on it. Then she grabbed a cold sugary coffee-based beverage from the fridge and plopped herself in front of the television in the den until Brendon and their mother came home and she announced, "Kayla killed the janitor."

Brendon was terrified.

Mrs. Hollins looked like she was going to choke.

Rex and Deschutes banged on the French doors outside the dining room.

Kayla stood at the top of the stairs and shouted down, "I had nothing to do with that, bitch!" She ran down the steps to explain the situation, *CREAKS!* and *SQUEAKS!* following her like flying monkeys as she descended.

"I was just joking! Gawd, Kayla!" Sheree said, still watching Oprah, turning the volume up due to the ruckus of voices and scratching of nails on glass threatening to overtake her program. Oh yes, she was definitely turning into her father.

"Mr. Riley… died?" Mrs. Hollins asked, hand on her heart as if she was trying to keep it in her chest.

"Yeah. Said hello then just collapsed," Sheree said, eyes held hostage to the television.

"Oh my gawd," Mrs. Hollins said, making her way to a chair in the living room. "Oh my gawd."

"I didn't do it!" Kayla cried, another pang creeping up on her like a clown in a haunted maze when you least expect it and makes you pee a little because you are terrified of clowns. True story.

Mrs. Hollins started to cry. "Mr. Riley was at the high school when I went there. I can't believe he's dead. I mean, he's so old, but still."

"Wait a minute, you went to Ravenwood High?" Sheree asked. Suddenly Oprah wasn't so important, even if it was an episode about people creating authentic power. She pressed the POWER button and Oprah disappeared into the blackness.

"Of course I did. I grew up here. You knew that, right?" Mrs. Hollins asked before adding. "I mean, we live in my great-great-grandmother's house for Christ's sake!" She spit on the floor, making the three kids perturbed.

"I know we live in Jessica's house," Sheree started to say, but Kayla cried out in pain again.

"Oh my fucking gawd! What the hell is happening to me?" Kayla asked the universe, the pain wrenching her stomach, worsening.

Mrs. Hollins rushed to Kayla's side and put her hand on her abdomen to feel what might be going on. She used to be a registered nurse before Kayla died and she got sloppy and something bad happened and she lost her license. She looked like she was going to pass out. "No. Th-th-that's not possible."

"What?" Brendon asked. What's not possible?" He put his hand on her stomach as well and then quickly retracted it towards his mouth. "How?"

Sheree just watched as her mother and brother looked horrified at what they felt. "Seriously, people, what the hell is going on?"

"Kayla is pregnant!" Brendon shouted as Mr. Hollins strolled through the door.

"She's… what?" Mr. Hollins asked, his lilac scrubs still showing evidence of blood that had at least one attempt of trying to be removed with hydrogen peroxide, or at the very least smeared like ketchup. Considering he was a medical examiner and only worked with dead bodies, this was somewhat disturbing.

I wonder if that's Mr. Riley's? Sheree wondered

"Seriously?" Kayla said as she realized her instincts were true, looking up. "I call bullshit, God."

Chapter 3
Funeral for a Friend

Seeing Sky's body without a wheelchair unnerved Sheree as she stared into the open casket and saw the porcelain doll face version of the friend she never got to say goodbye to before she left this Earth for what some say is a better place, but knowing that when her sister died at the innocent age of four she never went to a better place made her wonder if that was only for people who believed in something better on the other side. *Nonsense,* she told herself as she kept looking at the mask pretending to be Sky's face. There was no spunk. No sarcastic humor. No life. Just a body. Lump of flesh slowly decomposing. Right now she was nothing more than a waterbed filled with formaldehyde.

Sheree wanted so desperately to leave. This was not her friend. This was an imposter! But she didn't. Not even when Sky's mother gave her a hug and she wanted to punch her in the throat because deep down she felt like the actions she took probably drove

Sky to take her own life. Not even after two guys she knew without a doubt had called her a "Retard!" and a "Cripple!" to her face before pushing her out of the way so they could walk past her in a crowded school hallway cried as they entered the funeral home. Guilt? Remorse? No. More milking, straight from the cow's teats. Not even after the funeral started and all she could do was stare at her stylish-yet-affordable shoes and drip endless tears onto them as she hunched over. No, because Sky was her friend in life. Sky was there for her when she considered suicide herself because Evil Kayla was threatening to take over her body and she thought it was the only way to prevent that from happening. Sky was there for her when she needed more than just Jennifer could offer. It isn't true that one can never have too many friends, but it is true that a few really close friends can change your life for the better. Too bad some people don't know that.

Now all Sheree had left were memories and her own guilty feelings of not being there for Sky when she needed her most. True, Mrs. Hawkins cunt-blocked any effort to talk to Sky those last couple weeks, but Sheree was a smart girl. She could have figured out a way to either sneak in to talk to Sky or break Sky out of her prison slash bedroom that held her captive and slave to foreboding thoughts of despair and death. But what could she do about that now? How could she have known that Sky was serious when she said she wanted to seize to exist? Isn't that just how someone with depression talks? So many unanswered questions, and the bloated shell in a wooden box could no longer talk.

Brendon rubbed Sheree's back as she rained on her black pumps.

Jennifer decided to join her in the hunched-over-stare-at-your-shoes position.

No words.

Just a look.

Sheree could see that Jennifer was having the same conflicts in her head as she was. It was somewhat comforting knowing that someone else was going through the same pain as her. Their hands found each other. Sharing in pain somehow makes it tolerable. Not like sharing chocolate. That's intolerable.

Then it was over.

There would be no wake. There would be no invitation to the graveside service and subsequent burial. There would be no more anything where Sky was involved, except for her cheer she did during her audition that won her a spot on the team and made Sheree just a tad bit jealous because it knocked her out of the running. Courtney would insist it remained a regular part of their routines during games and practices for years to come. That cheer became part of Ravenwood lore; the thing of legends, almost on par with the wrath of Song's End, the son of an Oaxaciian chief named Ravenwood, who was credited with killing every last person in the tribe, save his father whom he spared for reasons unknown except for some white guy to name the town after. It wasn't even that good. Just a cheer. Probably a knock-off of another school's cheer like a majority of the ones used in high schools in every city across America back in the days before the movie *Bring It On* put the competitive cheerleading organizations in the spotlight, forever changing the sport. Okay, that may be a little generous. Then again, that movie is amazeballs. Seriously, yo.

At home, Jennifer and Sheree were staring out Sheree's bedroom bay window towards the cemetery, waiting for the cars to roll away. One way or another, they were going to have a graveside service for Sky. A torrential downpour pounded on the windows, blocking most of the view.

"I'm glad it's raining on them. Assholes," Jennifer said.

"Me, too," Sheree said, grabbing Jennifer's hand and squeezing it.

"I prayed for rain," Kayla said quietly at the doorway, causing Sheree and Jennifer to jump a little in the bench seat.

"You shouldn't sneak up on people, Kayla!" Sheree said loudly.

Her face was solemn. "Sorry. Habit."

The look made Sheree feel sorry for her. "Come here. Or not, since, you know, dead people out my window."

Kayla snorted out a chuckle, holding her stomach with one hand. "Yeah, maybe I'll just sit on your bed," she said before doing just that.

"How is…" Sheree started, then looked at Jennifer who she realized wasn't keen on the whole virgin pregnancy thing, and finished with, "stuff?"

"Cryptic much?" Jennifer asked, giving Sheree a perplexed look.

"Fine now," Kayla said.

Silence.

"Okay, uh, are you two having a Psychic Friends Network conversation?" Jennifer asked, remembering the days when Sheree and her would have those. Of course, those were also linked to Evil Kayla, so she was glad when the connection was severed. Forever.

"No," Sheree said.

"It's okay if she knows," Kayla said, staring down at the floor towards the air vent and getting a chill down her spine.

"Are you sure?" Sheree asked.

"Yeah. I mean, she's gonna find out sooner or later," Kayla said.

"What am I going to find out?!" Jennifer shouted, standing up.

"That I'm pregnant," Kayla told her, looking at her stomach that a hand was cradling as if this would bring further understanding.

"WHAT?!" Jennifer's lower jaw was stuck out so far, it reminded Sheree of both the family dogs and their massive under bites.

Kayla looked at Jennifer. "I don't know how, but I am. Well, that's not exactly true…"

"What do you mean?" Sheree asked. *How could she…?*

"Well, I knew that at some point in my life I'd have to carry a baby as part of my agreement with The Powers That Be," Kayla revealed. "I just thought it would be, I don't know, later?"

"Well that's a shitty bargain!" Sheree said loudly, hoping the noise wouldn't draw too much attention, but then she remembered it was just the three of them in the house. Brendon was off playing with Darryl and a neighbor kid named Kwirk at his house, and their parents were grocery shopping.

Kayla looked uncomfortable, not just preggers uncomfortable, but like she was hiding something that desperately wanted out. "I told you Easter Sunday that one day you and Jeff would be reunited."

Sheree just stared.

Kayla did say that.

She thought it might have been a threat.

Now she prayed it wasn't true.

Jennifer was still confused.

"Please don't tell me he's…" Sheree said, unable to finish.

"Yes," Kayla said, holding back tears.

Sheree put her hands to her mouth. She'd wanted her boyfriend that Kayla killed months ago back, but at what cost?

"Huh?" Jennifer asked.

"I'm pregnant. The baby is Jeff Mains. Only there is something wrong," Kayla said.

That last part was not expected.

"What do you mean something's wrong?" Sheree asked quietly, lowering her hands to her lap.

"I mean, there is something not right happening in here," Kayla motioned in a circle over her midsection. "I sense evil. Very powerful evil." Her eyes were wide and she was visibly shaking. She looked scared.

"You don't think…?" Sheree started to ask. "No, that couldn't happen. Could it?"

"Oh my Buddha, people! I'm the smartest one in the room and can't figure out what you are all freaking out about!" Jennifer yelled.

"I think I'm carrying twins," Kayla said.

"You don't think, you know, that you also have Evil Kayla in your, uh, uterus, do you?" Sheree asked, terrified at what the response might be to her query and fighting the image of Fetal Evil Kayla duking it out with Fetal Jeff Mains in a Battle for Womb Supremacy. Winner takes all.

"What? No! That's not possible. I'm a whole person, both evil and good and everything in between. No. That can't be it," Kayla assured. "Can it?"

Nobody had any answers.

Kayla looked at the vent again, sensing danger.

"The itsy bitsy spider went up the water spout…"

"What the fuck?!" Sheree and Kayla screamed in unison as Jennifer listened in terror.

"Down came Jeff's rain and washed the spider out…"

They listened, stunned, not knowing who or what was singing since Kayla was alive and well and flesh and blood and no longer an evil ghost witch hell-bent on tormenting her family. The voice was obviously different but somehow familiar.

Creepy.

Gravelly.

Childlike and elderly at the same time.

"Up rose Kayla with child on Easter Day,

"And the itsy bitsy spider will soon be out to play!"

A rush of cold air pushed its way out of the old iron air vent, filling the room with a sense of doom.

"How is this…?" Sheree said.

"I don't know!" Kayla said.

"I am seriously freaked the fuck out!" Jennifer said, her normally slanted eyes round in horror.

The front door opened and slammed shut, followed by loud footsteps running up the stairs on approach. "I got here as soon as I could!" Brendon said, his pudgy body out of breath from the jaunt. "What… was… that?"

Kayla looked at Brendon curiously. "You heard that?"

"In my head, but I knew it was happening," Brendon told her, taking another deep breath. "Don't ask. Probably witch-technology I'm still unfamiliar with."

"Sometimes I have serious regrets about you being my best friend, Sheree," Jennifer announced, hands balled into fists.

Sheree smiled at her hot little Asian mess. "I don't. I wouldn't be here without you."

"Well, that's true. You do owe me your life. I mean, I've saved it at least twice now, but who's counting?" Jennifer smiled back. "Still, I need answers to the singing crazy. That was you when Sheree claimed she heard singing from her air vent last year, right?" she asked Kayla, eyes full of desperation.

The way Jennifer said 'claimed' stung Sheree.

"Yes. But whoever is doing that now is not. I'm certain. I mean, I'm pretty sure I could dabble in the art of ventriloquism, but I promise it wasn't me," Kayla said, thoughts of being onstage with a dummy dancing around her brain, though the dummy was modeled after Brendon and she hoped for the love of all things holy he couldn't see this image she couldn't shake.

"I believe you," Sheree said, still recovering from Jennifer's unintended jibe and pretending not to hear Kayla's ventriloquist remarks.

"Me, too," Brendon said. "Whoever that was is much more powerful than you, Kayla."

"More powerful? Is that even possible?" Kayla asked with a cocked eyebrow, her voice full of arrogance.

"A. Lot. More. Powerful." Brendon was serious.

Sheree shrugged, laughed, made everyone uncomfortable, then said, "Maybe the house really is haunted! Yay!"

Kayla didn't like this theory. "That doesn't explain me."

"Maybe it does," Sheree said, nodding her head up and down.

"How?" Kayla asked.

"Think about it," Sheree said. "You never once tried to extoll your evil powers when we lived in West Seattle, and you actually lived there."

"And died there," Kayla added.

Jennifer pointed, nodding her head affirmatively.

"Precisely. Well, not precisely but in the street in front, but whatever. Details. But right after moving into this house, which just so happens to be in a town known for paranormal supernatural activity, on a street that was paved over a Native American mass burial site, that also, side note! said Native Americans all died of paranormal supernatural activity according to the legend told by practically every nation up and down the Pacific Coast according to you,"—she looked right at Jennifer who nodded in agreement before turning her attention back to Kayla—"you started your damned creepy lullaby singing that manifested into a sequence of deaths culminating in the four assholes you killed when we went back to West Seattle to pay the fuckers who gang-raped me a visit," Sheree said, suddenly regretting that she added the last part.

"You were raped?" Jennifer asked, her voice small and sad.

"Yes. And the bastards who did it got what they deserved," Sheree said confidently, deciding to own up to her actions, as well as those performed by others that she condoned.

Kayla looked broken.

Brendon looked torn.

"So when you were telling me about your friend…"

"I was telling you about me."

"Oh my gawd, Sheree!" Jennifer said, rushing over to hug her.

"I should have told you the truth, but I was too chickenshit," Sheree said, holding tightly, her long black hair tickling her nose and smelling faintly of lavender and tea tree oil.

"Okay, so let's get back to me and how this is all my fault," Kayla said bluntly.

Sheree let go of Jennifer and looked at Kayla. "I never said it was your fault!"

"But it is." Kayla looked certain.

Brendon asked, "Why do you say that?"

"I think I brought back whatever evil had been cast out before you moved in. I must have. No, I did." Kayla's body language was confident, but the look in her eyes spelled D-O-U-B-T.

"Don't say that. You know it's not true," Brendon said.

"Do I?" Kayla asked, a lone tear escaping.

"You're not as mighty as you think you are," Brendon told her, immediately regretting his choice of words.

"Damn, Brendon!" Kayla looked hurt, but also somewhat proud at how brave her little brother was turning out to be, even if she did at one point or another during her tenure as an evil ghost witch call him a fat faggot boy.

Sheree and Jennifer decided it was time to sit down and let the witches try and figure it all out. After all, they had no answers.

"Seriously! Hear me out," Brendon said. "I mean, I know you can sense that power. That you can feel it down to the bone that it is beyond anything you could possibly acquire in your lifetime."

"It is strong, but I wouldn't say it'd be impossible to acquire in a lifetime. You are also pretty talented for only displaying your gifts for a couple months now."

"I've got one-hundred-and-ninety-two people trapped in my head," Brendon said, referring to his insistence that he had multiple personalities and that the host body of Brendon was only allowed to pretend to be in control most of the time because one-hundred-and-ninety of those voices voted that there should be some sort of order in his brain so Juan Benito—the self-proclaimed Ruler of the Universe—wasn't allowed to execute his dictatorship over everyone and everything. Very complicated. Just go with it. "I'm pretty sure that gives me a boost in all things Wiccan."

"True," Kayla concurred as if she agreed that both he had one-hundred-and-ninety-two personalities and that having that many personalities would greatly increase Wiccan abilities. "But, while I was wandering the afterlife during my time in Purgatory," she said in a sing-song voice, "I discovered that this house sits upon

Chief Ravenwood's entire family. Well, the ones that weren't taken and never found, anyway."

Sheree and Jennifer looked puzzled as to the relevance.

Brendon looked frightened. "You don't think that Song's End could be behind this latest batch of crap, do you?"

"The thought has crossed my mind in the last few minutes," Kayla said.

"Well, isn't that just the frickin' cherry on top of the shit sundae!" Sheree said loudly. She laughed. "I mean, the irony of Song's End singing!"

"Yeah, irony. Like the rain stopping just as soon as the assholes are leaving the cemetery," Jennifer said, looking out the window as the cars drove off towards Main Street and whatever their next destination was. Probably a bar.

Secretly, Sheree wished they all would choke on the pills Sky took as she watched the last of the taillights disappear, imagining them celebrating the life insurance policy payment. "Awesome," she said. "Let's go say a proper goodbye to Sky."

"Sounds good to me," Brendon said. "But I need to grab my jacket." He opened his bedroom door and was immediately pounced by Rex and Deschutes, their Boxer-Boston Terrier-Pit Bull bodies jumping up and down so their ever-smiling faces could lick him to death. "Seriously, guys! Stop!"

"Ugh, it's a goddamned penisfest over there," Sheree said, thinking out loud.

"You really just said that, didn't you?" Jennifer asked, trying to contain her body's urge to laugh.

"Oh, apparently," Sheree said, her face flushing fuchsia.

Kayla's uncomfortableness could not be ignored. "If you don't mind, I'm going to stay here. I, well, I don't think my presence would be welcome. I feel responsible for the whole thing."

Sheree understood. After all, it was Evil Kayla who caused the car accident that killed Jeff and Sky's boyfriend Chad (not to be confused with Jennifer's ex-boyfriend Chad) and put Sky in a wheelchair that led to her depression that eventually was the death of her. Even if Kayla was whole again, part of her was indeed responsible, and who was Sheree to take away her decision to take ownership of that?

Chapter 4
The Twins

"You can't tell Courtney that I'm pregnant," Kayla pleaded before they left for school Monday morning.

"Of course not," Sheree assured, leading the way to her little blue sedan while the morning drizzled on them, dampening more than just their moods that it was, well, Monday morning.

"I'm hiding this pregnancy as long as I can," Kayla said, staring at her stomach as she waited for Sheree to unlock the passenger side door with about as much patience as a hyena after spotting a half-eaten gazelle leftover after the lions got bored with it and moved on. "I'm serious, Sheree. I really like her and don't want her getting the wrong impression about me."

"Yeah? So how long, because we kind of told her that you got kicked out of juvie, but were debating between that or a pregnancy scandal. Perhaps we should have gone with the latter given the circumstances." Sheree didn't bother looking in Kayla's direction, but could guess her reaction was not that of amusement.

"I hate you," Kayla said coldly.

"Hey, apparently Courtney doesn't care about that. Maybe telling her wouldn't be such a bad thing," Sheree said, doing a U-turn to head towards Main Street, nearly hitting a car parked in front of the neighbor's house across the street. *Jesus, Sheree!*

As if pondering this alternative, Kayla told her, "Maybe in a while. It can probably wait until I begin to show." She looked down at her abdomen again and sighed.

Sheree looked over to Kayla's belly as well. "So how long do you think that will last?" She could already notice a measurable baby bump. Small, yes, but decidedly noticeable. "I mean, sooner or later she will know that something other than post-resurrection weight gain is going on!"

Kayla rubbed her stomach gently before looking to Sheree's ever-so-slight midsection pudge for comparison. "Yeah, I have a feeling these bastards aren't going to be full term."

Sheree debated over whether to add salt to the fresh wounds, but only for a brief moment. "You know, Courtney is pretty cool." *Oh my gawd! What the hell, Sheree!*

"She's not going to know anything about my past. I am going to hold onto that forever." Kayla glowered out the passenger side window to avoid letting Sheree see her eyes welling up. "Or at least until I am ready to tell her everything."

"You really think that you should?" Sheree asked. "I mean, you did kind of kill a couple of her good friends, or at least people she tolerated socially in their roles as top-tier Wolf Wall Pyramid Cheerleaders."

"Oh my gawd, Sheree! You're right! Jesus," Kayla said, rolling her eyes and slapping her forehead to accentuate the sarcasm in her voice, the tears receding behind their orbital dam.

Sheree laughed.

Kayla laughed.

The laughter stopped as they turned down Main Street.

"I still hate you for putting spiders in my mouth that night," Sheree told Kayla, specifying that that was more terrifying than seeing broken cheerleaders splattered across the gym floor after popping like water balloons.

"You are never going to let me live that down, are you?" Kayla asked.

"Never," Sheree said.

"Thanks," Kayla said, both hurt and glad at the same time.

The remaining forty-two seconds of the car trip was silent as Sheree pulled into the student parking lot, finding a spot in the same general area she normally parked so she wouldn't have to think about where to find her car after a brain-draining school day. There is something to be said about silence. It allows time to process. Sometimes it allows time to heal.

Sometimes.

Entering the main doors to Ravenwood High, Kayla spotted Courtney and vice versa. They ran towards each other like old Hollywood stars in a poorly made studio-machine movie, collapsing into one another's arms and embracing.

"Can you believe she's pregnant?" Jennifer said, sneaking up on them.

"With twins?" Sheree said, adding gas to the fire with the intent that it would fuel a war then regretting said war because the war would be with a very powerful witch and she had no defenses and it would basically be like the Russian army against Liechtenstein.

"Fuck you both," Kayla said, pulling away from Courtney and starting to cry actual teenage girl tears.

Courtney pulled her head back into her hair, almost making it disappear. "Whatchew talkin' 'bout? Girl, you be pregnant with twinsies?"

"It's true," Kayla said, head staring at her shoes, or would be if her eyes weren't closed and leaking.

"I thought you said you ain't never dated nobody?" Courtney asked, posturing like a fashion model mid runway, bitch-face firmly planted.

"I haven't," Kayla said quietly.

"It's true. She hasn't," Sheree confirmed, but the damage was already done.

"Then, well, then how you 'splain the baby thing goin' on in there?" Courtney asked, twirling her finger wildly in front of Kayla's stomach accusingly.

"I can't. I mean, there may have been partial consent, but I was not aware the act had happened," Kayla said, dancing around the truth because the truth was more than she wanted to tell her or anyone or even admit to herself that she'd actually agreed to it.

"Gurrrrrl! You were raped!" Courtney shouted so loud her voice echoed off the halls, bouncing into every ear within a three-mile vicinity.

Nobody seemed to care.

Yell "Candy!" and everyone's ears perk up with curiosity, but yell "Rape!" or "Fire!" or "Crazy kid with semi-automatic rifles again!" and the halls are filled with indignant ignorance. High school.

"Thanks for letting everyone know that," Kayla said, crossing her arms, her eyes taking on a familiar fiery red.

Brace yourself! Sheree thought, wincing.

"That is bull *shit*, Lemon Meringue! We gettin' you an abortion. Ain't no way you need to be makin' no rape babies," Courtney told her, grabbing Kayla's hand out of her chest and copping a feel at the same time by accident, though she wasn't sorry she did, but did feel bad about it considering the conversation.

"No abortion. I'm carrying them. It's not their fault," Kayla said, taking on a pro-life stance that, perhaps after all the lives she had taken, was probably more about guilt than anything else. After all, being raped by God isn't such a bad thing. I mean, look at Mary and her rape-baby, Jesus, and how that turned out? On second thought...

"Well you ain't gonna go through this alone," Courtney told her, hugging her from the side.

"We are all here for you," Jennifer said, somehow pulling off a smile that didn't even look forced.

It was Sheree's turn. She hesitated, not knowing if saying she would be there for her sister would mean she condoned all the actions she took before coming back from the dead, but at the same time knew that was all in the past and now that Kayla was whole again and promised no more evil would come from her, where was the harm in showing support? The full gamut of emotions ran through her, flashing and sparking her brain with anger, compassion, hate, love, and the worst bastard of all: guilt.

Guilt.

Guilt.

Guilt.

Guilt.

Guilt stacked for miles and miles.

"Of course we will be here for you, Kayla," Sheree told her sister, lips curling into a slightly open smile.

Kayla burst into tears. "Thank you!"

They group-hugged her.

Chad and Nikki walked in as the hug was dissipating.

"What'd we miss?" Chad asked, holding Nikki's hand limply as if it was merely out of habit. Two-and-a-half months in and it was already old as the term "the aughts" was for the decade that had just begun. Wait until their relationship hits two-and-a-half years.

"Kayla. Rape. Pregnant. Twins," Courtney recounted the last five minute's events in a way that would make Ernest Hemingway proud because it was practically a full story told in four words without all that unnecessary extra verbiage clogging it all up like a toilet after a pasty poop that required an excessive amount of toilet paper. Don't lie. You know what I'm talking about.

"Oh my gawd, is there anything I can do?" Chad asked, letting go of Nikki's hand as if it offended him and walking closer to Kayla, making Nikki have angry eyes.

Kayla smiled. "Thanks, but I will be fine. I've got a pretty amazing family," she said, reaching out to squeeze Chad's hand and immediately retracting it as she accidentally discovered something about him that she'd have to keep secret, or more accurately, a few things.

"If you change your mind, let me know. We're practically neighbors!" Chad said, flashing his perfectly white toothy grin that looked shockingly like her own and made all the girls swoon. Well, most of them. A few boys, too.

Once Chad's hand was reconnected with Nikki's, her anger subsided. Chad, however, was beginning to lose feeling from her ever-tightening grip, but didn't dare let her in on that. The feisty Russian was prone to pummeling when she sensed weakness.

The bell rang.

"We should get to class," Sheree said, for once thankful that classes were about to start and take her away from the awkward situation she was partly to blame for.

"Lunch, bitches!" Courtney announced, kissing Kayla before walking away.

Jennifer and Nikki went in one direction. Sheree and Chad followed Courtney in another. Kayla stood by herself for a second, cried out in pain, let it subside, then walked to class alone.

Sheree and Kayla sat on the couch eating Tillamook Mudslide ice cream directly from the carton while watching Oprah when the door sprung open and a chorus of fourth graders piled inside. The twins in Kayla's uterus danced around violently as Brendon and his twin friends Kwirk and Wayne Werewolf made their way into the kitchen for after school snacks consisting mostly of multiple bowls of overly processed sugar-fueled cereal and highly-caffeinated soda pop for the twins and Sprite for Brendon, being followed around by the canine twins, Rex and Deschutes, as they waited for crumbs to fall. Sheree couldn't help but notice the plethora of Yins and Yangs while acknowledging that the distance between her own Yang to her Yin was quickly diminishing as she watched the mirror spoon chocolate ice cream into her open and awaiting mouth with ecstatic expectations.

Staring at the neighbor kids, Sheree pondered over whether Kwirk and Wayne were identical because they looked like it in every way except that Kwirk—the one who was over most because he was actually Brendon's friend—had fiery hair that made her mother irrationally jealous with its striations of blond and burgundy slithering through an oranger-than-orange mane, while Wayne—the one who was merely an acquaintance by extension of his twin brother—was practically bleach blond. *Genetics*, she thought. For the record, they're paternal, like Mary Kate and Ashley Olsen who were all the rage in 2000 with their teenage empire ruling the planet, or at the very least, the television and straight-to-video business and fashion industry and blah blah blah. Fucking child prodigies. Ptooey.

Things started getting awkward when Brendon started showing Kwirk pictures of the guys in the underwear catalog that was casually displayed on the living room coffee table along with *Better Homes and Gardens* and *Martha Stewart Living,* causing Wayne to roll his eyes and Kwirk to agree and disagree.

"Huh. I guess Kwirk is gay, or at least open to the idea that boys are attractive," Sheree said to Kayla as she stared.

"Wayne's not," Kayla said, lips dripping with brown.

"Do you think he knows that he is?" Sheree asked, unable to take her eyes off the scene to their left or get the image of Kevin, the local dairy farm boy slash junior varsity football team's quarterback slash male cheerleader, making out with Nathan, a fellow cheerleader and future class president. *Why do two guys making out turn me on?*

"Shut up, Wayne! I like boys in the same way you like girls! It's a thing. It's called being gay. Look it up," Kwirk argued as Mrs. Hollins walked through the door to spot the boy she hated with a red-hot passion over having naturally red hair she coveted.

"I know it's a thing and I know that you are! I just don't want to look at pictures of half-naked men, dork!" Wayne declared, throwing his hands up in the air and quickly retracting them towards his mouth when he spotted Mrs. Hollins behind him.

"Don't call him a penis!" Sheree and Kayla yelled in unison.

Mrs. Hollins shook her head, turned around, walked out and over to her friend Amanda's house two doors down. Amanda was Chad Walker's mom. They're best friends. They both work for the middle school. They have a past, present, and future relationship. They also like to drink an inordinate amount of wine and bitch about their kids, which likely was about to commence given the circumstances that just unfolded.

Just when the boys's conversation was getting lively again, the doorbell rang. It was Chad and Nikki.

"Um, this is weird. You never come over," Sheree said as she let them in.

"Yeah, well, Mom kicked us out and Nikki's house is too crazy right now with the Russian Mafia, aka, her nieces and nephews and brother and sisters, and I think her mom hates me." Nikki nodded her head in agreement. "You were my first thoughts of refuge and shelter," Chad said, seeing that Brendon and Kwirk were whispering to each other but unable to make out what they were saying because he left his hearing aids at home and didn't feel like having his mother's coal eyes burn into his soul during their retrieval.

The gays giggled.

"We're watching Oprah," Kayla said, sitting most unladylike on the couch with the mostly empty ice cream container resting on her not-so-empty chest catching the melted mess from her mouth.

"Thank God!" Nikki exclaimed, taking a seat next to Kayla and causing a 2.7 magnitude earthquake, leaving little room on the sofa for anyone else due to the sheer size of her ass.

Chad smooshed his face.

Sheree decided Oprah wasn't very interesting that afternoon anyway, especially now that her sister had total control over the Tillamook Mudslide. She walked to the kitchen and sat on one of the barstools between it and the dining room. Chad did the same.

Silence.

"I miss Sky," Chad said quietly, almost a murmur.

"Me too," Sheree said in barely a whisper before spotting the lack of hearing devices in Chad's ears, or at least the one she could see, and repeated herself louder.

The door opened and Mr. Hollins walked in to an energetic conversation about cute boys and girls to his right, his recently undeceased daughter and a vaguely familiar neighbor girl to his left sitting where he wanted to be sitting after he changed out of what he deemed to be the worst clothing ever: scrubs, and his other daughter and the neighbor boy straight ahead. At that, he smiled. "Hi, Chad."

Chad smiled back. "Hi, Mr. Hollins."

Mr. Hollins shook his head, but didn't shake the grin. "Call me…" He hesitated, almost blurting out what he really wanted to say. "Frank."

"I'll try, but can't make any guarantees. Mom said it's important to be polite," Chad said.

"You're in the wrong house if you're expecting politeness," Mr. Hollins said.

"Ain't that the truth!" Sheree said.

"Grrrnnnnnnnnggghh!!!" Kayla screamed out like a wild animal, the ice cream container dropping to the ground and creating its own chocolate crime scene as she stood up.

Nikki sat in horror.

Sheree and Chad stayed put as well.

Mr. Hollins rushed to her side, and assuming that nobody was the wiser about her predicament, asked, "What happened? Are you alright?"

"These goddamned twins are tearing me apart!" she shrieked, letting out another howl before collapsing into the couch.

"Your sister's pregnant?" Kwirk asked Brendon.

"Yeah," Brendon told him.

"Mom said we were the worst thing to happen to her figure," Wayne said bluntly, staring at the scene.

"We should go to your house," Brendon said.

The Werewolfs agreed, and the three of them went next door where they lived. Kwirk snagged the underwear catalog to take with him, mostly to watch his mother and father squirm like earthworms after a hard rain.

"I'm sorry, I know I should know your name," Mr. Hollins said to the girl sitting next to Kayla.

"Nikki," said the girl in question, still frightened and deciding then and there she was never ever EVER going to have kids so long as she lived.

Best. Birth. Control. Ever.

"Nikki, can you…" but before he could finish she was up and by Chad's side. Mr. Hollins took Kayla's hand and she squeezed it as hard as she could, but it didn't alleviate the pain or make the situation any better except that her father was by her side in this time of need and she was helpless to do anything about it and hated the fact that she brought this whole thing down on herself. "Tell me what I can do?"

Kayla forced a short-lived smile. "You are doing it."

And then it was over.

Chad broke the silence with, "Don't take this the wrong way, Nikki, but I don't want to have sex with you."

"I'm inclined to agree with you, Chad," Nikki said back, still recoiling from the horror that took place mere feet from her present location.

And they didn't. Ever.

Chapter 5
House of Horrors

"The itsy bity spider went up the water spout…"

Sheree's eyes ripped open so quickly she swore her lids were bleeding.

"Down came Kayla and sought the spider out…"

Brendon opened her door and was at her side.

"Up rose her buns and dried up all the rain,

And the itsy bitsy spider will soon roam free again!"

"Caaaaaaaawwww!!!" they heard from down the hall. It was from Kayla's room, followed by a horrifying *THUD!*.

The whole house was a flurry at this, as both Mr. and Mrs. Hollins rushed into Kayla's bedroom from the side door in their room, and Brendon and Sheree entered from the main door. It was the Spanish Inquisition in Barcelona and she was a Jew.

"Just labor pains and a frickin' nightmare," Kayla said to calm the storm.

The parental units looked uncertain.

"It wasn't just a nightmare," Brendon said.

"It was the voice again," Sheree told her. "You know the one."

Mrs. Hollins looked like she was about to burst. "We need to get out of this house, Frank. One of my sisters can look after it for all I care!"

"Now, wait just a…" he started, but was quickly shushed.

"No! I can't watch as my family is tortured anymore! I don't care what kind of guarantees my mother gave us, something is wrong here!" Mrs. Hollins was hysterical, tears streaming down her face like river rapids, her normally kempt obviously-colored-from-a-generic-brand-of-dye-from-the-grocery-store hair, frazzled.

The phone rang, causing the five of them to jump in place.

"Jesus! Who's calling at this time of night?" Mr. Hollins asked the ceiling as the telephone let out its incessant demands.

"I don't think it's Jesus," Brendon said bluntly.

Sheree suddenly realized the closest phone was in her room, and quickly went to answer it before the ringing became a permanent fixture in her ears. "Mom, it's for you."

Mrs. Hollins walked over to Sheree's room and yanked the pink princess phone from her hand. "Yes, that is a problem, Mother. No. You can't. What? How? No. That's not acceptable. No. Fine."

SLAM!

The sound of the receiver hitting the base echoed through the house. A faint ringing resonated in the air long after the event.

"I take it things went well with Grandma?" Sheree asked, her sarcasm an unwanted guest.

Mrs. Hollins looked visibly shaken like a bottle of Italian salad dressing settling. "She said that Kayla knows what to do."

"Bull *shit*!" Kayla said mimicking Courtney and recognizing her stylistic vocalizations were rubbing off on her, still in bed and afraid to get up for fear the pain will only increase.

Staring wide-eyed at her daughter for swearing but realizing she was both too tired and too worried to care, gave it a pass. Again. She was getting too old to let such things bother her anymore, she decided. "She said that you knew what had to be done and told me that since I'm not a witch I wouldn't understand."

Sheree could see the bee's stinger left behind after her mother spoke.

Sunlight crept through the Hollins house like a burglar; quiet at first then fast and furious before the clouds jailed it for trespassing. The coffee pot urinated the sweet nectar of the gods into the carafe as three of the five humans awaited the rewards of their patience. The witches were in the living room pontificating, irking their mother to no end every time her ears decided to listen in on their conversation.

Mr. Hollins stared out the kitchen window at a backyard in desperate need of mowing and was about to muster up the courage to say aloud his intentions when the clouds that rolled in quickly unleashed their watery wrath up the poor citizens of Ravenwood. "Son of a bitch!" he yelled, slamming his fist onto the counter, vibrating the brown-black liquid halfway full in the pot. He pulled it out early, letting a few drops sizzle and evaporate onto the hotplate as he poured coffee into his cup and the two next to it before replacing it back into its spot. A flurry of the backed-up brew burst in like a flash-flood. "All I had to do was think about mowing the goddamned grass and it starts to rain!"

"Stop thinking, Dad," Sheree said after drinking her black coffee.

"It'll give you an aneurism," Mrs. Hollins told him, taking a sip after adding cream and sugar. Her face looked bitter. She added more of both.

The Saturday rain ruined any plans for a happy Mother's Day weekend. The fact that all three of the Hollins children were clueless as to the holiday the following day was not lost on Mrs. Hollins as she stared scornfully towards the scheming brother-sister duo with supernatural powers she was never blessed slash cursed with. A suddenly silver strand of hair temporarily broke her attention as she attempted to free it from her scalp.

As the day passed and the sun kept breaking out of jail, the air became thick.

Stifling.

Hot and sticky like fresh out of the oven cinnamon rolls after slathering on the cream cheese frosting.

Humidity is a moist whore.

The afternoon brought Jennifer over to the Hollins house to escape her mother's clinginess she possessed every time her father was about to come back into town. She never understood her mother's obsession over the man who could barely stand to spend a few hours a month with his family, and resented her father's absence each passing year as his monthly visits became shorter and shorter.

"That man is going to drive me to drink one day," Jennifer told Sheree and Kayla as they decided to take a trip into the basement in hopes of getting to the bottom of the most recent cryptic lullabies.

"Don't become a statistic, Jen," Sheree said as she landed on the basement floor, this time with shoes just in case it was covered in millions upon millions of bugs. Again. Blech.

"Besides, you're Asian and can't hold your liquor," Kayla said coldly, but still causing Sheree to chuckle and wish she had been the one to think of that instead.

"Bitch. And. Bitch," Jennifer said, shaking her head as her eyes rolled into the back of it.

A silky cobweb clung to Sheree as she turned around without looking. "Gack!" she cried, wiping it off her face and trying desperately to detach it from her fore and middle fingers. Its ghost stayed behind for hours.

"What are we looking for?" Jennifer asked, her face scrunched up in a most unattractive way that made Sheree wish she had a mirror so her friend would never make that face again, but alas, she never had one handy in situations like these. *Note to self…*

"I don't know. Something," Kayla said, eyes searching, but for what she was uncertain, which was pretty obvious by her choice of words and casually annoyed demeanor.

"Oh! That helps! Not!" Jennifer wailed, shaking her head and shattering the scrunchy face with it. Praise Buddha!

A box caught Sheree's eyes. A large red shoebox she hadn't seen in years. What treasures lie within? Curiosity begged her to open it. She immediately regretted her decision.

Barbies.

Dozens of Barbies.

Naked Barbies with short sheared hair.

In a box, staring lifelessly.

It was a shoebox Auschwitz.

Sheree stared at it like she was Rudolf Höss, looking superior over his camp with indignant disgust. She quickly put the lid back on before her sister or best friend saw the contained horrors of her childhood.

"Find anything?" Kayla asked as she saw Sheree's hands resting on the red lid.

"Nope. You?" she asked back quickly.

Sheree's guilty lie was not lost to the abyss as she had hoped, but Kayla let it go.

"Nothing yet. Of course, it'd help if I knew what the hell we were looking for," Kayla said, returning her search. "Thanks, Grandma!"

Sheree sniffed the musty air, inhaling whiffs of mildew and mothballs and mouse droppings. She found the odor slightly pleasant much to her own horror. Then again, she also secretly loved to smell her fingers after wiping her ass. "Jesus Christ! That damn painting scares me every time," she said, hand on her chest as she tried to look away from the painting of a long dead relative.

"Well it should. That's Grandma Jessica," Kayla said matter-of-factly.

"I'm just trying to figure out how you could have possibly convinced me to be down here with the two of you!" Jennifer said. "I mean, the last time we three were down here,"—she pointed as she spoke—"you possessed me, made me knock Sheree out putting her in a coma for a week, then smashed my head against that post so I'd be unconscious too."

"True. This is all part of my evil plan," Kayla told them. "To scare you with hundred-year-old pictures and pre-corporeal form memories of me."

"That is Jessica?" Sheree asked quietly, shivering as a spine-tingling cold crept up on her.

"Yes. It can't leave the house, it can't be destroyed, and it definitely can't be stared at or she will jump out and kill you," Kayla said, no hint of sarcasm in her voice.

"Shit!" Sheree screamed, looking away from the painting. "Now you tell me!"

"I'm kidding about the last part," Kayla told her gullible sister. "I think I'm kidding, anyway."

"What's so bad about Grandma Jessica?" Jennifer asked.

So much she was clueless about.

"Oh, she's crazy. Had to be burned at the stake by her own family because she killed too many people," Sheree said, trying to find something to cover the painting with.

"Got it. So it runs in the family."—She looked right at Kayla who looked right back—"And this was her house so it has to stay here because it has some supernatural mojo, right?" Jennifer asked, filling in her own blanks.

"Yep," Kayla confirmed.

"Got it," Jennifer said again, shaking her head in affirmation.

Sheree went to throw a moving blanket over the painting as Kayla said, "Don't bother. Won't work."

She did it anyway and watched as it flew back at her in a ball and punched her in the stomach.

"Gaw. Why-ay-ay?" Sheree asked, doubled over and hugging her tummy.

"Supernatural mojo," Jennifer said, rolling her eyes. "Even I could figure that out."

Brendon strolled down the stairs and saw his sister hunched over. "Someone try to cover up Grandma Jessica again?"

"Yep," Kayla said, staring at her twin.

"Amateur," Brendon said, rolling his eyes.

Sheree straightened out. "Maybe we should move her over to a corner so…"

"Nobody puts Grandma in a corner!" Kayla and Brendon yelled. Then laughed and laughed and laughed. They'd just watched *Dirty Dancing* the night before, otherwise Kayla wouldn't have been able to be in on the joke, and that would have been sad. [Tear.]

"Are you being serious or just assholes?" Sheree asked her siblings, not finding their antics amusing.

"Both," Kayla said. "I mean, you're welcome to try."

"Yeah, it won't do any good," Brendon said, folding his arms across his chest.

"Well," Sheree said, picking up the painting. "I'm going to take a chance."

The mutual sigh hit Sheree like a brick, but didn't deter her. She walked over to a dark corner, turned the painting around, and watched as the painting's subject burned into the reverse of the canvas, somehow looking angry and alive.

"Great!" Jennifer shouted. "Now creepy grandma is in a dark corner and looks scarier than she was before. Way to go, Sheree."

"Are you kidding me?" Sheree asked the painting.

Grandma Jessica's smile widened and her face shook from side to side as if to say, "No, dear. I am not kidding. Not at all."

Sheree turned around. "We have to burn down the house."

"It's just a painting," Brendon said.

"That just shook its head and smiled at me. Its evil made of evil parts by an evil corporation for the sole purpose of committing evil," Sheree said. "Pack what you must. Leave the rest. There isn't time."

"Won't help. The painting will survive," Kayla said, trying to force a smile on her face but her stomach was obviously wrenching in pain.

"Son of a bitch." Sheree deflated.

"Wait wait wait wait wait. Someone please tell me how that crazy-ass old lady in the painting can move? This isn't Harry Potter!" Jennifer shrieked.

"Well, it is a magical household and you two are muggles and she wasn't very fond of them," Brendon said with a faux-British accent. Being gay was making him far more fancy than he ever intended.

"Fuck me," Sheree said.

"Fuck us," Jennifer said.

Chapter 6
Mother's Day

The morning held such promise. Too bad everyone slept in.

"Oh my gawd, Sheree. It's already noon," Jennifer said as she rubbed the sleep from her eyes after glancing at the alarm clock.

"Barely dawn. Go back to sleep," Sheree said, pulling the covers over her eyes to avoid the pathetic excuse for daylight the Pacific Northwest had to offer that day.

Loud footsteps rushed to her door that opened to reveal Brendon in a panic. "Crap! It's Mother's Day!"

"Crap!" Sheree said, covers flying off in a flash, almost taking the Asian girl with them.

Thunder began rolling in, shaking the windows.

Rex and Deschutes cowered, despite needing to go outside to potty. They refused. Instead, they opted to relieve themselves in the kitchen. This wasn't the first time. It certainly wouldn't be the last.

"Brendon!" Kayla yelled from the stove where she was attempting eggs and sausage but failing miserably. "Clean up after your dogs!"

"Son of a... Why?" Brendon asked his canine companions, both of whom simply looked at him with sad ASPCA eyes and held a frightened stance like they were afraid he was going to beat them, which only made their position that much stronger because Brendon would never beat his dogs because he was a decent human being. Only assholes beat their dogs. Don't be an asshole.

Another clap of thunder shook the house.

"It smells like burning," Sheree noted as she walked into the kitchen. Sure enough, the eggs were black as thick molasses.

Jennifer followed. "Oh, Sweet Buddha! Make the stench go away!"

Kayla looked them straight in the eye with a stoic expression, snapped her fingers, and *POOF!* the smell was gone. Magic. Actual magic, none of that air freshener crap that makes the house smell like artificial versions of whatever fragrance it says on the can. Okay, so in reality the smell was simply moved to the forest outside their home.

"Can you do that with my Algebra homework?" Sheree asked, taking in a hefty whiff of the fresh air.

"Yes," Kayla said.

"Really?" Sheree asked, eyes perking up.

"Yes. But I won't."

"Bitch."

"That's what sisters are for."

"I hate you."

"No! It's love! You love me!" Kayla said far creepier than when she was a ghost-witch with a vendetta to kill her, giving Sheree a hug.

Sheree stayed still as a possum playing dead.

Jennifer just shook her head and stared at the piles of poop and pools of piss on the puke-colored linoleum. "And to think this is preferable to being at home with my parents."

"Your mom wants to chop off my hair to make herself a wig and I would say that is preferable to this!" Sheree said, still being squished by her twin who suddenly started petting her hair like Lennie Small, almost hoping her neck would snap in the process so she wouldn't have to suffer the indignity of it all.

Brendon giggled.

Mrs. Hollins walked in to find her daughters hugging, Brendon sitting on a barstool, Jennifer leaning against the counter, Rex and Deschutes wagging their tails and smiling profusely, and a crime scene of excrement all over her floors. "I'm leaving and never coming back." She actually got to the front door before her children stopped her.

"Don't go!" Brendon pleaded.

"We made you breakfast!" Sheree said.

"I made breakfast," Kayla corrected.

"I don't even live here," Jennifer said, stating the obvious.

She reluctantly agreed not to abandon them. "I could swear I smelled burnt eggs just a minute ago."

"Yeah, Kayla burnt the shit outta them! Hehehe!" Sheree said.

"And made the smell go away. And look! No more crusties!" Kayla said, revealing a platter of beautifully fluffy scrambled eggs, piles of buttered toast, sausage links galore, and halved grapefruits.

"Magic?" Mrs. Hollins asked.

"Only a little bit," Kayla admitted.

"Remind me to talk to you about the kitchen color scheme," Mrs. Hollins said.

"No!" Sheree screamed. "I love avocado!"

"Avocado must die," Mrs. Hollins said.

"Shouldn't we ask dad?" Sheree said. "Dad!"

"He's at work," Mrs. Hollins told her.

"Oh gawd, who died now?" Brendon asked, rolling his eyes.

The town's death toll was becoming a habit.

Mr. Hollins had recently become Ravenwood's Chief Medical Examiner, no longer just the assistant, so his hours weren't as regular as they used to be. The previous one just up and quit after Easter. Too much death, which, you know, is quite ironic for a coroner. You'd think he'd've been happy about the job security.

"He said the police found John Upcock's parents," she told them bluntly, hoping none of them knew the couple. She did. From high school. Didn't care for them much then either. Still, she never wished death upon them, though it might be better all the same as she would never wish having them live with the death of their child, an unspeakable pain she was far too familiar with, even if her daughter was back from the grave now.

"What the hell happened?" Sheree asked, suddenly digging up the sadness of losing Sky all over again.

Her mother was silent. Not silent like one who doesn't have the answer to the query in question, but silent like one who has the answer and can't tell anyone about it. Secret. "I'm sure the news will cover the story."

Sure enough, she was right. Six o'clock. Breaking News. The trials and tribulations of Ami's murder spree were quickly gaining national attention. Who else on the list of missing persons could be attributed to her? Who else would they find?

Mr. Hollins walked in the door not long after his brief interview by the local news and well after dinner, collapsed into the living room sofa, and started crying.

Something bad happened. Oh shit. Something very bad happened, Sheree thought as she watched the scene unfold like accordion-style Post-its from the comforts of the den.

"What is it, Frank?" Mrs. Hollins asked, rushing to his side.

"Annie," he said quietly. It sounded like he had peanut butter stuck to the roof of his mouth.

Annie. Annie. Why is that name so familiar?

"My nurse?" Brendon asked, holding his left arm.

Shit! That's right! Annie was Brendon's nurse when he fractured his arm after falling… no, after Kayla pushed him out of a tree. Annie Myer. Kori Myer's mom. Dead Kori Myer's mom.

Kayla walked down the stairs. "Dad's crying. This can't be good."

Mr. Hollins shook his head. Mrs. Hollins gave her a scolding look on par with a public spanking.

"Annie… she… she…" Mr. Hollins kept trying to say, but couldn't get the words out over his tears.

"She didn't do something bad? Something like I did after Kayla… died?" Mrs. Hollins said, suddenly regretting her glare and motioning for Kayla to come in so she could hold her like a baby.

As Mrs. Hollins hugged Kayla, Sheree and Brendon crept in closer to hear what Annie did.

"She tried to kill herself today."

❦ ❦ ❦

"Mom, you of all people should know how magic works. I mean, you grew up surrounded by witches," Kayla said, an unintended air of superiority and smugness floating around her like dust motes as she spoke.

"I know what they let me know," Mrs. Hollins told her daughter. "Which, quite honestly, wasn't much."

The bitterness in her mother's tongue saddened her. "I'm sorry. I don't know why they treated you like a pariah," Kayla said, reaching over to hug her mom. "I promise not to perpetuate the stereotype that you just won't understand because you aren't one of us."

The "us" hurt Mrs. Hollins more than she cared to admit, especially since it consisted of practically every female relative in her family except herself, and also two of her own children. She was acutely aware that she was considered a "them." An outsider in her own family.

"How can I explain this simply?" Kayla said, scrunching up her face.

"As Sheree would say, use small words and enunciate," Mrs. Hollins suggested.

"That's so Sheree," Kayla said, rolling her eyes.

"Hey!" Sheree yelled from the living room sofa.

Kayla ignored her. "Okay, so there are living things and non-living things."

"What about zombies and vampires?" Mrs. Hollins asked.

"Seriously?" Kayla asked.

"Yes."

"You're tangenting."

"Indulge me."

"I'll attempt to. So, non-living things can't change by use of magic. I mean, I can break this glass and put it back together, but physically, chemically, nothing has changed. I can't turn this glass into a purple vase or a diamond ring. Are you following me so far?"

"Attempting."

"Anyway, living things have living cells that can be manipulated. Pliable. Moldable. Cells that can be told to change shape or do your evil bidding or whatever."

"Where do zombies and vampires fall into this?"

"Well, zombies aren't real. And as far as vampires go, I guess I could ask any number of our neighbors on this street if they are up for an experiment to satisfy your inquiry."

"Ugh, never mind."

"Okay, so take this kitchen for example," Kayla said, spreading her hands out like a game show model.

Mrs. Hollins's eyes lit up like Christmas, hopeful that perhaps this Mother's Day wasn't going to be completely ruined after all. "Yes?"

Kayla shifted. "Do you know if Amanda or Chad are home?"

Perplexed, Mrs. Hollins failed to understand the seemingly random question, but played along anyway. Her hated kitchen might finally be getting the makeover she'd been dreaming about since moving into the old house on Song's End. "No. They're at some cheerleading thing with Courtney until ten or so."

Hearing her mother say her girlfriend's name aloud made her swoon and smile uncontrollably. Mrs. Hollins did not fail to take notice.

"Excellent. Okay, so, the way our power works is by, uh, replacement?" Kayla said, suddenly befuddled at exactly how to explain the process.

Sheree's ears perked up at this. She merely pretended to read her celebrity fashion slash gossip magazine while she waited for her sister to continue.

"Now, I can take one thing from somewhere else, like this…" Kayla said, and suddenly the kitchen was orange instead of avocado.

"Oh gawd. Ew!" Mrs. Hollins said, her face a lemon.

"But I can't transform it into your dream kitchen," Kayla said, returning the avocado back into its proper place.

"Well that sucks," Mrs. Hollins said, her disappointment beyond obvious.

"Unless you want to encourage me to steal…" Kayla said mischievously, a slight grin and twinkle in her eye awaiting a response.

"I'll live with the avocado for now."
Alas, hope is but a fantasy.

Chapter 7
Strange Things Are Happening

"The itsy bitsy spider went up the water spout…"

"Jesus Christ, you've got to be kidding me," Sheree said, still awake as the lullaby vibrated through the old iron air vent, echoing through her bedroom.

"Down came the rain and washed the spider out…"

Brendon and Kayla had joined her, their annoyance beyond apparent.

"Seriously?" Brendon asked.

"We need to figure out who's singing this time," Kayla said, knowing, at the very least, it wasn't herself. "I really need my baby sleep."

"Up rose the babes to take Kayla's place…"

Panic struck Kayla harder than she ever thought possible, and she fell to the hardwood floors as her legs quit.

"And the itsy bitsy spider was out to rule again!"

Laughter filled the air.

"No! No no no! This can't be happening!" Kayla cried, staring at her stomach in horror, her eyes ready to leap and abandon ship to save themselves.

Sheree flew out of her bed and rushed to her sister's side. "What? Oh gawd, what?" she asked, holding Kayla.

"That laughing!" Kayla shrieked.

"I know. It won't stop," Brendon said, clasping his ears to no avail.

Kayla burst into tears. "It's coming from me. From inside me!"

"Well, shit," Sheree said, shaking her head and beginning to laugh herself.

"What?" Kayla asked, perplexed by the reaction as the twins kicked and thrashed.

Brendon was too horrified to speak.

"Congratulations! You're going to give birth to my dead boyfriend and our great-great-great-grandmother!" Sheree squealed like she was a child experiencing Disneyland for the first time.

Kayla looked like someone let the helium out of her balloon.

"I hope I at least get to kiss a boy before I die," Brendon said in all seriousness.

"Brendon!" Sheree and Kayla said together.

"Don't talk like that," Sheree said.

"Nothing's going to happen to you!" Kayla assured loudly, even if she didn't believe it herself. Part of her was certain she wouldn't survive childbirth like all those pre-twentieth century women before her, only bloodier. Gorier. Picture the most horrific, awful, crappiest way to be torn apart from the inside out. Now multiply that by infinity. Still not even close to what she had in mind.

Mr. Hollins rushed into the room, his pajama bottoms only a formality as he normally slept in the nude, and was quite obvious that they were haphazardly thrown on in haste at the last outburst. "What the hell is going on in here?" he demanded, his eyes squinting as they attempted to adjust to the fire-hazard wattage light bulbs he insisted on.

"Kayla's babies are Jeff and Grandma Jessica!" Sheree announced, bubbles still permeating the space between them.

"She's... huh?" Mr. Hollins asked as his wife joined his side.

"I don't understand. And don't give me any of that you're-not-a-witch-so-you-won't-get-it crap!" Mrs. Hollins said sternly, though she was trembling with fear on the inside.

"I... I... I knew that Jeff was part of the bargain," Kayla said, her tears recycling into her mouth as she spoke. "But... but Jessica?"

Deer in headlights, that's what Mrs. Hollins looked like. She shook her head after the car passed. "I'm going to brew a strong pot of pennyroyal tea."

"You can't," Kayla said, calming down as much as she could.

"What's...?" Brendon started, but was interrupted by his mother.

"I can and I will." Her drive was iron.

Kayla started crying again. "They are too attached. Any attempt to abort will kill me along with them." Then she suddenly stopped as a thought lit up in her brain. "That's it. I'll do it. Kill me. Save the world."

"Not going to happen," Mrs. Hollins said. "We will figure out another way."

"And if there is no other way?" Kayla asked, surprised at how readily she was willing to throw her life away so shortly after regaining it.

"We will find another way," Brendon said, patting her shoulder in a way Kayla couldn't be certain if it was genuine or mockery, but knowing Brendon it very well could have been both.

Kayla smiled. "I hope you're right."

Brendon smiled. *Me, too.*

The morning was ruined, thanks to Grandma Jessica. Bitch. Mondays are the worst. As the Hollins family attempted to resuscitate themselves for the day ahead, grogginess weighed them down like a tombstone. Kayla looked the worst of the bunch, as her pregnant belly grew quite noticeably over the last few hours.

"FRANK!!!" the household heard, pictures trembling on the walls as the name reverberated across the home from the basement.

Mr. Hollins ran down the stairs in boxers, hair wet and matted. "What?! What is it, Beth?" he asked, trying to locate his wife.

"Basement. Now. I need you to move Jessica so I can start a load of laundry," Mrs. Hollins said from the bottom of the stairs.

"Are you serious?" he asked, droplets raining from his hair over his toned body all Sheree's friends (even Courtney, the lesbian) coveted to the point of calling him a DILF and making no qualms about wanting to fuck him like an animal.

"Do I look like I'm kidding, Frank?" she asked.

Even in the darkness at the base of the stairs, despite the 150-watt bulb mere inches from his face blinding him, he could feel his wife's eyes burn into his chest and threaten to rip his heart out. "No?" And with that, he went down to the basement to do his husbandry duties. Like kill the spiders, trap the mice, swat the moth.

"Who put Jessica in a corner by the washer and dryer anyway?" Mrs. Hollins asked as she watched her husband pick up the painting and, using only his eyes, ask where she wanted it put. After the painting was securely out of the way of staring at her while doing laundry, she snatched up Mr. Hollins, pulled him in for a kiss, and said, "My hero!"

Sheree closed the door after that because she could hear banging against the washing machine and didn't want to know why. After pouring herself a bowl of Lucky Charms, she cursed each marshmallow before swallowing them. After the string of bad luck over the last nine months, she was beginning to wonder if the cereal had lost its magic. Red balloons, purple horseshoes, and green clovers danced along oat shapes of fish and diamonds and spades… and a lone black marshmallow in the shape of a spider.

At first, she thought her eyes were deceiving her. Playing tricks. She was, after all, quite sleep deprived. Had it been closer to Halloween, she would have merely passed it off as being a seasonal addition, though admittedly an odd one to boot, to the cereal's lineup of good luck charms.

She swore it started moving.

Swimming.

Leaping onto her spoon and begging for her to swallow it.

She felt compelled to obey.

She lifted the spoon to her mouth.

Closer.

Almost to her lips.

"Don't!" Brendon shouted, knocking the spoon away and watching in horror as the marshmallow spider scurried away into the crevice beneath the pantry door. "What were you thinking?"

"I wasn't," Sheree said, and it was true. She wasn't. Like Princess Aurora, her hand was on autopilot and her mind was along for the ride to touch the spindle.

"You've got to be careful. Now that we know that Jessica is behind the latest Radio Air Vent Pop Sensations, we have to be on extra alert," Brendon said, his eyes still focused on the crack between the pantry door and linoleum floor.

"You really just referred to those damned deadly rhymes as 'Radio Air Vent Pop Sensations?' " Sheree asked, trying not to laugh, but only a little.

"Well, it's true! Crazy ol' witch!" Brendon said, sounding more ten-year-old boy again as his gaze was broken. "I can't get her tunes out of my head!"

"Maybe I should find the marshmallow spider and use the spade shape from the cereal to dig a hole and bury it," Sheree said, fingering her cereal.

"Spade? There aren't any spades in Lucky Charms! This isn't a deck of cards!" Brendon said, face scrunched up at the absurdity.

"Yes there is," Sheree said, digging one out. "See?"

Brendon doubled over laughing. "Oh my gawd!"

"What?"

"That's an arrowhead!"

"Oh."

"Why did you think it was a shovel? What kind of good luck charm is a shovel?"

"Well…" She let the word linger on her tongue longer than she meant to. "If you need to dispose of a body and lo and behold, a spade appears by your side to assist you, then it would be good luck."

"It's an arrowhead. Sorry," Brendon said after his laughter died down.

"My childhood is a lie," Sheree said, wondering what other shapes she misidentified.

Kayla walked into the house carrying a mason jar, entered the kitchen, pulled out a jar of pickles, ate one, and washed it down with a swig of red. She drank again from the mason jar full of thick red liquid, and followed it up with another dill pickle.

"Bloody Mary?" Sheree asked, laughing at the sight.

Brendon looked merely amused.

"Not sure if any of this is Mary, but blood, yes," Kayla said, slurping down the last of it.

Disgust fell to the pit of Sheree's stomach like a three-day-old scone. "You're not joking, are you?"

"Nope," Kayla said, licking her lips.

"That's disgusting, even for you, Kayla," Brendon said, face as green as the kitchen and the recently consumed pickle.

"The fetus demands it," Kayla said, before starting to sing and dance. "Whatever Fetus wants, Fetus gets. And little man, little Fetus wants you!"

"Stop!" Brendon shouted, pushing his hand out as far as he could, his eyes full of rage.

"I was just joking with you, Bren! Geez!" Kayla said, laughing. "Seriously, let me go."

"What?" Sheree asked.

"Our little brother has me bound to a bubble and won't let me bounce out of it," Kayla said. "He's such a wonderful witch! Oh! Let's call him that! Wonder Witch!"

Sheree started giggling uncontrollably, and Brendon put his hand down and released Kayla from her invisible prison.

"Don't call me Wonder Witch. It's bad enough I get called a fat faggot at school," Brendon said quietly.

Now Kayla's eyes were full of rage. "Who calls you that?" she asked, even though she had called him the same only a few short months before.

"Tommy," he whispered, voice filled with pain and heartbreak and disappointment.

"Tommy's a narcissistic asshole who's probably in denial about his sexuality and taking it out on you," Sheree assured.

"I know," he said, head bowed in prayer.

"If you want, I can turn him into a toad," Kayla offered. It was a lie, but still, there was sentiment behind it. Okay, so it wasn't a complete lie.

"I can handle Tommy," he said, though his voice suggested otherwise.

Sheree lit up. "Have Kwirk handle Tommy. You know he'd be up to making someone's life miserable! He irritates mom to no end without even trying!"

"All because she is jealous of his hair," Brendon said, voice returning back to normal. "How petty is that?"

Rex and Deschutes started banging on the French doors in the dining room, begging to be let back inside the house. Their forest romp and poop sessions must have ended. Brendon let them in and they immediately smothered him in muddy paws and wet kisses. He laughed as he tried shooing them off.

"Breakfast?" he asked.

They immediately stopped and sat in place. Well, as much in place as two easily excitable terrier mixes could be. Actually, they looked like heroin addicts rocking themselves from withdrawals as they (not so) patiently waited for their meal to be scooped.

Brendon stopped at the pantry door, hand lingering on the knob.

"What is it?" Kayla asked, wondering why he was paused.

"Marshmallow spider went in there," Sheree said matter-of-factly.

"Dammit, Jessica! No more tricks you naughty, wicked little girl!" Kayla scolded the bulge in her stomach.

The sight was quite comical. It was also enough for Brendon to gain the courage to open the door, scoop out kibble from the bag of dog food, and feed his canine companions. They whimpered with anticipation as they couldn't see their bowls they knew were filled with delicious meat-flavored kibble.

"Okay!" Brendon said, slapping his thigh.

Rex and Deschutes broke through the dining room, nearly toppling a chair or two, as they rushed into the kitchen and swallowed their breakfast so quickly it was gone before a blink. They drank a little from their respective water bowls, then were back at the door begging to be let out because apparently they have Irish bladders. Brendon let them out again and waited by the door to let them back in, knowing this would be a quick trip.

"Actually, maybe I should ask Wayne to pay Tommy a visit," Brendon said, watching the dogs urinate on his father's perfect lawn and hoping it didn't burn it. He prayed for rain, but knew it wasn't in the forecast that day.

"What? Why Wayne?" Sheree asked, confused like the blond girl she was and perpetuating that stereotype, though, admittedly, this was one where anyone else would also be curious as to the relevancy. And besides, she was strawberry blond. Technically a ginger. Well, maybe diet ginger.

"Uh, because he's a werewolf?" Brendon said, an air of duh-you-stupid-bitch in his tone. He turned back toward the door just in time to watch Rex and Deschutes disappear into the forest again.

"So is Kwirk. They are both Werewolfs. I don't get why Wayne would be the better choice. Kwirk is the gay one," Sheree said.

Kayla sat back and watched, eating another dill pickle and sad she didn't have any more blood to drink.

"No. He's a werewolf. An actual werewolf. Like, he turns into a wolf-boy," Brendon clarified.

"Huh?" Sheree said.

"Oh for God's sake, Sheree! He's a fucking werewolf, and that might scare the fucking shit out of a fucking asshole like fucking Tommy Gufflebacht!" Kayla shouted, dropping her half-eaten pickle onto the floor where muddy paw prints were smeared like car tire tracks after doing cookies in the school parking lot. "Sonofabitch!" She picked it up and ate the rest anyway.

"Oh. Huh. Didn't know. Now I do," Sheree said, suddenly aware that Ravenwood was much stranger than she had originally thought it to be.

"He's also got a magic genie," Brendon told her.

"Now you are just playing on my gullibility and societally passable blondness," Sheree told him.

"Whatever," Brendon said, shaking his head as he put on his shoes to retrieve his ADHD dogs, deciding it might be too soon to let her in on all of the other various supernatural parts of their quiet little haunted town.

Chapter 8
The Tragedy of Adam and Eve

While Sheree was chatting with Jennifer about shoes, a girl she recognized but couldn't place a name with the face kept saying, "Yes, Adam, we should finally have sex while my parents are out of town," while the boy she presumed to be Adam kept responding with, "No, I'm not ready." He looked like he was going to cry. Broken. Her yesses wearing down his noes until it became unbearable to withstand the pressure.

Pop.

Instinct kicked in before Sheree had a chance to realize it, and she was in the girl's face in a flap of a hummingbird's wing. "You need to back off."

"Who the hell do you think you are?" the girl asked, the ugliness she possessed on the inside evident on the out.

"I… it's…" Adam tried to choke out.

"He said no. Get that through your thick skull, missy," Sheree said, her eyes fire, her glare ice.

"Listen, bitch. He's my boyfriend. This isn't any of your business, so just walk away," the girl told her, arms across her chest.

"It's…" Adam started again, but failed to finish, tears streaming down his red-hot cheeks.

The girl looked at him with disgust.

Jennifer continued being the casual observer.

The boy looked torn and confused.

Sheree continued to fume like a volcano.

"I don't care if he's your frickin' husband and you've been married for fifty goddamned years. He said no, and that means no," Sheree told the girl through gritted teeth, hands solid rocks ready for pummeling.

"He's a boy. Unless he's a faggot, I don't get why he won't fuck me!" the girl yelled, hands thrown in the air as the accusation settled.

"I'm not…" Adam started to say, but Sheree cut him off.

"You do realize rape goes both ways, right? Just because you're a girl doesn't give you a free pass to pressure a guy who isn't ready for sex into doing it," Sheree told the girl who just stared at her in disbelief that anyone would think that way.

"Who said anything about rape?" the girl asked, unable to comprehend the correlation.

Jennifer rolled her eyes and started walking towards Sheree in case things got ugly. Sheree punched the girl in the face, breaking her nose, which began flowing like a red waterfall down the front of her white shirt.

Too late.

"What the fuck?!" the girl cried, holding her head towards the ceiling, eyes catching a pencil stuck in one of the paper tiles, swallowing the metallic red stuff her body offered up with abandon.

So much red.

Sheree started shaking, her hand starting to bruise from the blow.

Adam was about to rush to the girl's aid, but Jennifer stopped him and said, "Leave her. She's not worth your while."

He looked frayed. Hurt. And then the disappointment that someone he cared about, someone he thought he might actually love, could do something like force him into a life-altering act he wasn't prepared for, sank in. He finally saw the girl for what she was: a predator.

"I'm done. We're done," Adam said, walking away. Sheree watched as Jennifer followed, but he shook his head no and whispered, "I really need to be alone right now."

POP!

Adam fell to the ground, a red puddle spilling out from his head like someone dropped a bowl of ambrosia with melting Jell-O chunks.

"Nooooo!" Jennifer screamed, face and shirt covered in back spatter.

"Oh God, what'd I do?" the girl asked, the Glock 26 still pointing to its own guilt.

Seeing that Jennifer was still in the trajectory of the girl's gun, Sheree turned around and used her body to shield her from any bullets hitting her friend as she ran in her direction.

Fear in Jennifer's eyes as she was frozen in place, covered in someone else's blood, staring at Sheree.

Round instead of almond slits.

Sheree running.

Running towards her.

Away from the shooter.

It all played out like a silent movie without the live orchestra.

Sheree was close enough to grab Jennifer and blanket her completely from danger…

POP!

Sheree collapsed into Jennifer's arms.

"No! Sheree, no!" Jennifer cried. "Oh gawd, nooooooo!"

"I'm fine," Sheree said, annoyed. "Just tripped over my shoelace." She stared at the offending strand and cursed it silently.

"I know you're okay, but that girl and Adam!" Jennifer bawled, her tears washing away the red from her face.

After turning around, Sheree saw what the girl had done. Her mouth was open like a sleeping mouth breather. The splatter on the ceiling and floor behind her, however, suggested that she wasn't sleeping. At least, not sleeping from a slumber she would ever wake up from. The pencil dropped into her lap; a #2 Dixon Ticonderoga. The best.

"Uuuhhnnnnnhhh," came a groan from Adam's direction.

"He's still alive!" Sheree shouted, but when she turned around, she found her sister hovering over his body, a teal light draping it.

"What are you doing?" Jennifer asked furiously.

"Trying to save him," Kayla said quietly, eyes closed as she concentrated. "He can't be dead. No. Not dead. Not Adam."

Sheree was perplexed as Kayla kept repeating "Not Adam" over and over again, watching as her sister was obviously losing strength as the force within her continued bathing the body in light.

"We have to stop her," Jennifer said, noticing how emaciated and sickly Kayla was making herself.

"I know," Sheree said, getting up off the floor and slowly walking towards her sister. "Kayla. I'm sorry."

"Not Adam," Kayla said again, eyes black and bloodshot, skin so pale it was suddenly translucent.

Putting a hand on Kayla's shoulder, Jennifer said, "You've done all you can. Please for the love of Buddha, and I can't believe that I of all people am saying this, but don't destroy yourself over something you can't control."

The teal light faded, flooding back into Kayla until it trickled in like a faint fog reversing; like sucking in cigarette smoke. She fell over onto Adam's body and began sobbing, banging the mismatched vinyl tiled floor with her hands. "Why did Eve do it?"

Eve. Of course that's her name, Sheree thought. "Some people are just crazy," she said as the new janitor walked around the corner with a mop bucket.

"I'm really getting tired of death following me everywhere," Kayla said stoically on the drive home after the bodies were documented and transported by their father for further analysis.

It was true. Sheree couldn't help but notice the formulaic pattern. Even if alternate hypotheses were entered into the equation, Kayla was still the common denominator. But random chance must also be considered as well. It was also true that school shootings were quite the fashion trend circa the year 2000, but could this really be considered such? Mr. Hollins would more-than-likely write MURDER-SUICIDE on their death certificates in the CAUSE box.

Gunshot wound to the head.

Crime of passion.

Crimes of passion are bullshit. "I killed him because I loved him, then killed myself because I couldn't live without him!" Just let that ridiculousness linger on your brain for a bit.

As for Kayla, Sheree also couldn't help but think back to the previous Christmas, back before she was corporeal, back when she was just a terrifying ghost-witch getting ready to kill her once and for all, and her claim that she was Purgatory. Now Kayla was in Purgatory as well as Purgatory for the souls she devoured and that live inside her until final departure, all aching to get out, eating away at her own soul.

"Me, too," Sheree finally said, squeezing Kayla's hand as it rested on her thigh and offering up the best, least painful, convoluted smile she could muster.

"I think I should lie to my mom if she asks how my day was," Jennifer said, filing her nails in the backseat.

Sheree had almost forgotten her friend was there, which made her realize she needed to remember to check her rearview mirror more often as their eyes met in the reflection. "I don't think we have that luxury, and you should probably shower to get rid of the blood in your hair," she said.

"Agreed," Jennifer said, nodding.

An irrational fire burned in Sheree as she spotted the headrest behind Jennifer starting to redden. "Even though Dad's not supposed to talk about work stuff, word travels fast via alternate routes."

"Lucky," Jennifer said, rolling her eyes as she dropped the emery board into her purse.

"Lucky?" Kayla asked, turning around. "What the hell?"

Jennifer looked almost as frightened as she did on the swing set last Christmas.

Frozen in fear.

Kayla's eyes burned with fury.

"I… uh, I only meant that I wish my parents talked to me about important stuff. All they really want to know is my grades, and how they will help me get into college, and have a successful career before I marry a rich man who is never home, and I'm forced to leave that dream job they wanted for me to raise the children he insists on having because that is what a good Asian wife is supposed to do, so that I can look back on my life when it is all over and tell myself that I wasted it on the dreams of my parents."

"Huh," Sheree said in response. "I see you've never reflected on this before."

Kayla laughed, snorted, cried, then farted. "Goddammit, I hate being pregnant!"

Chapter 9
Ouijas and Mediums

"That's it! I need answers. Time to break out the Ouija board," Brendon said, getting off the floor and heading toward the cabinet where the games were kept. The defeat in his voice was not unlike rooting for the home team when the opponent had a sizeable lead. And by sizeable lead, I mean our team has nothing. Nada. Nil. You know, like, c'mon, guys, just score once so we don't look like total pathetic losers.

"You seriously believe that is going to help?" Sheree asked, the quizzical expression on her face displaying her doubt like, uh, she doubted it would help?

"Don't knock Ouija. Board knows her shit," Kayla said, dead serious.

"Or it knows it *is* shit," Sheree said, rolling her eyes.

"Shush yo' mouth, girl. We doin' this," Kayla said.

"Courtney is affecting your vocab," Jennifer said, stating the obvious.

"Bitch be affectin' more than dat!" Kayla said with a perfect head snap.

"She be all like up in yo' snatch!" Brendon said also with a perfect head snap.

"Brendon!" Sheree and Kayla and Jennifer screamed in unison.

"What?" he asked, playing the innocent.

"You shouldn't say words like snatch," Sheree said.

"Yeah, it's not nice," Kayla said.

"And a little gross," Jennifer said, but really didn't have to since her face was all distorted into an unnatural state of being that could make a grown man cry. Except for her father. He would just look at her and ask how she ever expected to get A's and a husband with that face.

"So I shouldn't snatch the board? Maybe I should snatch Yahtzee instead? Snatch snatch snatch snatch snatch!" Brendon yelled gleefully as he pulled out every game he could snatch while their mother walked down the stairs.

"What in the snatch is going on down here?" Mrs. Hollins said before apologizing. "I meant to say hell! Sorry! Oh gawd, why are you saying that word? I thought you were gay which means you shouldn't be getting anywhere near a girl's snatch!"

Kayla and Sheree just stared, horrified at their mother. Jennifer looked like she wanted popcorn.

Brendon said, "Oh my gawd! That's what snatch means?" He started crying, then motioning like he was going to vomit, heaving up an invisible hairball. "Why does Courtney say it so…" He looked at Kayla and put two and two together and failed to reject the null hypothesis and finished with, "I got the Ouija board. Ready, Kayla?"

"Since when do we have a Ouija board?" Mrs. Hollins asked.

"Since Grandma Lowell got it for me for Christmas!" Brendon said, all smiles. "Hey, you don't think she knew about me, do you?"

"Yes. She knew about the witch thing, but as usual waited until after the fact to let me in on anything," Mrs. Hollins said with unabashed animosity.

"Why does your mom treat you like that?" Sheree asked without thinking, but it was too late to backtrack her words so she let the fishing line dangle.

Mom took the bait.

"Because I am not a witch and she is terribly disappointed in me," Mrs. Hollins said while Kayla said at the same time, "Because she is not a witch and Grandma doesn't know how to treat her."

Sadness filled the room like an old bassoon.

Mrs. Hollins started crying. "I thought she would love me and let me know about what was really going on if I looked after the house."

"What?" Sheree shrieked.

"Grandma loves you!" Brendon said.

"She just doesn't know what to do with you because you're different," Kayla said.

"Since when is being normal different?" she asked.

"Wait, Mom's got a point," Sheree said. "And what do you mean about the house?"

"I mean someone has to care for it so it doesn't destroy Ravenwood."

The words stayed in the air long after she spoke, like pot smoke.

"The… who-whole town?" Jennifer asked, suddenly shivering despite the pleasantly comfortable seventy-three degree indoor temperature brought to them by modern conveniences.

"Yes," Mrs. Hollins said, the tears coming to a close.

"Son of a bitch," Sheree said. "There goes my social life when I'm your age!"

Mrs. Hollins told the kids she was going to Amanda Walker's house to pick her up and take her to a bar so they could do their magic stuff without the non-magical mother in the house, and the bar so Chad and Nikki wouldn't be let in on the supernatural slash paranormal events about to take place as they wouldn't be displaced and tempted to take refuge at the Hollins house. Smart thinking, Beth Hollins. Too bad Amanda Walker already opened the wine.

After she left, Brendon, Jennifer, Sheree, and Kayla sat around the coffee table, each with fingertips on the planchette, hoping to find an answer. Jessica, however, was not willing to give it.

"Damn it, Jessica! Tell us what we want to know or no more blood!" Kayla scolded her stomach.

Jennifer's eyes darted towards Sheree. "Oh gawd, do I even want to know?"

"No," Sheree said quickly to the letter J, unable to look Jennifer in the eye when she did.

Brendon let go. "I don't know how much longer we should bother. She just keeps giving the same answer, and that answer isn't very helpful."

It was true. For half an hour they asked what Jessica wanted, and each time the board replied with DIE. They figured that much out, but every time they rephrased the question for specificity, DIE was the only response. Grandma Jessica didn't want to play forward; she was stuck on repeat.

Jennifer let go and said, "Well, if this isn't going to produce results, maybe we should focus on homework."

"Ehhhuhhn," Sheree and Kayla groaned.

"Why do you always revert back to homework?" Sheree asked.

"Why are you trying to ruin my life?" Kayla asked.

"Why is your gay ex-boyfriend dating a girl?" Brendon asked.

"What the hell?!" Jennifer cried, standing up and throwing her arms in the air. "Is this gang-up-on-Jennifer time?"

"Yes," the three Hollins siblings said.

"Fuck my life," Jennifer said nonchalantly before adding, "Sonofabitch. Angie says that."

"Angie?" Sheree asked.

"Kevin's best friend."

"Kevin?"

"From cheer."

"Cheer?"

Jennifer rolled her eyes. "And football."

"Oh!" Brendon cried. "The cute one from the dairy farm!"

"Oh! I know him! Yeah, he is cute," Sheree said.

"And gay," Brendon said.

"Just because he's cute, doesn't mean he's gay," Sheree told her brother, half sticking her tongue out at him.

"He's right. Kevin's gay," Jennifer said.

"Chad-gay or gay-gay?" Sheree asked, suddenly aware that Kayla had been silent during this entire conversation.

"Like super out and proud gay. His parents are like co-presidents of PFLAG," Jennifer said, looking at Kayla as well.

Kayla appeared to be in a trance.

"Brendon, can you put Kayla back in a bubble in case she's possessed or something?" Sheree asked, her eyes showing no fear, just the reality of her life.

Brendon chuckled. "She's not possessed, she's sleeping."

Deciding to test that theory, Sheree took her forefinger and pushed Kayla's shoulder. She toppled over and hit the floor like a Weeble, waking with a start as she flapped her wings and let loose her talons upon the world around her. Once she calmed down, she said, "The fetuses are not well pleased with you."

"The fetuses can kiss my ass. I have Algebra homework," Jennifer told Kayla.

"Ugh. Advanced Algebra is the bane of my existence!" Sheree said loudly, throwing her head back over her shoulders in a quite unnatural pose that made her look like someone snapped her neck.

Just then, the front door swung open and a vulgar voice asked, "You bitches playin' a game and you din't invite me? Oh *hell* no!"

It was Courtney. Her minions were behind her, and by minions, Chad, Nikki, and her brother Darryl.

"C'mon, Bren! Let's go to Wayne and Kwirk's!" Darryl said. He was a splitting image of his sister if she didn't have such a ginormous Afro.

"Okay! Come on Rex, Deschutes!" Brendon said, running next door with his friend and dogs.

Chad closed the door behind him. "Whatcha playin'?"

"The dumbest game in the world," Jennifer said coldly.

"Then why you playin' it?" Courtney asked, mimicking Chad's childish inquisitive tone. "Especially when we got other things to do, like plan a bee-day party an' figure out a way to convince Anna she ain't quittin' cheerleading next year."

"What?! Anna can't quit!" Jennifer screamed. "We need her!"

"Preachin' to the goddamned choir, gurrrl!" Courtney said, raising her hand up to Jesus.

Jennifer slapped it. "Oh my Buddha. What are we going to do without Anna? I am the worst friend ever, Sheree. It's your birthday and I totally forgot. Kill me now."

Sheree shrugged.

Kayla simply said, "Maybe we should call up the Lifetime Channel and ask if they have any ideas for a Seventeen and Pregnant birthday party."

Courtney laughed so hard she went silent.

While Courtney struggled to breathe, Sheree said, "It's not until Sunday. We've got plenty of time to ponder a lame ass birthday party."

"Speaking of lame ass," Chad said. "Our moms are at my house commiserating over how shitty we children are. Something about being mothers on Mother's day or something."

"Figures. I knew she'd never make it to the bar. How many bottles of wine have they gone through?" Sheree asked.

Chad sniff-laughed. "You mean boxes," he informed her. "Mom's a tightwad in the financial department."

Sheree laughed harder than she expected to as her father walked through the front door wearing a tie and dress shirt and slacks and not the usual scrubs. Nobody must have died today… yet. Or he had to meet with the families of the recently deceased. Or he was busy being interviewed. Or all of the above. She couldn't help but see the annoyed look on his face until he saw Chad and lit up like the Fourth of July.

"Hi, Chad!" Mr. Hollins said. "My wife at your house?"

Chad smiled. "Yeah. Her and Mom are busy getting their drink on."

"I should join them. Let you kids have the house to yourselves." His smile was electric until he saw the Ouija board and it disappeared into the abyss. He quickly grabbed the Ouija board, boxed it up, put it away, and said, "If you're going to play a game, play a better one than that piece of shit." His eyes burned into his daughters.

"Yes, Daddy Dearest," Kayla said mockingly, causing Courtney to go into hysterics like a Baptist on Pentecost.

"I swear to God, young lady, if you weren't pregnant…" Mr. Hollins said.

"What? You'd beat me?" Kayla asked, a smug smile on her face.

"What?! No! I'd get you a shot of tequila! The good stuff! That was a pretty amazing comeback for… you!" Mr. Hollins said, catching himself from adding: "being dead for so long." Good catch, Frank.

No wonder all the kids wanted him to be their dad.

Or fuck him.

Or both.

Ew.

"What do I have to do to get that shot?" Chad asked, obviously joking.

Mr. Hollins looked dead serious. "Be twenty-one. I'm changing and going over to your house," he said, before running up the stairs.

"Damn. Just when I thought your dad liked me," Chad said, wrinkling his mouth into a most unsexy formation.

Sheree realized her mouth was doing the same thing, so she relaxed it. "Whatever. My dad loves you for some reason or another."

Should I tell her why? No. Not now, Kayla thought, fake smile plastered while the babies battled in her belly.

Mr. Hollins ran down the stairs in a tight fitting T-shirt and polyester shorts that showed off the fact that he wasn't wearing underwear. The form of his penis beneath left nothing to the imagination as it wobbled to and fro hypnotically, causing Nikki to spontaneously collapse into the nearest chair and Jennifer to swoon. "I'll be back later. Don't burn down the house."

"Why's yo' daddy so hot?" Courtney asked after Mr. Hollins left. "I mean, I know I be all lesbian an' shit, but, daaayyyummmmmmmn! He's such a DILF!"

"Court, I think we should break up," Kayla said, no hint of sarcasm.

Nikki and Jennifer were still mentally orgasming.

"Lemon Meringue, you know I only got eyes fo' you!" Courtney told her, snuggling beside her on the floor and placing a hand over her obviously pregnant stomach. "Now tell me what you want yo' Chocolate Mousse to getchoo fo' yo' bee-day?"

Kayla knew that lemon and chocolate were not complimentary, but she was determined to make it work for as long as she could. She smiled. "I'll tell you what I want, what I really really want!"

Without missing a Spice Girl beat, Courtney sang, "So tell me what you want, what you really really want!"

"I wanna, I wanna, I wanna, I wanna, I wanna hotdog real bad!" Kayla finished. "Gawd, these babies are going to be the death of me!"

"That sounds great!" Chad said, heading towards the kitchen where he was unable to see Jennifer mouth 'figures' as she rolled her eyes. "Do you have any in the fridge?" The phone rang next to his ear, causing him to jump in place and scream in a high pitch voice, "Jesus Christ!"

"Not Jesus, just the phone," Sheree said, getting up to answer it. "Uh, okay. Thanks. That was Dad. He ordered us pizza for dinner."

"Is it a twelve-inch sausage?" Jennifer asked, trying desperately to contain the laughter that was clawing its way out.

"I hate you," Sheree said as she slammed the phone onto the charging base.

"So, hotdog appetizers?" Chad asked, putting his hearing aid back into his ear after rubbing the sound away.

"Jennifer says. You need to talk. To the dead," Anna said after cheer practice the next day, her voice punctuated between her excited smiles.

"Uh, yeah," Sheree said. "Ouija was a bust."

"Ouija boards. Only work when the person. On the other side. Wants to talk. Most don't," Anna said, small nose trying to crinkle as her upward slanted eyes twinkled.

"Really? How do you know?" Sheree asked, head tilting to the right like a dog, face still questioning.

Anna rolled her eyes and looked annoyed as her tongue fell out of her mouth. "I have Down Syndrome, bitch. I'm not stupid."

Sheree's eyes widened and her mouth turned into an O. "What? No! I never…"

"I'm just giving you shit," Anna said. She giggled. "I'm a medium. I talk to the dead. Mr. Riley says hello."

"Well that's creepy," Sheree said, adding, "Mr. Riley, not you being a medium."

She giggled again. "He says to tell. Kayla that it wasn't. Her fault. He's old. It was his time."

"Well, that's reassuring."

"It is."

"Don't quit the team."

"I'm weighing my options. Not really sure. If cheer will work. With my schedule next year. I'll be a senior. And have a lot. On my plate." Her smile was radiant and consistent as it kept reappearing during each pause.

"Courtney's pretty sure the team won't work without you."

"She's wrong. With me off. You're in."

"You think?"

"Yes!" Anna practically floated like she was filled with helium.

"Wait, no, I'm supposed to convince you to stay."

"And I am supposed. To do what's best. For me!"

"I tried."

"You failed."

"I fail at life."

"When do you want. To talk to the dead?"

"ASAP."

"I need a witch. In case things get bad. Jennifer said she's. Pretty powerful."

"I've got two."

"I'll drive," Anna said, walking away.

"I'm not leaving my car," Sheree told her.

"I'll follow."

"Okay."

Sheree prayed that Brendon and Kayla were home and her parents were not. Her prayers were not answered as she parked in the street in front of the house and saw both cars in the driveway. Anna parked behind her.

"Do your parents know?" Anna asked as she walked up to Sheree.

Sheree was hesitant. "Yes, but they don't know about this plan to talk to Jessica."

Anna's smile suddenly faded as the blood drained from her face. "Jessica isn't happy. That I'm here."

"Jessica isn't happy about a great many things," Sheree said. "It isn't too late to back out of this."

"No. I want to help. Just don't tell Courtney. What I am. Okay?"

"Why?"

"Because. Then I'd be forced. To tell her who killed. Kylie and Monique."

Kylie? Monique? Oh shit! The cheerleaders Kayla killed in January! "I agree. I wouldn't want her to find out that way. Kayla should be the one to tell her."

"Yes. That is one reason I want. To quit the team. I blabber."

Sheree chuckled, and then got serious. "How did Jennifer know that you are a medium, then?"

"She was talking quietly. To herself while warming up. And I overheard."

"What?! She was talking about our family problems openly?!"

"Whispering. Barely. Away from everyone. I snuck up on her. I think she pooped a little." Sheree didn't think Anna's smile could get any bigger, but now she was practically the Cheshire Cat.

"I guess I can forgive her. She likes to work out everything in a logical fashion, and I guess part of that has to happen out loud." Sheree started walking towards the front door, but Anna stayed in place. "Are you coming?"

Anna's smile was gone again, pale as death. "Get Kayla. Jessica doesn't want me. To come in."

Sheree went to the front door to open it, but it wouldn't budge. The handle turned, but she couldn't get it to give way as she pushed, like there was something blocking the other end. She could hear voices inside, so she banged on the door.

Nothing.

She banged again, harder.

Nothing.

She started screaming so loud that the neighbors across the street peeked out their front windows from behind the drapes to witness the commotion, but it was pointless. The house didn't want her in, and the people inside didn't know she was on the outside.

Then a hand touched her shoulder.

Cold.

Cold as death.

"Jesus!" Sheree shrieked as she turned around, trying to keep her heart in her chest.

"Sorry, just your brother, but I suppose I could understand the confusion," Brendon said, letting his hand fall to his side. "Forget your key?"

"No. Can't get in," Sheree told him.

He opened the door with ease. "You need to start working out. Being off cheer is affecting your muscle tone," he teased, walking into the house. "C'mon, Anna. Jessica can't keep you out now."

Anna smiled. "You didn't tell me. Your brother's the other witch!" She flew inside. "That's so cool!"

Yeah. Cool. Sheree put on her fake smile. "Now let's figure out what that bitch wants."

"I WANT YOU ALL DEAD!!!"

"No shit, Sherlock! Tell us something we don't know," Sheree said to Anna, who at the moment wasn't really Anna, but her long dead multi-great grandmother, Jessica.

Foamy bubbles around the mouth and dilated pupils overtaking the whites of her eyes made the sweet face of Anna look like a rabid dog as she shot back, "Die! Die!! DIE!!!"

If Kayla and Brendon weren't keeping her trapped in a bubble, Sheree knew that she'd already be dead. Thanks, magic. Thagic.

"Jessica, there has to be a reason for your anger!" Mrs. Hollins shouted, no longer willing to be a bystander.

Anna's face turned to her direction, and sniffed. "You most of all should die. Disgrace to our entire family line. You are nothing but an anomaly that would have been eradicated had I lived to make sure my daughter married into a proper family."

Mrs. Hollins tried to hide the hurt, but it slithered through to the surface.

Anna/Jessica then looked at Brendon, and her face fell into utter revulsion. "And you. Dirty, disgusting deviant. You shouldn't even exist."

Brendon didn't falter, but instead smiled and said, "But I do exist, and will go on existing long after we destroy you forever."

Sheree couldn't help but be proud as she heard her brother say those words. He had become such a brave young man in such a short time. A glance at her father showed that he was thinking the same thing while he held her mother who had become a wet blanket.

Laughter suddenly sprang out in all directions, causing the windows to shake, pictures to shudder, and the chandelier in the dining room to shiver in horror. Kayla fell to the ground as her body gyrated and her stomach looked like it was about to burst. It was *Alien* all over again.

"You say that now, little deviant. But not for long! Once I am born, the world will have no time to prepare for my rightful place as its ruler!"

Brendon suddenly looked like he was struggling. Sheree realized why. He was holding Jessica by himself now while Kayla struggled to regain control of her body. She was about to rush to her side, but her mother beat her to the punch. Picking Kayla up, she held her hand, which gave Kayla enough strength to regain her end of the bubble bargain.

Kayla glanced at Brendon.

Brendon glanced back at Kayla.

Suddenly a blinding flash of light shattered the room.

Anna shook her head and said, "Jessica is a. Crazy ass bitch."

"You've got that right," Sheree said.

Then Anna looked directly into Kayla's face and said, "And I'm quitting. The cheerleading. Squad."

"What? Why?" Sheree asked, trying to understand the seemingly rash decision to end her cheer career after being possessed by the house's former owner.

"Because I can see. How good Kayla is now. She's not the same. Person who killed. My teammates," Anna said. "And because Courtney. Is going to need her."

Her eyes were drowning in sadness.

"What do you mean?" Kayla asked.

"I mean that I hate. That the dead talk to me. And I can't tell the living. What they say most of the time," she said before walking out the door, down the driveway, getting into her car, and driving off.

Chapter 10
Mean Girls

A seemingly new girl rolled into the main entrance of Ravenwood High Thursday morning and immediately caught Courtney's attention. Sheree's eyes followed her as she approached the girl in a wheelchair. She watched as the girl yelled, "Get away from me, freak! I don't want to be seen around a dyke, especially a black dyke!" She almost felt sorry for her as the girl in a wheelchair who wasn't new at all told her, "Fuck off!" as she rolled down the hall, turned, and was quickly out of sight. Sheree knew she had to comfort Courtney when her face turned into a sprinkler system as she fell to the ground.

"I don't understand?" Courtney asked the universe. "I just wanted to be a friend." Her usual brand of Ebonics was missing.

"Not everyone wants a friend," Sheree said, kneeling and rubbing Courtney's back and noticing a lack of a bra strap, which made her instantly jealous that those large breasts were naturally that perky.

"But why'd she gotta be so mean? Why she gotta hate?"

"Some people are just filled with the stuff."

"But I thought…"

"She's not Sky. Nobody will ever be like Sky."

"I know. I just… I just…"

"I miss her, too."

"Depression is some fucked up shit, yo."

"Fo' sho' MoFo."

"And that skanky ass ho who just dissed me like she all dat needs to pull the stick outta her ass 'fore someone drops a house on her."

"I hate her fucking guts," a voice said from behind them, causing a panic.

"Seriously, Anna! You can't be all sneakin' up on people!" Courtney told her fellow cheerleader and Fashion Committee member.

"Sorry Courtney. I hate her. She's so mean. All the time," Anna said.

"Maybe she's mean because she's in a wheelchair now," Sheree said, still not recognizing the girl in question.

"No. I don't think so," Anna said. "Angie's just a. Fucking bitch."

"That was Angie? I be all tryin' to make friends with Angie? Oh hell no! Why she got wheels now? What'd she do to her hair? Why her face be all like that?" Courtney asked rapid-fire.

Sheree was confused. "Huh?" she somehow muttered involuntarily.

Anna was not. "Bitch tried jumping. Off her roof into the pool. And panicked. After she started. And landed on her feet. On the patio. And broke both her ankles."

"But her hair?" Courtney asked again, noticing it was much shorter than it used to be, and not in a good way.

"Kevin said her friend. Cut it off as a joke. While she was passed out. With broken ankles. Another reason not. To drink, right?" Anna said, giggling afterwards with a mischievous smile on her round face.

"That's disturbing. I'd buy better friends," Sheree said, envisioning the scene and cringing as her ankles swelled up with white-hot pain every time that part replayed. Which it did. Over and over and over. For days.

"True. But still. It's Angie. Bitch had it comin'."

Anna kept giggling.

"Girl, you know you ain't Kevin's type, right?" Courtney asked, her head wiggling as she stuck out her face as far as it could go towards Anna.

Sheree was about to be offended and say something but Anna beat her to it.

"I know I don't have a dick. But he's still cute!" More giggles.

Sheree just shook her head. Then her face scrunched up in a most unsexy way. "Wait, that's Kevin's Angie?"

"They're best friends," both Courtney and Anna said in unison with a not-so-subtle-duh-you-dumb-ass-white-girl connotation.

"Wait wait wait, what?! So Angie's best friend is gay and she doesn't want to be seen around you because you're gay?" Sheree asked in hopes of clarifying the absurdity.

"Angie's just a stuck up bitch whose shit's about to get real, yo," Courtney said, crossing her arms over her braless perky-yet-quite-ample breasts as if to unconsciously make Sheree jealous at their defiance of gravity.

"Mmm hmm," Anna said, mimicking Courtney's stance.

"Oh my gawd!" they heard from down the hall. "I can*not* be seen with you until that grows back!" Laughter echoed loudly, increasing in volume, which could only mean that the person it was emanating from was walking towards them. "Court! Please tell me you saw how freaking awful Angie looks?"

It was Kevin, junior varsity football quarterback and male cheerleader the rest of the school year. Sheree remembered that his parents owned and operated a local dairy farm, and couldn't help but notice milk did his body good. Neither could Anna, whom he waved to with a slight wink and caused her to giggle again, blushing profusely.

"Mmm hmm. Bitch be dissin' me an' my black dykeness like she got moral authority or some shit like dat," Courtney said with her head snapping from left to right and back to the left before it stopped to reveal her resting bitch face.

"I gotta pee!" Anna squealed as she ran towards the girl's bathroom being followed by giggles bouncing off the mismatched vinyl-tiled floors.

Sheree watched and wondered if she really had to urinate or if she had to take care of something else. That something else was masturbate in case you didn't catch that, something Sheree was contemplating as well since she couldn't shake the image of Kevin making out with his boyfriend shirtless and sweaty from a long, hot day on the farm. With his cowboy hat still on. And a tall glass of milk in one hand. Damn.

"Have you seen Harry Wood?" Kevin asked.

Oh, Jesus! Sheree squealed on the inside, until her brain remembered Harry Wood was a person and not just a metaphor.

"Ain't seen him yet," Courtney said. "Was hopin' we could go over a couple routines real quick before tonight's game."

"Me too. Gawd, I hope my dick cooperates. Boys in soccer kit. Drool," Kevin said, melting like butter.

"Oh, Sweet Lawd Geeeezus! What'm I gonna do wit' you?" Courtney asked before busting out, "Ha HA!" so loud, it knocked over a nearby trophy locked up in a case. Down the hall. And to the left.

Now all Sheree could think about was a locker room scene with the entire soccer team and Kevin having an orgy. "I gotta pee!"

"This isn't anywhere near as sexy as my brain thought it would be," Sheree said to Brendon as they sat in the bleachers and watched the soccer boys kick the black-and-white ball around the field.

"What?! This is so sexy!" Brendon yelled.

"Like, really sexy!" Kwirk yelled, revealing his jacked-up-to-Jesus bangs as he bent forward to give her wild eyes.

"I'm with you, Sheree," Wayne said, also revealing his jacked-up-to-Jesus bangs as he bent forward even more.

"I love soccer!" Darryl squealed. "It's my fave-fave-fave-fave-favorite!"

"Ugh. How did I get stuck with a bunch of ten-year-olds on a Friday night?" Sheree asked the air.

Brendon shrugged. "Just lucky, I guess."

Ravenwood's cheer team was the only one because, well, soccer is a nonstop sport. Okay, so mostly nonstop. There is a halftime. Mandy and Courtney insisted on having at least a few quick routines before the game and in case of an injury while they carried the broken player off the field. At the moment, they looked like statues waiting to crumble. Suddenly they scrambled into position as Chancellor called a rare timeout.

"Kick it!
Kick it!
Kick it down the green!
Kick it!
Kick it!
Kick it like you're mean!
Kick it!

Kick it!

Kick it in the goal!

Kick it!

Kick it!

Kick it for us all!"

Then the girls curled up into balls, and the boys kicked them in every direction. Not really kicked them, because that would be bad. The girls tumbled around, somehow all rolling up to the same place before springing like shooting stars and shouting, "Go Crows!"

Sheree stared at Kevin to see if he had a boner as the soccer players ran back onto the field. The disappointment on her face did not go unnoticed. Anna caught her glance and flashed her a caught-you-in-the-act look and grimace that morphed into a full on smile the size of Texas. "Oh my gawd," Sheree said as she covered her reddening face.

"Oh my gawd is right! Kevin is dreamy! I want to pet his Moobs," Brendon said before he melted into a puddle of goo.

"Me too!" Kwirk said before he melted into a puddle of goo.

"Everyone wants to pet Moobs!" Wayne said.

"Yeah!" Darryl said.

Sheree just stared, horrified at the fourth graders's conversation unfolding before her. "What? You can't just say things like that out loud, people!"

"Why not?" Brendon asked, perplexed as usual.

"Because moobs are private," Sheree said.

"What? Are those like boobs?" Brendon asked.

"Gross!" Kwirk and Darryl shouted in unison.

"Moobs is Kevin's calf at the dairy. He's way adorable," Wayne told Sheree.

"Yeah, curds and whey adorable!" Brendon said, squealing.

"How was the game?" Mr. Hollins asked when Sheree and Brendon walked through the front door, finger on the mute button about to depress, eyes looking like he was being tortured from lack of volume on the program he was watching about some war that they were too young to understand the importance of.

"We tied," Sheree said blandly while Brendon shouted at the same time, "Soccer boys are so cute!"

Mr. Hollins smiled uncomfortably.

"I'm sure our team would've preferred a win for the last game of the season, but alas, it was not meant to be," Sheree said.

"I want to be in soccer this fall, Dad!" Brendon said gleefully as he bounced into the seat next to his father in the den.

Mr. Hollins smiled uncomfortably.

"I mean, we probably would have won if Jeff was still alive, but Kayla had to go and kill him to piss me off, so, yeah," Sheree said.

"Hey!" Kayla said from behind them, peaking her head off the living room sofa. "I'm right here!"

Mr. Hollins smiled uncomfortably.

"I know," Sheree said.

Machinegun fire filled the house.

Mr. Hollins smiled uncomfortably. "Sorry guys, but I had to unmute the TV."

Sheree rolled her eyes and walked into the kitchen. Kayla followed, hugging her from behind. Both of them jumped out of their skin when they caught sight of another person in the kitchen with them.

"Jesus, Mom!" Sheree screamed.

"How long have you been in here?" Kayla asked, holding her heart to steady it. The babies were also not amused.

Mrs. Hollins swallowed the last gulp of wine in her glass, set it down, and said, "About half an hour. Came in for a glass."

The empty bottle on the counter let them know that glass turned to four.

"Oh great. Mother is becoming an alcoholic," Kayla said, crossing her arms.

"Becoming? Where have you been for the last dozen or so years?" Sheree asked.

"Dead."

"Oh, that's right."

"Don't remind me."

"You were so transparent then."

"I know, but now I have feelings."

"Feelings are stupid."

"Feelings *are* stupid."

Mrs. Hollins's eyes started welling up, about to burst.

"Shhh," Sheree said, pressing her fingers to her mother's lips and taking her off guard. Then she casually lifted her fingers up, ran them through her mom's hair, and tossed her bangs to one side. "There, that's better."

"Oh my gawd, Mom! You look hot!" Kayla said, wide-eyed and slack-jawed.

This revelation pricked Mr. Hollins ears and he had to get up to investigate despite what he might miss on the all-important boob tube. "Honey, you need to go take a look in the mirror."

"Really? Jesus, Sheree, what'd you do?" she asked as she walked out of the kitchen and into the downstairs bathroom beneath the stairs, not even caring about breaking Catholic rules and regulations about name usage. "Oh my gawd! I'm young!"

"What made you think to do that?" Mr. Hollins asked, all smiles.

"It came to me in a vision," Sheree told him, giving Kayla a wink.

"When do you think you'll be old enough for us to have sex?" Sheree asked Jeff bluntly.

"I haven't even been born yet, so you're just going to have to be patient," he told her.

"Damn. I hope you grow at hyper speed."

"Me, too."

"I mean, I want you to stop where you left off, otherwise that'd be an awful waste of a life."

"I agree."

"I mean, it would be amazing if you could just grow like Spock on the Genesis planet but stop at the age he pon farrs Saavik version 2.0."

"You only wish I looked like him."

"Puhleeze. You know I prefer you to be like you."

"I know. We're not alone anymore."

"I know."

"The itsy bitsy spider went up the water spout…"

The eye roll emanating from Sheree's head could be heard for miles as she opened them from her awkwardly peaceful slumber.

"Down came the rain and washed the spider out…"

Sheree decided to conduct the tune with her index fingers, hoping her great-great-great-grandmother got the hint that she was an annoyance to her very existence. Towards each other. Away from each other. Towards. Away. Towards. Away.

"Up rose a plan to kill the aberrations…"

Sheree's fingers froze.

Her eyes widened.

Her breath stopped.

"Then the itsy bitsy spider will rule once again!"

Hideous laughter escaped the air vent as Kayla walked in. "You know she's lying," she lied.

"I know," Sheree lied.

Chapter 11
Birthday Weekend

Sheree relished the return of Ragu. After her mother's failed attempts at homemade spaghetti sauce, she was ecstatic the boring was back. No more salting to the point of stomach-churning sickness. No more extra glasses of milk to wash down the film left behind that clung to the roof of her mouth like Saran Wrap. No more lying to her mother. Kayla's return was already proving to be a positive influence, at least where dinner was concerned. Of course, Kayla wasn't afraid to tell her mother exactly how she felt when that first bite of homemade pasty goo hit her tongue and made an immediate reappearance onto the table with a horrified, "Blehck! Are you trying to kill me? Again?"

That was weeks ago, and now it seemed that, in spite of spaghetti being one of Sheree's least preferred meals, her mother insisted, despite all efforts to the contrary, that it was indeed her favorite, and therefore would make an appearance during the grand spectacle that was hers and Kayla's birthday weekend. Joy. At least she finally got the hint about the mushrooms.

Mushrooms.

Sheree had a sudden curiosity to make sure that the shriveled mushroom that had found a place beneath the dining room table, lurking in the shadows for months like something Sylvia Plath might write, was finally disposed of. She felt around with her feet until a marble-size object caught her bare toes. She looked at Rex and Deschutes who both cowered as they skedaddled into the living room behind the sofa. Her face turned green. She tried to cover up her discovery by putting her napkin over her face to faux-vomit into, but it was no use. She'd have to cover it up with words.

"I heard Chad say that he was coming to our birthday party. Are you sure that is such a great idea considering how sensitive Jennifer can sometimes be to the subject of ex-boyfriends?" Sheree asked. *That was the lamest cover-up you've ever conjured. You're losing your touch, bitch.*

"But we already invited him. It'd be rude to uninvite him now," Mr. Hollins said before slurping a forkful of saucy noodles.

"But…" Sheree started, but her mother interrupted.

"You wouldn't want to be a Rude Regina, would you?" Mrs. Hollins asked, her glass of red wine like a second head.

"But…" Sheree started, but her brother interrupted.

"You shouldn't be such a Negative Nancy," Brendon said with a mouthful of cheesy garlic bread.

"But…" Sheree started, but her sister interrupted.

"Why you gotta be a Debbie Downer?" Kayla said before downing the rest of her milk.

"I'm failing at life. Check please," Sheree said, letting the napkin drop onto her plate, smothering the remainder of her dinner.

"Cheer up, Charlie," Mr. Hollins sang.

A smile crept onto her face. *Damn you, Dad.* "Fine. Chad can come. I just hope Jennifer isn't on her period, because otherwise I won't be held responsible for the shit show."

There was a knock at the door before it opened to reveal Jennifer. "I need chocolate."

The Hollins family stared at her from the dining room.

"We have chocolate cream pie for dessert, and Dad invited Chad Sunday," Sheree said.

"Awesome. About both. Buddha, being a woman sucks. Any way Nikki can be evicted from the celebrational activities? I need to get Chad back," Jennifer said, closing the door behind her with her foot and walking towards the table.

"Uh…" Mrs. Hollins started, but finished with a long gulp of merlot instead.

"Mind if I dish up? Mom's a raging bitch right now and forgot to feed me," Jennifer said as she grabbed a plate from the cupboard, fork from the drawer, and sat down next to Mrs. Hollins across from Kayla.

"Help yourself," Mr. Hollins said, scooting the spaghetti platter towards her.

"Thanks," Jennifer said, piling her plate high before dumping the salad on top. She took a huge bite and said before swallowing,

"I don't understand why parenting is such an inconvenience to my mom and dad."

Sheree and Kayla just stared. Mrs. Hollins offered a consolation smile. Mr. Hollins was about to say something but Brendon beat him to the punch. "Some people just aren't meant to be parents. I'm sorry, Jen."

She smiled. "Thanks, Bren."

"So…" Sheree said, starting to eat again after removing the red-stained napkin off her plate. "We have to hook you back up with Chad again?"

"If it's not too much of a hassle," Jennifer said, the insides of her mouth filled with lettuce and noodles bearing the remains of slain tomatoes and cows.

"It's not that it's too much of a hassle, I just don't see the point. Boy's gay," Kayla said bluntly.

"But that mouth! Ugh! I miss that heavenly mouth!" Jennifer cried, causing Mr. Hollins to cringe and Mrs. Hollins to snicker as she held his hand, squeezing it tight. "Can you give me a ride home, Sheree? I think the atmo is threatening rain."

"Leaving without chocolate?" Sheree joked.

"Leaving because I leaked a little. Like I said, being a woman sucks. I hate periods. Have a pad I can borrow?" Jennifer asked, dropping her fork onto the now empty plate, the clatter echoing throughout the house.

"Oh gawd," Mr. Hollins said, face turning green.

"Uh, not to borrow, but to have. I don't want that thing back when you've finished bleeding all over it," Sheree told her friend as she got up and grabbed one from her purse sitting on a chair in the living room while giving the dogs the stink eye, throwing it in her direction, smacking her in the face.

"This family is disgusting," Brendon said with a mouthful of spaghetti, shaking his head as the noodles wagged like tentacles.

Jennifer smiled. "This family is perfect."

"Why does Jessica want blood?" Sheree asked, staring at the rounding belly of her sister Saturday afternoon, half expecting the fetus to answer.

"She just does. Can't explain it." Kayla took another swig from her jar of O-positive.

"She wasn't a vampire, was she?"

"A vampire witch! Preposterous!"

"Oh really, that's preposterous?"

"Yes."

"Need I remind you, dear sister, that only a couple months ago you were a ghost witch. Who's to say one can't be a vampire witch?"

"I'm not saying it's not possible, I'm just… Oh, gawd…"

"What?"

Kayla stayed silent for what felt like eternity, or at least the span of time it takes to microwave a Hot Pocket.

"Sheree, I'm scared."

"Why? Besides the obvious part about giving birth to your own great-great-great-grandmother and my dead boyfriend."

"What if… What if I'm not?"

"Not what?"

"Carrying Jessica and Jeff."

"What do you mean?" Sheree's voice was barely above a whisper.

"What if this feeling I have inside is all another illusion." Kayla's face went green.

Silence.

"Preposterous!" Sheree said, laughing heartily.

"Song's End was a vampire witch."

"Don't fuck with me."

"I'm not. I mean, I don't know for sure, but it would explain a lot about him."

"Please explain before my head explodes."

"Witches burn."

"Uh huh."

"Vampires burn."

"Uh huh."

"And legend has it that Chief Ravenwood burned Song's End which caused him to become immortal."

"I don't get it."

"If he was just a vampire, he should have died. If he was just a witch, he would have died. But what if the combination created an anomaly in the supernatural realm?"

"And inadvertently caused the birth of a race of atomic supermen who desire nothing more than to conquer the world?" Sheree's smile was eerily reminiscent of a mad scientist.

"You've watched too many B-movies."

"I love B-movies. Don't judge."

"Fine. I'll only judge you in secret."

"So how does this relate back to you now thinking my dead boyfriend won't be passing through your vagina?"

Kayla spit out the blood she'd just taken a drink of, splattering it all over Sheree's face, and watched in horror as it slid down her nose, cheeks, and chin. "Sorry!"

Sheree's painted face looked like Christmas before she projectile vomited onto Kayla's, and watched in slow motion as her partially digested ham sandwich masked the anger she knew her sister's face held.

Brendon, Mr., and Mrs. Hollins walked in the front door to find the twins covered in body fluids and excrement.

"Oh, gawd! I'm going to my room to claw my eyes out!" Brendon cried as he ran up the stairs, slamming the door to his bedroom when he got there.

"Frank, I'm done. Good luck," Mrs. Hollins said, walking back outside and heading towards the Walkers.

"Beth, I think I should go to work in case I missed a body, or just wait until one shows up," Mr. Hollins said as she kept walking, not even acknowledging his comment. He got into the station wagon and drove off.

"Great. We've torn this family apart." Sheree was afraid to look at how bad her face was.

"Only took seventeen years." Kayla's eyes remained firmly shut.

"Can you use your witchy-poo magic and clean this shit off?"

With a wave of her hand, Kayla made the blood disappear from Sheree's face, got up, and said, "I'm going to wash this off the traditional way. I don't want to get magic cancer."

"What?!" Sheree screamed, standing up, eyes wild. "You mean magic can give me cancer?"

"No, I just wanted to get another rise out of you," Kayla said, revealing a smile as the vomit disappeared with another wave.

The next morning, Sheree awoke to find herself looking at a mirror, a reflection of her golden sleep-tossed hair, no makeup face, shimmering aquamarine eyes. It was her, only harsher. Different. Like a dream… or nightmare.

"Don't hate me," the reflection said.

It was Kayla, staring at her with a sad smile. This was no nightmare. Then again…

"I don't hate you, but you are seriously creeping me out now," Sheree said, no hint of fear in her calm voice as she kept her head firmly glued to the pillow.

Kayla stared.

Sheree stared back.

Kayla kept staring.

Goosebumps skipped all over Sheree's body as she waited for a reason, a response as to why her sister was in her bed in the middle of the night like a rapist. Kayla of all people knew Sheree's shattered emotions in that particular realm. Hell, she'd been coconspirator in the revenge plan against the four guys who violated her body the previous year, taking turns at her innocent weakness. But that was last year, and if anything held true, it was that Kayla made her stronger. Kayla made her callused. Kayla made her practically bulletproof.

"I've been lying to you," Kayla told Sheree bluntly as her face watered like a faucet left on while the family vacationed during Christmas to prevent the pipes from freezing over and bursting and flooding the whole damn house.

"I've been wondering how long it would take you to tell me why I physically can't get mad at you since you've been back," Sheree said just as bluntly, face dry as a desert complete with cactuses.

"You… you knew?" Kayla asked, her frame suddenly small and vulnerable.

"Yes. I think. I guess I decided to just give you a chance because Brendon believed in you so fully," Sheree confessed, surprised at how easily she accepted the lies as necessary.

"Brendon's gullibility is going to be the death of him," Kayla said, turning the faucet off.

The humidity between them was like what Sheree imagined daily life in Florida to be: STIFLING.

"Between that and his utter determination to procure a boyfriend, he's doomed," Sheree said, her face softening.

One smile spurred the other.

"He's going to kill me for this, but I am giving you back your free will to hate me if you want," Kayla said, laying her hand on Sheree's cheek as if it was the final time she would ever be able to.

"That act alone tells me that I can trust you implicitly. Like when we were little and you protected me from Jeremy."

"You remember that?"

"I remember he wanted me to touch him, but you gave him one look and he was never seen again."

"I didn't kill him if that's what you're insinuating. We were only four for Christ's sake!"

Sheree laughed. "That's not what I meant. I meant that you used some sort of magic and made him go away."

Kayla laughed. "I made his dick burn so bad for a week that he had serious thoughts of cutting it off."

"You really don't like penises, do you?" Sheree asked as images of what the news reports said about the four guys who were found mutilated and dead over Easter in West Seattle flashed before her; the four guys who gang raped her; the four teenage boys who would never become men.

"I guess that explains the lesbian thing." Kayla shrugged, then pulled off the cloak that had been hiding Sheree's ability to feel any bad emotion towards the recently undeceased sister, and tossed it into the abyss.

Suddenly Sheree felt like she could breathe again, like that invisible plug was a thousand-pound bull sitting on her brain. You know, like when Benadryl wears off.

"Happy birthday, Sister."

"Happy birthday, Sister."

"Good. Gooooood! Let the hate flow through you," a gravelly voice said, shocking them both.

"Jessica?" Sheree asked quietly, too frightened to turn around and investigate.

"No, it's someone even worse," Kayla said.

"Hey!" Brendon shouted in faux offendedness, Rex and Deschutes on either side of him like Zuul and Vinz Clortho to his Gozer.

"I'm just kidding, Brendon," Kayla said, her half-smile not convincing.

"You're not mad at me, are you?" Brendon asked Sheree, wincing, preparing himself for a certain purple pillow Sheree had taken a partiality to pummeling him with.

Sheree turned to Kayla and said, "He tasks me. He tasks me, and I shall have him. I'll chase him round the Moons of Nibia and round the Antares Maelstrom and round Perdition's flames before I give him up!" then flew off the bed and chased him down the stairs laughing maniacally before she screamed in the octave of a banshee or when Mariah Carey hits that high E note for no reason whatsoever, "Jesus!" before she gathered herself together and finished with, "What the hell are you doing here?"

A red balloon floated to the ceiling as the person in question let her grip loosen.

"Fool! It's yo' bee-day! I ain't leavin' that partay to chance! Ha HA!" Courtney said with such force it shook the room, her hair somehow stayed put no matter where her face went. Physics be damned.

"Darling, the place looks fabulous!" Brendon feigned as he and Courtney kissed each other's cheeks like old British friends.

Rex and Deschutes were not as fancy with their kisses.

Standing behind Sheree, all Kayla could do was smile as the girl she liked saw her sans makeup, hair scattered from sleeplessness, and looking quite pregnant in an old T-shirt that barely covered her ass, who smiled back at her while she rubbed dog ears.

"Lemon Meringue, get over here and give yo' Chocolate Mousse a kiss," Courtney demanded playfully, her nose scrunching on the last word.

As Kayla raced past her and proceeded to make out with Courtney, Sheree couldn't help but be amazed at the transformation the living room had undergone. Streamers and balloons danced around the room under the mirror ball hung in the middle of it, forming a fantastic jump, jive an' wail space with the usual sofa and chairs removed. The further down the steps she walked the more she noticed, like the photographs. Pictures from Fashion Club Meetings where they were mostly posing in trendy outfits to be published in the school newspaper and make the student population feel inferior in their clothing choices, or goofing off in spaghetti straps with plunging cleavage lines and tight fitting leather pants pretending to be vampire slayers with their pencils; the time Sheree dressed like a penguin and Jennifer dressed like a cheetah to raise funds for the zoo (a lie she would take to the grave); from Valentine's Day after the dance when they went out to Ravenwood Bar & Grill and commiserated over the losses with pizza. Then one picture caught her eye and broke her heart. It was Sky; larger than all the rest and placed in a chair, her smile radiant and full of life. It wasn't the dressed up fancy version from the dance or the cheerleader from the squad, but just Sky like she was in life before her life fell apart and crumbled into nothingness.

Sheree sat on the stairs and stared at that picture and cried and cried and cried until the tears were pointless, like her eyes suddenly realized that no amount of reservoir releasing would bring Sky back from the dead. After all, she died by her own hand, not supernaturally like Kayla or Jeff or Jessica. Part of her wished that Sky had died that night of the accident that stole Jeff from her life, because if magic killed her, magic could bring her back. But then the reality of the situation that she never would have even known Sky existed stabbed her brain, painting it red with the obvious.

"I think it's right she here," Courtney said quietly as she approached Sheree on the steps.

"Me too. Thanks, Court," Sheree said, squeezing Courtney so hard she thought she might pop her Afro off and send it bouncing down the stairs and across the room like a tumbling tumbleweed.

Fortunately the only bursting was from Courtney's mouth.

"Bitch checked out early, and we all gotta pick up the tab? No. Hell no. She don't get off that easy. Mmm mmmmm."

"Thanks for keepin' it real, yo'," Sheree said before her lips formed a toothless smile.

Courtney smiled back the same toothless grin. "Yo' welcome, sweetie. Is Nikki comin'? Chad's prolly comin' which means my Russian Teacake'll be like ass cancer to him. Should we tell her he gay? He gay, right? Course he gay. I known since grade three he gay. Jen know he gay? She gotta know. That why they broke up, right? Answer me woman when I talk at you!"

"Yes, yes, no, yes, uh huh, figures, moot, yep, shoes, waiting for a gap," Sheree said.

"Don't you wait for a gap, guurrrll! Just squeeze yo'self in! Ha HA!" Courtney winked. "Now, lemme get this place deco'd 'fore the limo come'n take us shoppin'!" she said, powerfully whispering the last word as if it was forbidden.

"Limo?"

"Fuuuuuuuck, I ruin everything. May wanna get dressed. It comin' soon."

The doorbell rang.

"Too late. Lezgo," Courtney said, pressing her lips tightly while grabbing Sheree's hand and pulling her down the steps.

"No. Uh uh. Not like this," Sheree told her, eyes wide, pulling with all her might, but Courtney was too strong.

Jennifer opened the door. "We gotta go!"

"No shit, girl!" Courtney shouted back, dragging Sheree behind her.

"Courtney, we cannot take them out in public without bottoms on!" Jennifer shrieked. "Screw it! There isn't time! Shove them in the car and we'll figure it out!"

Kayla looked confused as hell. "Wait wait wait wait wait. What is going on?"

"Move, woman! Ain't got time to 'splain nothin'!" Courtney told her, pushing her out the door with her free hand, still pulling Sheree with the other like she was luggage.

Sheree turned around as her bare feet squished in the moist grass and watched as the front door to her house grew smaller and smaller and Brendon shouted back gleefully, "Have fun!" before slamming it shut. She turned to face the black limousine and was blasted with Montel Jordan's "This is How We Do It" as the chauffeur opened the door for her and Kayla to get in. Jennifer and Courtney followed.

To avoid a boring seven-hour shopping extravaganza…

M O N T A G E ! ! !

First Stop: Starbucks for Caramel Macchiatos all around, followed by laughs and slurps and a little spillage on Jennifer's part caught by Sheree's cleavage.

Second Stop: Regal Nails for Mani/Pedis. "Does this pink polish make my teal eyes pop?" "Totally!" "Like, for sure!" "Jealous!" "Hahahahahahaha!!!"

Third Stop: Violet's Vintage, where Violet's enthusiasm over customers was quickly diffused upon the typical teenage girl shenanigans that ensued. "That hat looks like ass!" "Oh my gawd, take that nasty fur coat off! It probably has fleas!" "Take back your minks! Take back your pearls! What makes you think, that I was one of those girls?!" Then they all got strands of pearls and joked about the shower scene in *St. Elmo's Fire* and laughed and laughed and laughed, even Kayla who was clueless as to why that was as hilarious as the others found it for lack of having seen the movie.

Fourth Stop: Fabulous Freddy's Formalwear and Further for party outfits, where Courtney was once again the Clearance Queen, snagging the four of them amazing ensembles for a fraction of their retail value. She also may or may not have busted the seams on part of her own dress that was not on clearance, but made a scene at the counter that ensured a steep discount. That's so Courtney.

"I'm hungry!" "So am I!" "We gotta eat pronto!" "Bitch bitch bitch bitch bitch! Fine, bitches! Let's eat then!"

Fifth Stop: Ravenwood Bar & Grill where they stuffed their faces full of their collective favorite pizza, a magical piece of heavenly deliciousness concocted from pepperoni, pineapple, Italian sausage, and pepperoncini topping an indescribably crunchy-yet-soft-and-chewy crust. There is no need for dialogue when this pizza is being hand-delivered into one's mouth.

"SHOES!!!!"

Sixth Stop: Payless Shoes for stylish yet affordable sole-covering options, which, after ransacking the entire store's selection of dress, formal, and classy casual styles, looked like the Tasmanian Devil himself had spun through the aisles. "This is so beautiful, I want it in every color!" "Ugh, why don't they have my size?" "Who the hell would wear these shit-squirts?" "Do you have these in fuchsia?" "I love these but they'll cover up my fabulous toenails!" "Why is it so much to ask for fashion forward-yet-completely-comfortable shoes?" "I know, right?" "Hello, it's like, the new millennium and stuff. Get with the program folks!" "Will these shoes help me get Chad back?" "FUCHSIA!!!"

Seventh Stop: Hair & Flair to get a style and makeup for the finishing touch to unify the nails, dresses, pearls, and shoes. "Jack those bangs up to Jesus!" "Cornrows!" "Oh gawd, I'm having regrets about that decision. Can you fix it?" "Just give me random crimps mingling with chunky curls!" "I'm only here for the flair."

When they were finished, they took one last look into the full-length mirrors sporting new hairdos, old pearl necklaces, tight-fitting party dresses that made Kayla look like she was four months pregnant or ate one-hundred-forty-four doughnuts or so and it all ended up in her midsection, and cheap shoes, but they all felt like a million bucks.

"Party time," Courtney said, and with that, they strutted to the limo and had the driver take them back to the Hollins house.

"Hot Boyz" greeted them as only Missy Elliott (and guests) could do when they opened the front door. Not the actual Missy Elliott because Ravenwood is a small town nobody has ever heard of and likely never will, especially not famous R&B singers, but instead the digitized compact disc audio version. "Happy birthday!" rang through the air, temporarily overtaking the song blaring through rented speakers from a rented DJ.

"Grandma!" Sheree cried as she spotted her mother's mother.

"Kayla!" Grandma Lowell cried as she rushed past Sheree's open arms to hug her twin.

"And apparently I'm invisible now. Yay me," Sheree said, shrugging her eyes, and taking in the magic Courtney whipped up for their birthday party. Suddenly she regretted her dress choice as the fabric began clawing at her bare skin.

Grandma Lowell reached in for a hug from behind, dragging Sheree completely off-guard. "Kayla, Sheree, together again!" she cried before whispering into Kayla's ears, "This is not your fault. This is not your mother's fault. Make sure she knows that."

"You should tell her," Kayla whispered back with a forced grin, holding back the urge to snap her grandmother's neck as one of her unborn children demanded.

"She won't listen to me. Too much anger in her, and that's my fault," Grandma Lowell whispered.

Sheree just listened, hoping that somehow she'd be able to solve the underlying problem, the faulty foundation of a relationship between her mother and her mother's mother that was only one earthquake away from crumbling apart. For now, they faked congeniality.

"Maybe if you talk to her, explain why, she'd understand," Kayla said a little louder, forgetting this was supposed to be a hush-hush conversation to avoid prying ears.

Grandma Lowell smiled a toothless grin. "Sweet child," she said, putting her hand on Kayla's growing babies bump, which suddenly had a calming effect on the more violent of the twins. "One day you will understand. Being a parent is all about sacrifices." Her smile faded. "I don't envy the sacrifice you are going to have to make." Her choked voice told Kayla all she needed to know.

As a new song pounded through the speakers, Courtney shouted, "LADIES!!! Get yo' asses out here an' twerk it!"

"Um, I think I missed something being dead. What is 'twerk'?" Kayla asked her grandmother, but before she could get an oral answer, a visual one presented itself in the form of Courtney and Sheree who began thrusting their hips and bouncing their butts up and down at an alarming rate while the Ying Yang Twins's new song "Whistle While You Twurk" played.

"Sheree! We need to get yo' grammy out here and teach her dis!" Courtney shouted.

"YES!!!" Sheree responded.

And they did.

Much to the delight of Kayla, and the horror of Mrs. Hollins and Brendon who both looked like they were going to vomit or cry or both while Mr. Hollins and Chad laughed so hard they went silent, Grandma Lowell twerked like the best of them, even getting low to show how they used to do it back in the 80s in New Orleans when she visited a couple girlfriends who liked to party and to this day probably don't remember the 70s but the 70s sure remember them. Then, pushing Mrs. Hollins to exit the house and get a little fresh air outside with Rex and Deschutes, Grandma Lowell queefed so loud it also made the DJ pause.

"What the hell ya'll lookin' at? If you don't queef, you ain't doin' it right! Sweet Lawd Geezus, niggas never hearda pussy farts?" Courtney queried loudly. "Pay no 'ttention to dem, Grammy. They jus' jealous 'cuz you got the moves they only wish they had."

The DJ decided it was time to divert the attention away from pussy farts and back to dancing. "Alright, we're gonna change things up a little. Who's ready for The Verve?"

Sheree's friends were excited, but she was frozen and felt like somebody was about to stab her as her gaze turned towards Sky's picture in a chair. And then the song started and the stabbing began, the knife firmly wielding itself into her heart and head over and over while the violins plucked out the tune of "Bittersweet Symphony" until the drums kicked in and she had to get away.

Out.

Anywhere but where she was.

She quickly made her way to the front door and away from the words that made her sick to her stomach. It used to be their song; hers, Jennifer's, and Sky's. They'd sing it in the car every time it came over the radio, every time they watched *Cruel Intentions*, and every time something sparked a memory about the song. Some good memories, some bad, and some Sheree wanted to forget. It also used to be their song, hers and the boy; the boy who changed her life forever; the boy who raped her; the boy who still had power over her long after Kayla took care of him; the boy she vowed never to even say his name again, which, as she walked, she suddenly realized how impossible that was going to be to sustain considering how common it was.

Walking, wandering aimlessly towards the sidewalk like one procrastinates their math homework on a Sunday night, something she realized she was doing by partaking in her own birthday party, Sheree spotted a lone black feather—a crow feather—standing out against the green grass and a yellow dandelion. She picked it up, twirling it between her thumb and index finger and smiled.

"This. This is it," Sheree said quietly.

"What?" Jennifer asked, sneaking up from behind.

"I need to let go of the past," Sheree said.

"Huh?"

"I need to let go of my excess baggage. I thought Easter was it, but it's not. I have so much more I need to shed from my life. So much I need to eradicate from my presence: my beliefs, my so-called friends, my family. All of it."

"You're scaring me, Sheree. Seriously."

"I am being serious, Jen! I've had enough of this shit show! I'm sick and tired of being life's pawn. I have to let it all go. Start over. Or give up. In the end, it's all the same."

Sheree continued twirling the feather, watching as it picked up green and purple hues, no longer smiling.

Stoic.

Jennifer stared at her friend in disbelief. How could she think this way? Letting go of the past is one thing, but giving up? That didn't sound like Sheree.

"I sincerely hope you aren't planning suicide, because that is too selfish, even for you," Jennifer said bluntly.

"What? No! Jesus, Jen! What the hell? I'd never kill myself."

"Our song came on and then you bailed. I assumed."

"You assumed wrong."

"Then what did you mean by your little Crow Feather Revelation?"

"About giving up?"

"Uh, yeah?"

"I meant giving up my grudge on life. My grudge against Kayla I keep trying to stuff away into a cracked bottle in the far reaches of my brain because of that tiny glimmer of hope that she isn't going to go all psychopathic-bitch-witch on my again. My grudge against my parents for basically erasing all memory of her through therapy and omission. My grudge against Courtney for being… Courtney. My grudge against you for being so goddamned perfect. My grudge against my brother for knowing who he is and fully embracing it. My grudge against Chad for being my father's favorite non-bio child in the entire fucking universe that you for some unknown reason is also held hostage to his charm. My grudge against Sky for leaving me. My grudge against the bastards who raped me, and, yeah, sure, they're all dead now and shit, but my weak mind and weaker body still remember every unforgivable thing they did to me. My grudge against my own grandmother for basically putting me in harm's way in order to fulfill some shitty prophecy."

Sheree shut up after her bottle spilled its contents.

The silence that followed made Jennifer's ears bleed.

"Are you sure you didn't miss any grudges?" Jennifer asked.

"Probably missed a dozen or so, but who cares? I'm letting them all go. Shit, that feels good to get off my chest!" Sheree said, smiling a full open-mouthed smile that made her eyes pop that she usually reserved for when she took her bra off at the end of the night.

"I bet. I mean, when one is in the presence of perfection," Jennifer said before breaking into a cackle that made Sheree picture the stereotypical Looney Tunes witch.

"Sorry, Jen. I shouldn't hold a grudge against you for being perfect. It's just, you're my pillow," Sheree confessed.

"Your pillow?"

"Yeah."

"What the hell does that even mean?" Her confusion was evident by the contorted look on her face, especially after the whole feather fiasco.

"It means you're my pillow. You comfort me and support my head when it wants some rest and make me feel safe and loved and home."

"Goddamn you, Sheree. You're gonna make me cry."

"Oh shit. Please don't. Gawd, that breaks your perfection. Big time."

"Fine."

"Hug me."

"Okay."

And they hugged and hugged and hugged until Jennifer just couldn't hug anymore.

"Unhug me!" Jennifer cried, voice cutting the air like a knife.

As if in slow motion, their bodies became two again. The feather flittered down to the ground, nestling quietly amongst clover and crabgrass that her father would surely curse as soon as he spotted it.

"You dropped your feather," Jennifer said.

"I'm letting it go. It's all in the past now," Sheree said.

"I guess it's time to face the present again, huh?"

"Yeah, I suppose."

"I mean, we did kinda duck out of your own birthday party."

"True."

"Besides, if we don't make it back soon, I'm afraid Courtney will be teaching your grandma something worse than twerking!"

"Oh gawd, you're right! Hurry up, let's get back in there."

"A lady never runs in pumps and pearls!" Jennifer laughed.

But it was too late. Sheree opened her front door to find Chad and Courtney teaching her Grandma Lowell a different way to twerk as Sir Mixalot's "Baby Got Back" shoved its way out of the speakers. Nikki did not look amused, even though she decidedly had the largest butt of them all. Sheree decided they must have missed a possible reenactment of the beginning of the song and she must have been the object of Becky's friend's gossip.

"Well, if you can't beat 'em, join 'em!" Sheree said, shrugging and making her way to the center of the floor.

Jennifer followed, making sure to squeeze herself in front of Chad.

"You girls are going to be the death of me!" Grandma Lowell declared.

And they twerked the night away.

After the party, after cake and presents and everyone else had left, Jennifer sat slouched on the sofa in solemn solitude. She resembled any number of the helium-filled balloons that lost their power to stay afloat surrounding her.

"What's up? Need a ride home?" Sheree asked, spanking a sad balloon onto the floor, sitting next to her best friend, and then rubbing her back in the most platonic way possible even though she really wanted to rip off the party dress she was wearing and slip into something that didn't feel like cat nails shredding her skin.

"No," Jennifer replied.

"Need to stay over?" Sheree asked.

"Yes," Jennifer replied.

"Okay."

"Thanks."

"Sorry your efforts to lure Chad back into your mouth were moot," Sheree said as she let her hand fall from Jennifer's back.

"The fact you just said moot is moot," Jennifer said, a smile creeping onto her face that seconds before was threatening an ugly cry version.

The front door opened to reveal Mr. Hollins and Kayla, both of whom looked positively glowing—Kayla for being so blindly in love with Courtney, and Mr. Hollins for his daughter being so happy.

"You staying over, Jennifer?" he asked as he closed the door, depositing his car keys onto a small table next to it.

"Yeah," she answered quietly.

He smiled back. "I'm going to check on the wife and see how well she's doing erasing the vision of her mother dancing with you girls."

"What about your son?" Brendon cried from the top of the stairs before adding, "Why, Daddy? Why?!" as he ran down and clutched his arms around his father.

"There, there, Brendon," Mr. Hollins said, soothing his son while petting his head.

"I don't think I'll ever get the sound of Grandma's pussy farts out of my head!"

Chapter 12
School's Out for Summer

The last few weeks of school flew by so fast that the only reason Sheree knew it was the end of her freshman year at Ravenwood High School was because of all the finals she was ill prepared to take. Even Jennifer, the obviously more studious of the two of them, had become laxed on test preparation, instead spending her free time stalking Chad outside his bedroom window unbeknownst to anyone else. Her obsession was quickly becoming unhealthy. So was her home life.

"Ugh, so I'm pretty sure I failed ASL," Jennifer admitted as she walked alongside Sheree to the little blue sedan she'd become accustomed to riding shotgun in.

"And I'm pretty sure you're full of shit," Sheree shot back.

"What was I thinking signing *Green Eggs and Ham?*"

"You did fine!"

"I was drooling and spacing off!"

"What? Why?"

"Because all I could think about was century eggs! Curse you, China!"

"Wait, huh?" Sheree's face was so contorted, there sadly is just no way to describe it.

"Century eggs have green yolks."

"On purpose?"

"Yes."

"How? Wait, do I even want to know?"

"No."

"What does it taste like?"

"Stinky cheese."

"Sounds delicious."

"Oh, it is."

The car waited for her people to enter, but instead they just rubbed their bodies on her like she was a drunk sorority girl at a frat party. Jennifer stared up at the sky and thought for a brief moment a sliver of blue was trying to leak through the clouds. Sheree suddenly had a craving for some cave aged Roquefort. Courtney and her entourage burst onto the scene.

"Bitches ain't shit but hoes and tricks! Lick on the nuts and suck the dick! Gets the fuck out after you're done! And I hops in my ride to make a quick run!" Courtney rapped as if she was Snoop Dogg about to pass the mic to Dr. Dre. The microphone she was using, however, was simply Dr. Dre's *The Chronic* CD.

Chad and Nikki had blank expressions. Kayla looked like she was about to explode into laughter. Sheree and Jennifer just stared in mutual confusion.

"What's a nigga gotta do ta getta ride in this ghetto town?" Courtney asked in a way only Courtney would, squeezing Kayla's hand hard like she was afraid that if she lessened her grip her girlfriend would float away like a balloon.

"I only have room for four. Sorry Chad and Nikki," Sheree stated bluntly.

"Puhleeeeze, bitch. We can squeeze into yo' backseat no prob," Courtney said, shaking her head but not her hair.

"It's not safe. We might get pulled over," Jennifer piped in.

"Then you best make sure they ain't no cops follow'n ya'," Kayla snapped back.

A loud *THUD!* echoed throughout the parking lot amidst honking horns, screaming teenagers, and diesel engine busses daisy chained in front of the school as Sheree's forehead hit the top of her car. Without protest, Sheree got into the driver's seat, unlocked the rest of the doors, and waited for her passengers to test the little blue sedan's weight limit. Jennifer promptly sat in the front passenger seat, Nikki and Courtney sat in the back where their hips merged, and Chad and Kayla sat on their respective counterpart's laps like babies, craning their necks in an unnatural way to fit while their shoulders and cheeks grazed the car's fabric-lined ceiling, making it impossible for Sheree to use her rearview mirror.

"You can sit on my lap if you want, Chad," Jennifer offered as she turned around, but the look on Nikki's face said the only way that was going to happen was through death by combat, and that would only be assuming the combat was mathematical in nature as hand-to-hand combat would yield favorable results towards Nikki.

She slowly turned back around and pretended she never made the suggestion as she sunk into the seat.

The piercing sound of scraping metal overpowered the radio as the back half of her little blue sedan treaded the asphalt with the grace of a camel. The disappointed look on her mother's face as Sheree pulled up to the house was worse. Her brother, on the other hand as he exited their mother's car, looked gleefully mischievous and resembled the Joker from the Batman cartoon.

"Do you really think that song is appropriate to listen to, young lady?" Mrs. Hollins asked Sheree as she opened the door to get out of her car.

Crap. "Uh…"

"It's my CD," Courtney fessed up.

Mrs. Hollins's demeanor changed slightly. "Do your parents really let you listen to music like that?" she asked, placing air quotes around "music" as she said it to emphasis her bias.

"Mrs. H, my daddy's dead and my momma don't give a shit what I listen to. Hell, the good Dr. Dre prolly wrote that whole song 'bout her! Bitches ain't shit but hoes and tricks! Ha HA!" Courtney sang as she danced her way up to the front door, dragging Kayla behind her who simply shrugged and smiled at her mom.

There was a heavy bass pounding the pavement and visibly shaking the windows as Sheree made the walk of shame with Jennifer while her mother's eyes burned into the back of her skull and her brother's smirk made her want to punch him in the throat. She knew her father was home as well, even though it was only the middle of the afternoon. Death must have taken a holiday.

"School's out for summer!" Mr. Hollins sang along with Alice Cooper as Courtney opened the front door, wearing his usual tight fitting t-shirt and polyester shorts that showed off his junk, playing an air guitar.

Courtney flashed an approving open-mouthed smile and high-fived him, Kayla did the same, Jennifer couldn't stop staring at his shapely veiled penis along with Nikki, Mrs. Hollins shook her head like she was annoyed but still displayed a coy smile that said: "You're totally getting laid tonight," Chad bobbed his head to the beat while sticking out his tongue and making the sign of the horns with his hands, and Sheree and Brendon both said in unison, "You need eyeliner."

Later that night, after the embarrassing parental shenanigans subsided, after Courtney and Kayla finally stopped checking to make sure the other was breathing by discontinuing their seemingly incessant mouth-to-mouth, after Mrs. Hollins finished her bottle of wine and made sleepy-slutty eyes at her husband, after Chad and Nikki had long left, after Jennifer had already passed out on Sheree's bed, Brendon rolled his head back and announced to the ceiling, "I'm bored."

"Shiiiiiiiiiit," Mr. Hollins said slowly. "This is going to be a long summer."

Chapter 13
Father's Day Blues

"Bitches ain't shit but hoes and tricks! God damn you, Courtney!" Sheree screamed to the surrounding trees, sending a few songbirds into a flurry.

Breathing in the forest air felt refreshing as she paused to catch her breath, the smell reminding her of the grapefruit she had for breakfast. A heavy rain had passed through the day before, leaving everything in that damp-dry spectrum beneath the canopy where the ferns were spreading their wings amongst the caterpillar-eaten salal and blooming bunchberries. She closed her eyes and let nature fill her.

Tingling.

Rejuvenating.

Relaxing.

It was the first time she allowed herself to be alone in the woods since the previous April. Her reasons were valid. Her resolve to undo that fear was also valid. Her next step almost made her vomit as her foot crushed a wild mushroom, the flesh of which was now firmly glued to the soles of her Nikes.

SNAP!

Sheree turned towards the sound, but couldn't see anything. "Probably just a branch falling. Oh great, a branch falling in the forest where nobody can hear me scream if one should decide to land on my head. Then again, I'd probably be passed out or dead so my scream would never be let out. Jesus, Sheree! Get a grip on your crazy imagination before it turns into reality!"

CRUNCH!

Sheree turned toward the opposite direction, but didn't see anything there either. Just more forest. More Douglas firs and sword ferns and disgusting white mushrooms playing follow the leader along a partially worn path.

"CAW! CAW!" a crow shrieked from some hidden place above, causing her to jump and have to pull her soul back into her body as it threatened to leave.

CRUNCH! CRUNCH! CRUNCH!

Sheree turned once again towards the sounds, but there was nothing, at least nothing visible. The footsteps were getting louder. Louder and louder as whatever it was got closer and closer.

Louder.

Getting closer.

Pick up your damn feet and run, Sheree! Now!

Without carefully planning a route, she bolted, looking in all directions in hopes that she could catch a glimpse of what was following her or something familiar that would take her back home. Nothing registered. North, south, east, and west were merely words without meaning to her at this point in time.

The footsteps sounded like they were picking up speed, gaining on her.

Sheree ran faster.

Faster.

Faster and faster until she tripped over a fallen branch, possibly the very one that snapped just moments before. As she tried to pick herself up, the soft loam pulled her in deeper, dragging her into its decaying flesh to become nourishment for the fungus. The more she pulled, the more it pulled back.

Sinking.

The footsteps got louder.

The dirt pulled her in deeper.

So this is how I die, Sheree thought, finding the scenario humorous. *If only Courtney could see me now, stuck in the dirt, unable to pick myself up, and covered in filthy forest foliage. Gawd, Sheree. Even when you're about to die you can't help but alliterate?*

The footsteps stopped mere inches behind her.

She clenched her teeth so hard she could hear them cracking like ice.

She closed her eyes as tight as she could and waited for Death to make a mockery of her short life.

"Fool! Why you all bent over a log? An' why you runnin' from me?"

"Courtney!" *Of course.* "Jesus Christ, you scared the crap out of me!" Sheree said as she slowly turned to face her friend who, even in jogging attire, looked like a fashion goddess.

"Yeah, I see dat. Yo' ass covered in it," Courtney replied, her face in pre-vomit mode as she snapped her head back, crossing her arms under her perky-yet-sizeable breasts.

"Help me up," Sheree said.

"Hell no! I ain't gettin' my clothes all covered in yo' filthy ass! Time fo' you to pick yo' own damn self up, woman!" Courtney told her, then added, "Right. This. Second," snapping her fingers after each word for emphasis in a Z-formation.

Sheree rolled her eyes as a sigh escaped her mouth. "I've been trying, but the dirt is too soft and my muscles are too soft and I am just too damn soft." Without control, Sheree started bawling. "I am sick and tired of trying to be strong and failing and finding out I am just getting weaker and weaker! Why the hell can't life just stop being so fucking difficult for a goddamn second so I can, literally, pick myself up for once? Why does God hate me so much?"

Sheree's tears flooded the ground her hands had disappeared into.

"Bitch, God don't hate nobody! At least thazzwut my sistah keeps sayin' to me as she tryin' to save my soul an' shit. Hell, even the White Devil playin' Daddy in my house got God's love 'ccordin' to her, an' he a straight up dickwad! Quit yo' cryin," Courtney said, kneeling down behind Sheree and reaching her hands around her stomach. "Now, I may cop a feel gettin' yo' ass outta the mud, but it don't mean I wanna go down on you, comprende?"

"Got it."

"I hope that's mud all up on yo' ass and not shit, or we gone have words."

"Me, too."

And with a swift pull, Courtney lifted Sheree up off the forest floor as if she were an Amazonian warrior princess, steadying herself to avoid falling. Sheree saw she had a slight smile on her face as she turned around and flashed one right back.

"Thanks, Court."

"Yo' welcome. Now let's get you home 'fore you end up on *Unsolved Mysteries*."

"Agreed!"

The walk back to Sheree's house was filled with laughter and a few surprises as she and Courtney had a chance to get to know each other a little better without other people vying for their attention. It was just like Spring Break when the absence of their real friends forced them to hang out, only better.

"So Anna be all like 'Next year, I am taking, too many A.P. classes, to cheer. I quit!' and I be all like 'You can't quit, gurrrrrrl! We gonna be shit without yo' ass!' an' she be all like 'Sorry!' an' I be all like 'da fuck?' and she, I shit you not, goes all Ice Cube on my ass an' says 'Bye, Felicia!' Can you belieeeeeeeve that shit?" Courtney said, pulling her face into her hair as her lips went pouty.

"So, there's an opening on the cheer squad next year?" Sheree asked in reply.

"Bitch, you know you already got that slot! Mandy graduated and now I Queen Bee. High five me, wigga!"

Their hands slapped each other mid-air. That's a high-five, you know, in case you were confused. Somehow I doubt it. You seem like an intelligent person.

As the backyard came into view, Courtney turned to Sheree and asked, "So what's the plan for Daddy Day?"

Panic struck her. Father's Day. It was Father's Day and she had a father and instead of being a good daughter she was taking a selfish fear-facing walk in the woods. "Oh, crap!" She heard a lawnmower and assumed it was coming from the front yard. "Crap!"

Sheree sprung into a full on sprint, followed closely by Courtney who decided it was a race. As anticipated, Courtney won, giving Sheree a sly self-congratulatory smile as she wiped her feet on the mat and walked into the backdoor, through the laundry room, and met up with Kayla for smooches and cuddles. Sheree, however, was forced to strip to her underwear after being hosed off by her mother before being allowed entrance due to the sheer amount of mud encrusting her body. As she ran through the dining room, she watched her brother frosting cupcakes like Martha Stewart. *You're not helping the stereotype, bro.* After changing into a casual but not too casual outfit that said, "See, I put a little effort into this just for you, Daddy!" she walked down the steps in hopes of greeting her father. Instead she was met with snarkasm.

"If you are trying to impress Dad with that outfit, ew," Brendon said as he licked buttercream off the spatula in his hand.

Mrs. Hollins smacked the back of his head and said, "Don't listen to him, honey. You look very nice."

"Thanks, Mom," Sheree said while glaring at Brendon. "Please tell me Dad isn't mowing the lawn right now."

"He's not," Mrs. Hollins replied.

"Whew!" Sheree said, letting out a sigh of relief.

"Chad is," Mrs. Hollins said.

"Son of a bitch," Sheree said quietly as she deflated at the bottom of the stairs.

Mrs. Hollins rolled her eyes.

"Just because Chad doesn't have a dad, doesn't mean he gets to mooch off of ours!" Sheree thought out loud. "Oh! Crap! Shit! Fuck! Goddammit, I'm just digging myself into a bigger hole here."

Kayla lifted her face off of Courtney's long enough to say, "That was mean," before she hooked their tongues back together again to continue their wrestling match.

"Very insensitive, young woman," Mrs. Hollins told her.

"Bitch!" Brendon said loudly before breaking into a full on giggle-fest as he ran around the house expecting to be chased by his mother with a wooden spoon with the intent of spanking him with it. Secretly he was hoping she would. Well, truth be told, secretly he wished Tommy Gufflebacht would spank him, but Tommy's an asshole. He stopped running when he realized he was merely wasting his energy. His mother had given up scolding cuss words.

"I'm sorry. I didn't mean it, I... just... I guess I'm jealous about how much time Chad has been spending with him lately,"

Sheree confessed before adding, "And how much that makes Dad happy."

A little piece of Mrs. Hollins died after that, unable to live after witnessing her daughter's pain. However, before she could swoop Sheree into her arms and try her best to comfort her, Chad and Mr. Hollins walked into the house laughing heartily about something neither of them would admit to. A chunk of matted grass clung to the entryway rug, making her cringe as if she was Joan Crawford and that grass was a wire hanger. Alas, before she could beat Chad with it, he quickly realized his error, gathered up the evidence, the mat, and disposed of it all in the trashcan with a quick shake. Faux running—a pathetic signature trademark of Chad's—he made his way back to the front door where he replaced the rug. Her pleasantness was restored as she flashed a smile as fake as her obviously-colored-from-a-generic-brand-of-grocery-store-hair-dye copper hair.

He flashed her one that eerily reminded her of her husband's that made her nether regions tingle, which made her instantly uncomfortable until she remembered she had no blood relations to this child, which made her instantly uncomfortable again as his fifteen-year-old age factored into the equation, which made her instantly think that sixteen was legal age of consent, which made her wish she could shut her brain off because she didn't like the ride it was taking her on. At least she would never let these thoughts turn into action, unlike some people in this world.

"Cupcakes!" Brendon said, carrying a tray of freshly frosted treats for his father to indulge in, who promptly picked one, unwrapped it, and shoved it whole into his mouth.

"Mmm! Delicious, Bren!" he said, crumbs falling to the floor that he ungracefully tried to catch as they tumbled down, leaving Rex and Deschutes to attack them with their tongues.

Kayla hopped off Courtney and presented her father with a wrapped flat square, which after unwrapping revealed a vintage vinyl of The Mamas and the Papas *If You Can Believe Your Eyes and Ears* album. With the toilet.

"Where did you even find this, Kayla?" he asked, tears welling up in his eyes.

Kayla never answered, only smiled a toothless grin that told him he was never going to find out the answer to his query.

"Open mine, Mr. H!" Courtney demanded, shoving a box into his hands and practically opening it for him.

He unfolded the heather grey t-shirt inside that had the words "Real Men Make Twins and Gays" ironed onto the front in rainbow colors. "Thanks, Courtney!" he told her, giving her a hug before taking his shirt off and putting it on. "It fits perfect!"

Great. I've got nothing. Thank you, everyone, for making me look like a douche, Sheree thought as she walked over to her father to give him the only thing she could: a hug. "Sorry I don't have anything for you, Dad," she whispered into his ear as they embraced.

"Don't apologize, Sheree," he whispered back. "You've given me more than I could ever have asked for."

And with that, Sheree burst into tears. Her tears were short-lived, however. Jennifer walked into the house carrying a platter of Vietnamese spring rolls she made and walked a mile to give to Mr. Hollins.

"Thank you, Jennifer!" Mr. Hollins said before setting the platter down on the dining room table, dipping one in the sauce, and taking a bite. "Oh my gawd, these are amazing."

And they were.

Later, after Courtney was summoned home by her mother for family dinner (or what Courtney called "Eatin' Shit With The White Devil An' His Minions"), after Jennifer and Sheree had retired to her bedroom to gossip and bitch, after Brendon was in his room playing the latest Super Samurai Slugs video game (Shogun Slime Wars, in case you were interested), and after Chad left the house to go back home, Mr. Hollins got teary eyed. He really liked Chad and felt bad for his father not being around. He'd already made up his mind that as long as Chad wanted him in his life, he would try to fulfill that role as best he could.

"What is it, Frank?" Mrs. Hollins asked, noticing her husband's pain.

"We need to tell him the truth, Beth," he said, trying to force the tears to stay in his eyes, but they had other plans as they dripped all over his heather grey shirt, staining it with dark blobs.

Rubbing his back, she said, "We have to respect Amanda's wishes. I'm sure she will know when the time is right."

"I hope so. I need a beer."

"Coming right up."

Seeing her father distraught as she walked down the stairs, Kayla said, "I know."

"Wait, what?" Mrs. Hollins asked.

"What do you know?" Mr. Hollins asked, drying his eyes with the palm of his hand and trying his damnedest to plaster on a smile, but the plaster was too thin and kept dripping off the wall that was his face.

"I don't know, what do you know?" Kayla asked, suddenly regretting bringing up the subject for fear they weren't on the same page.

"About Chad?" Mr. Hollins asked.

"Yes," Kayla said.

"I know. His mom knows," Mr. Hollins said.

Kayla became nervous as she waited for the obvious.

Sensing her eye shifting, he added, "Yes, your mother knows, too."

"But Chad doesn't know," Kayla affirmed

"No."

And that was the last time the subject was spoken of until September 10, 2002.

Chapter 14
Fourth of July

Ransacking her closet for something that screamed AMERICA! for the Independence Day party she and all her friends were going to that night at some random rich girl's house in the hills, Sheree had a sudden realization that summer break was passing her by like a bullet train to heck. "Ugh! I've got nothing to wear!" she growled, her legs buried in a mountain of unworthy tops and bottoms, any number of which could have been combined to form a patriotic ensemble.

"You have plenty to wear. Quit trying to outdo Courtney. You'll fail," Jennifer said as she poked miniature American flags into her bun instead of chopsticks while staring at her reflection in the mirror of Sheree's vanity, frowning.

"You're right," Sheree said, letting her arms fall to her side. Her face followed, and caught a red and white striped top that would go great with her super short cutoff jean shorts with the pockets hanging out while revealing a little ass without being full on slutty, but more than enough to make her father cringe. "Oh my gawd, Jen. How's this?"

"Love the top, but I'd go with your side-lace-up jeans. Only supposed to max out at sixty today," Jennifer said authoritatively before tossing her a chunky blue scarf that had made its way to her feet. "Put this on, too."

"Thanks, Jen!" Sheree said, her eyes lighting up as she started dressing.

Jennifer simply smiled back, still unsure of her own choices.

"Why won't you go see *X-Men* with me when it comes out next week?" Sheree asked with a hint of bitterness and an assload of frustration as she squeezed her thighs into her jeans, too lazy to loosen the laces.

"Uh, because it's a comic book movie and I don't like comic books and it doesn't come out until the fourteenth which is more than a week. Ten days." Jennifer's response was full of duh-you-stupid-bitch tonal inflections.

That irked Sheree to no end, which spurred more irking as she surrendered to the fact that she would indeed have to loosen the laces because her body had obviously grown since the last time she wore the jeans… or they shrank. She decided the latter was the most plausible theory.

"But it has Captain Picard!" Sheree cried, hoping this revelation would spur interest because, c'mon, who doesn't like Patrick Stewart?

"Captain who?"

Sheree stared at her best friend in disbelief with her pants around her knees. "I can't be friends with you anymore."

"You don't mean that. Ask Chad. He loves that sort of stuff."

"But he's your ex-boyfriend."

"And he's your friend by extension of Courtney. I swear those guys are two turds in a toilet."

"You calling Courtney shit?"

"No. Expression."

Sheree nodded, finally able to pull her jeans over her ass to the point she could tighten the laces. "So Chad likes sci-fi, fantasy, comic book, et cetera movies?"

"Loves them. And romantic comedies."

"That's scary. Me, too."

"Yeah, you two are really similar. I'd use the turd expression, but would prefer to not get bruises from you. Bet you are a fantastic kisser, too?"

"So I've been told."

Jennifer rolled her eyes as she nodded her head. Then, for what seemed like forever, she watched Sheree sausage-case herself into size-too-small slacks.

"Finally!" Sheree cried as her jeans were firmly in place. "Crap!"

"What?" Jennifer asked, frightened a lace popped and they would have to start The Outfit Game all over.

"I forgot to change my thong," Sheree said, staring at the American flag underwear mocking her as it sat on her bed.

Looking for what color Sheree was wearing and hoping it would work, Jennifer noticed a super-thin hot pink line peeking out along her waist. "Here, I'll start unlacing this side, you get the other," she offered and began.

"Thanks. I'd be lost without you," Sheree said.

After fixing the panty fiasco, Sheree took one last look in the mirror, flopped her hair to one side, and decided she was finally ready to party. "Thanks for letting me borrow these hoops, Jennifer," she said, making sure the earrings were hooked to avoid falling off and getting lost even though she knew how much they cost because she bought them for Jennifer's Christmas present at Everything's A Dollar.

"Any time. Shall we go?" Jennifer asked.

Just then, Courtney burst through the door and shouted, "You bitches ready yet? We gonna be late."

Shaking her head and shaking on a smile, Sheree said, "Bitch, you late. We done."

Kayla shook her head and shook on a smile and said, "Sheree, no. Please, just no. Don't try."

"What? Why?"

"You're white."

"I'm white?!" Sheree shrieked, slapping her hands onto her cheeks like Macaulay Culkin in *Home Alone*. "Does mom know?"

"Yes she knows. Now go have fun! Don't drink anything questionable, and if you do, call me!" Mrs. Hollins said as she walked up the stairs before rounding the corner to her room. "Buh bye!"

Sheree rolled her eyes, but then understood just how lucky she was to have the parents she was born with. Parents who were actually more concerned with safety after making bad decisions than punishing those mistakes; parents who she could tell anything and wouldn't have to worry about repercussions; parents who knowingly withheld vital information about Kayla and Jessica and the evil that still resides in the place she called home. Her love quickly turned to bitterness.

"Let's get out of here," she said, pushing her way past Courtney and Kayla and heading down the stairs, out the door, and towards her car parked on the street.

Her entourage followed.

"Sheree, I think you've had enough," Jennifer said, her hand over the red Solo cup Sheree was holding and about to take another drink from.

Sheree pushed her away, swallowing the remainder in one gulp. Tossing the cup aside, it hit Courtney's hair as she was telling someone how she spent the previous Fourth of July calling 9-1-1 because her uncle caught fire and made Courtney become the one thing nobody thought possible: silent.

"I think you need to keep your superiority complex out of my business, bitch," Sheree told Jennifer inches away from her face, close enough for their tongues to high-five each other had the situation not been hostile.

"Sheree…" Jennifer pleaded, face softening as one of her flags fell from her bun, landing on the floor as if surrendering to the enemy, and causing her to wonder if she was supposed to dust it off and replace it back into her hair or burn it due to desecration.

"No, Jen! I'm sick of listening to you. I'm sick of looking at you. I'm sick of…"

"Sheree, I think…" Courtney started, but Sheree didn't allow her to finish.

"Shut your fucking trap, Courtney! I'm so sick of listening to how perfect you think you are. You know what? Newsflash! You are just as messed up as the rest of us, only you think hiding behind all the shit you do, all those before and after school meetings and committees and clubs, is all because you are afraid to be alone. Guess what? You keep pushing everyone away by being the bitchy ho you are and you'll die alone. Eventually Kayla will see you for the worthless trash you are."

The music stopped.

Courtney looked stone-faced.

"Come on, Sheree. Let's go home," Jennifer offered, still not willing to believe what her ears were telling her, picking up her miniature American flag off the carpet and scraping up something foreign into her fingernails in the process.

"No! I'm just getting started." Sheree turned around, picked up her cup off the floor, and asked, "Where's the keg? I need a refill."

"You need a lot of water and a couple aspirin," Jennifer told her, taking her hand.

Sheree threw it off. "Why don't you go home to your daddy, Jennifer? Oh, that's right. He's not home. He'd rather pay for a handjob from some random stranger than have to be around you."

"Now you're just being a dick," Jennifer told her, trying to hold back her own emotional baggage about her father's lack of parenting and possible preference for handjobs from sketchy foot massage parlors with black curtains because nobody gets that many foot massages in a week.

"Fuck off. The only reason I wanted to be friends with you was because I thought you were popular and would make me popular as well. Apparently I chose poorly," Sheree said, turning around and walking out of the room to find the keg she knew had to be somewhere.

Jennifer was about to go after her, but Courtney stopped her. "She don't deserve you. Damn, what's got her cunt all bruised? It's like cheer tryouts all over!"

Jennifer wanted to explain everything, all the reasons Sheree could possibly be acting the way she was, for all the horrible reasons that would make her act like she did. But she couldn't. And worse still, she knew that hurt was not going to go away.

Neither of theirs.

"I need something stronger than beer," Jennifer said quietly.

Kayla walked up to Courtney comforting Jennifer, a cup of Sprite in each hand. "What'd I miss?"

"Your sistah bein' a fuckin' bitch, that's what," Courtney told her, taking a cup from her hand and wishing it was stronger than just lemon-lime soda, but knowing that it couldn't be for fear of Sheree's words coming true.

Kayla shook her head. "I'm gone for like two seconds and the world falls apart around me. Fuck my life."

"Hey, that's my line, hooker," a girl told her, feigning offense or poorly displaying actually being offended, her hair painfully obvious that it was between styles.

"Shut up, Angie!" Courtney yelled, accidentally spitting in her face. "Oh! Oh hell! I so sorry, bitch!" she said, grabbing the closest thing to wipe Angie's face with.

Angie swiped Courtney's hand away as she took the used napkin from it. Walking away, she said nondescript curses while furiously trying to get saliva off her face, smearing her mascara and lipstick into something reminiscent of Liza Minnelli's coked out 1970s face.

"I should talk to her," Kayla said, looking around. "Where'd she go?"

"Keg," Jennifer told her quietly, still waiting for liquor to make its way into a cup and into her hand and into her mouth, down her throat, then straight to her head to numb the pain.

"Crap. She's our ride. How much has she had to drink?" Kayla asked.

"Too much," Jennifer said, barely above a whisper in the crowded room, music making it almost impossible to hear.

Kayla handed Courtney her cup and searched for her sister. She wasn't by the keg in the kitchen as anticipated, so she checked every other room, even the host's parents bedroom only to find that they were both in the room having sexy time with balding and sagging friends and suspicious white powder on mirrors while their house was filled with underage drinking. She wasn't in the upstairs bathrooms. None of the three she knew of, that is. Deciding Sheree couldn't be on the upper level of the house, she continued her search again downstairs, starting back at the keg and working her way from there to the basement, then back to Courtney and Jennifer, who seemed to be feeling a little better as she drank from a bottle of something amber-colored and too large to be a beer and smelling faintly of lighter fluid.

"I'm going to check out back," Kayla told them.

Courtney nodded.

The backyard was just as crowded as the house. The pool, despite the colder than normal weather that year, was full of kids around her age. The hot tub was full of people as well, most of whom decided clothing was optional. Kayla rolled her eyes as she thought, *Apparently high school parties have evolved into shameless orgies.* With the backyard a bust, she checked the large front yard, hoping that the fading light the soon-to-be-setting sun had to offer was enough to guide her. Cars were parked all along the heavily tree-lined driveway, a private road really that went a quarter mile until it met with another street that connected to the main highway that led home to Ravenwood where her warm and comfortable bed was and where she wanted to be even if the room itself was the size of a closet. Okay, so it was about a ten-foot square space, but still, it was half the size of her siblings's rooms. Ashley Heights was filled with private estates like this, where even a four-bedroom house like the one she called home had breathing space in any of their living rooms. Ashley Heights also seemed to attract people who were trying to compensate for something they lacked, and were spawning grounds for entitled children who don't like to be told no. Spotting her sister's little blue sedan and seeing that it was unoccupied, she made her way back to the house to let her girlfriend and Jennifer know that Sheree, at the very least, didn't ditch them.

"Who the fuck do you think you are?" Kayla heard a girl say as she opened the front door, pointing a gun at someone.

That someone turned out to be Sheree.

Kayla panicked.

Froze.

"Fool! I'm Sheree Hollins!" Sheree informed the crying gun-toting girl, half her drink spilling down her arm, onto her chest.

"And I'm Eve's sister! It's your fault she's dead!" she cried, gun wavering in her shaking hand.

Sheree laughed, dropping her beer onto the hardwood floor where it bounced and released its contents onto the large Persian rug in the middle of the room. "Let me guess, your name is Lilith, right?"

The girl seemed taken aback, the gun slowly lowering until the barrel pointed at the floor. "Yes," she said, her voice small and broken.

A snort escaped Sheree's nostrils. "Figures."

The girl regained her drive, pointed the gun directly at Sheree's head, and fired.

"Noooooooooooo!" Kayla screamed for what seemed like forever.

The cartridge sped towards Sheree.

Savage Garden's "Gunning Down Romance" played in the background.

Just when Sheree figured her life was over, the bullet changed course, passing her ear so close she could hear it scream until it found another target. It felt like it took half her face with it as it sped past her ear before coming to a screeching halt inside Nikki Boloski's upper right arm.

"Graaahhhwww! Fuck! FUUUUUUUUUUUUUCK!!!" Nikki screamed as she held her biceps, blood gushing between her fingers.

"Oh my gawd! Nik! Nikki!" Chad cried, too horrified to move anything but his mouth as he watched, seemingly hypnotized by the thick red liquid pouring out of his girlfriend.

Sheree touched her ear, certain that blood and brains would be there, but was mildly annoyed that the pain she felt was nothing more than air. Pneumatic air. Ear. Squish!

Another shot went off, followed by a third. Realizing that none of the bullets were hitting her, Sheree looked to see if anyone else was bleeding. Her eyes locked onto Lilith, and the bits of Lilith's skull that made their way into the clownfish-filled saltwater aquarium behind her, slowly sinking and tainting the bright blue water red as Lilith slowly fell to the floor.

A crowd rushed to Nikki.

Another rushed towards Lilith.

"She's still alive!" a blond girl shouted.

"Call nine-one-one!" another blond girl screamed, but Courtney was already talking to an operator and calmly explaining the situation. After all, this wasn't her first run-in with disasters on the Fourth of July, and certainly would not be her last.

"Nikki! Please tell me you're going to be okay!" Chad cried, tears streaming down his blotchy face as he watched her bleed out, too afraid to touch the wound, trying not to throw up or pass out.

"No! My mother is going to kill me! Хуёво!" Nikki screamed, too angry to allow tears to form.

"Why?" Chad asked as Courtney made her way to Nikki to investigate her arm.

"Cuz she said she be stayin' the night at my house an' didn't tell her we goin' to be at a damn party, that's why. Fuck, girl. You gonna need a doctor," Courtney told her bluntly, remaining calm.

"Tis but a scratch!" Nikki said, somehow able to joke despite the pain.

"Teacake, you need to suck it up. Maybe we can get you to my house an' I can blame it on the White Devil? He gotta gun. Shit. That ain't gonna work. Ballistics won't match. Sorry, girl. You fucked," Courtney said rapid fire.

Nikki slumped, causing Chad to go into a panic. "No no no no no! Don't pass out!"

"Don't worry, Chad. I am just, Jesus Fucking Christ! this burns! I'm just, well, trying to figure out how best to break the news to my mother that I lied to her," Nikki told him.

"Tell yo' daddy then," Courtney said.

"He's in Thailand with his boy-toy," Nikki said.

"Shut it, girl. You love Chi-Chi," Courtney reminded her.

"FUUUUUUCCCKKKK!!!" Nikki cried again as the cartridge lodged into her arm began growing limbs as it slowly spun. Clawing, digging into her flesh with cat claws soaked in acid and set on fire, stabbing her in pulses as it tapped her humerus, which she found anything but humorous.

Suddenly Courtney realized Kayla wasn't by her side. "Kayla!" she shouted before spotting her on the floor, holding her stomach, and crying out. "Oh shit shit shit, no!" she cried as tears the size of her Afro leapt from her eyes. "Baby! Please say you all right?"

Looking up to meet Courtney's eyes, Kayla half-lied and told her, "Just pregnancy pains. Bad timing. Where's Sheree?"

As Courtney looked around from the vantage point of Kayla's side, Jennifer walked up to them. Still holding the bottle of Black Velvet, she informed them that Sheree left. Then she sat down and funneled the remaining whiskey into her throat without even the hint of a wince from the burn.

BOOM!

BOOM! BOOM! BOOM!

Everyone looked around for where the shots were coming from. A drunk girl peeked her head into the open living room window from the backyard, dripping wet and completely naked. "Fireworks!"

"Mind if I join you?" a man whose years were obvious in his eyes asked Sheree as she sat alone on a bench at Ravenwood Park rethinking her life choices while methodically flicking the wheel of a BIC lighter she stole from some kid at the party after he lit a joint and dropped it.

Hesitant, but also not wanting to come off as a bitch to a complete stranger even though she apparently didn't have a problem doing so to her best friends, Sheree nodded. "There's room."

The man smiled, revealing even more of his oddly attractive features; high cheekbones, alabaster skin that shimmered like pearls (but didn't sparkle like glitter because that would be stupid), and piercing blue eyes. While the man was definitely a stranger, Sheree couldn't help but feel at ease with his presence. A spell? She didn't sense danger. She didn't feel fear. She did, however, instinctually know that this person was somehow... family.

"Have we met?" Sheree asked.

"No."

"But you seem so familiar."

"Yes."

Sheree was beginning to wonder why she wasn't uneasy at the cryptic responses. She wondered why this stranger made her feel so comfortable. She wondered if he was...

"I have been watching you for some time now, Sheree."

My name. He knows my name. "How do you...?"

"Like I said, I have been watching you."

"Okay, creeper."

The stranger laughed, penetrating the night air that, even in the wee hours before dawn, was still punctuated with randomly timed fireworks. His laugh seemed to ignite a string of them all at once just to the north where her car was hopefully still parked at that one girl's house that was now covered in brains. Sheree stirred in her seat, debating whether or not to make a run for it. She knew she'd regret leaving her car at the party, but also knew that she was in no condition to drive it then.

"I have wanted to approach you for many months now."

"You're not helping the creeper thing."

"Allow me to explain," he said, placing a cold hand on her thigh that felt more grandfatherly than child molester-ish.

A couple hours earlier and Sheree would have been furiously ripping this guy a new asshole. Now that she was sobering up, her anger was turning into guilt.

Guilt

Guilt.

Guilt.

Guilt stacked for miles and miles yet again.

A smile told the stranger to continue.

"Jessica is my wife."

The smile disappeared.

What was this man telling her? Maybe he just lost his wife to cancer and needed to talk to somebody, anybody, even a stranger in the park at two in the morning. Maybe his wife just left him and he's lonely. Maybe he...

"Which makes me your great-great-great-grandfather."

"Holy shit!" Sheree shouted, involuntarily standing up. "But how? You were murdered!"

He laughed again, igniting more fireworks in the near distance. "No, I was not murdered. Changed, yes. Dead, yes. But murdered, no."

"So…" Sheree started, taking in a deep breath and collecting her thoughts before continuing with, "…you're a vampire?"

The smile in his eyes told her all she needed to know. "You are not afraid?"

"Should I be?"

"Yes."

"Truth be told, a year ago I'd have been terrified. Now, not so much. Too much has happened. I've been exposed to too much paranormal that it's beginning to feel homey. Huh, maybe my neighbor really is a werewolf after all?" Sheree ended, pondering the notion that her brother was actually telling her the truth about Wayne.

"I am also a witch, like your brother," he revealed.

Suddenly Sheree wondered if Brendon was doomed to the same fate. Male witches were rare. Exceedingly rare. An anomaly according to Jessica via the medium-slash-former-cheerleader Anna. Unless Jessica was talking about the anomaly being his sexuality?

"Okay, so let me get this straight. You are a vampire witch, meaning you weren't murdered. Why, then, is it that everyone says Jessica went off the deep end because you were killed?" Sheree asked, hoping he had an answer.

Although his eyes never blinked, the slight nod of his head made it appear so. "The tale was to protect me. Me and my maker to be more precise."

"Are you saying you made the choice to become a vampire?"

"Yes."

"Why?"

"Because we were in love. It was the only way to guarantee we could stay together forever."

"Wait wait wait wait wait. You fell in love with a vampire? But you were married to Jessica! Didn't you love her?"

"In a way."

Sheree was beginning to lose patience, but quickly regained it for the sake of having a conversation with somebody who had firsthand knowledge of her evil ancestor. "Without going into too much detail, do you mind explaining that?"

"Not at all. My dear, sweet Jessica and I were arranged to be married by our parents from the time we were toddlers. Our families decided that a union of witches would create a powerful bond, hopefully conjuring enough public sympathy in this here small town to allow us witches to come out of the closet, so to speak as they do today. However, I was still trapped in my closet. Your brother and I share another trait as well."

"So your maker...?"

"Is also male. A very powerful vampire. And even more so, a very powerful witch."

"Serious?!"

"Yes."

"What's his name?"

"We are getting off track. The reason I came to speak with you tonight is because I must put a plan into action to defeat Jessica once and for all. Your sister, Kayla, on the day she gives birth, will likely die."

"But she can't! She just came back!" Sheree cried hysterically.

He smiled. "Sweet child, this is why I am here now. Jessica has ruined too many lives to be allowed a second chance. She stole most of Kayla's already by possessing her body, making her go into that street in front of your childhood home, and allowing herself to get hit by that truck."

Sheree fell into the bench as shock punched her in the gut. Could this be true? Could Jessica really be the one responsible for Kayla's death, and not the actions she took by throwing Kayla's beloved baby doll into the busy street? Suddenly the events of the last ten months began to make sense. The puzzle was finally revealing the picture hidden within its jagged pieces.

"Tell me what I need to do?"

And he did.

After he revealed everything she needed to know, he said, "We need to tell the rest of your family."

"But it's late."

Staring in the direction of her house—his old house— towards Song's End, he appeared to listen for a moment before saying, "They are awake."

"Crap. They're probably waiting up for me. Jennifer or Courtney or Kayla or all of them probably told my parents about my erratic behavior at the party."

"It is about your brother, Brendon. He is hurt."

Before he had a chance to say anything else, Sheree started running home, carefully placing the stolen lighter into a pocket. Wedges were not made for running, Sheree decided as she contemplated tossing them aside and making a go at it barefoot. However, she ditched that notion for fear it would ruin the pedicure she just spent the remainder of her birthday money on. That and the thought of running barefoot on pavement was like when the lunch lady plops a lazy piece of peperoni pizza onto a platter with her bare hands. It's just unsanitary. However, Sheree also mentally calculated how quickly microbes could multiply on bare hands versus plastic gloves, and came to a frightening conclusion that gloves grow bacteria seven-hundred times faster than bare hands in a single hour, and suddenly she understood the lunch lady's reasons for defying the practice. Hopefully she at the very least washed her hands. Then she cursed Jennifer for making her do math on summer break. Then she cried for cursing her best friend since she was taking out her own personal anger on everyone around her and suddenly she wondered if she ever wanted to go home again.

Maybe she should run away.

Leave.

Go somewhere else and never come back.

But then she realized how much she'd miss her family. Her friends, assuming they'd still have her as a friend. Her town she'd grown to love despite its apparent loathing of her. Hell, even her brother's dogs.

The laces of her jeans burned, threatening to catch her thighs on fire as they chafed. The backless wedge heels she ever-so-gracefully ran in began to take their toll on her calves. The lack of exercise in general made her lungs feel like they were about to explode.

But there was her house.

The light was on in the living room.

She could see her mother.

She could see her brother.

She could see her sister.

She could not see her father.

But she could see his car, which meant that he either hadn't been called into work to examine Lilith's body, which, as she thought about it, made her wonder if he quit or got fired or if he was dead or… "SHUT UP!" she shouted to her brain as it spiraled out of control, stopping just short of the front door.

"I'll try to be quieter," a man's voice said from the shadows.

"Dad!" Sheree squealed, quickly walking over to the side of the house by the maple tree her brother fell out of the previous fall.

Sheree went in for a hug, but he protested. It took a second to register why, but when she caught sight of the blood-tinged knuckles, she understood he didn't want to ruin her clothes. However, she didn't care at that particular moment in time, especially since they were already soaked in beer, and wrapped her arms around her father and told him how much she loved him and apologized for being a shitty daughter and cried as he tightened his grip on her and apologized for being a shitty dad and cried as blood dribbled down her back and onto the jeans she'd already sworn never to wear again as long as she lived.

"Some kids beat up Brendon today while we were at Fort Vancouver," he told her, keeping his grip firmly in place even if it meant talking into her hair and eating it while he spoke.

"What the hell? Why?" Sheree asked, her voice muffled against his chest where she could hear the soft beating of his heart.

"His shirt."

It took a moment to figure out what Brendon decided to wear that morning, but then she clearly remembered how diligently he worked on it. The shirt. Sharpies and Crayola markers boldly announced "That's Mr. Faggot To You!" with "Mr. Faggot" in rainbow stripes. He was so proud of being gay, even at ten. The world, however, had different views.

"Where were their parents?" Sheree asked, unwilling to let go even though her father was showing signs he was.

The gulp her father took hit her ear as it traveled down. "Perhaps 'kids' is too loose a term. They were like twenty-something's."

"What?!" Sheree screamed, causing the maple tree to tremble. "Please tell me that is their blood all over your hand?"

The blood.

Mr. Hollins melted into the grass as he sobbed, "I wanted to! But I didn't want Brendon to see that part of me. I had to show him what you are supposed to do. I had to be a better man."

"But your hands?"

"Ask Mr. Maple over there."

Sheree nodded. "Brendon will understand. He thinks that tree is out to get him anyway."

He chortled. "Stop making me laugh. I need to feel like shit for a while."

"Can we feel like shit together?"

A smile managed to come out of the darkness that had overtaken his soul. "Two fucking turds in a can, the two of us."

"Okay, where are people getting these expressions from and why am I apparently the last person to find out about them?"

A low whistle in the wind caused her father to perk up like a guard dog. He grabbed Sheree and placed himself in front of her. "We're not alone."

She turned to see a familiar face. "Dad, meet Jonathan."

"If he's your new boyfriend, we are going to have to have a very uncomfortable father-daughter talk," Mr. Hollins said coldly.

"Um, ew! He's like a hundred and forty years old, Dad!"

"He looks good for his age then. If I was gay, I'd do him."

"Groaty!"

Of all the things her father could say, this was not what she wanted to hear. Any other guy saying he'd have sex with another guy and she'd want to watch the action, but her father? No. Never. Not in a million years for a million dollars. She knew her friends felt differently. Of course, deep down she also knew her friends wanted to be the other man.

The man in question stepped forward. "Frank, it is, correct?"

"Yes?" her father replied, soccor-momming Sheree.

Sensing Mr. Hollins's fear, Jonathan said, "I'm your wife's great-great-grandfather."

"No shit."

Chapter 15
Exes and Ohs

"You really should go see *X-Men* with Chad," Kayla said quietly.

"Really?" Sheree asked back, somewhat shocked, but the more she thought about it, the more she realized Kayla was basically Switzerland when it came to the subject of Chad.

"Yeah. It might be good for you guys to get to know each other," Kayla responded, causing Mr. Hollins's ears to perk up as he listened in. Kayla saw his interest and decided to make her intentions clear by adding, "Since you're going to be cheerleading together."

"Hmmm. You make an excellent point. Jennifer basically said the same thing," Sheree said.

Jennifer.

Saying her name aloud felt like she was Julius Caesar on the Ides of March. Shaking off the knives repeatedly stabbing her,

Sheree sat down next to Kayla in silence. Her mother read silently. Her father stared silently. Her brother ate silently.

Silence.

Achingly.

Painful.

Silence.

"That's it! I'm taking a bath! Phobia be damned!" Sheree announced.

"Okay," her mother said behind the veil of some ridiculous home magazine.

"Awesome," her father managed without removing his eyes from the sexy glow of televised historical violence.

"About time, you're getting ripe," Brendon said while chewing a banana, half of it somehow defying gravity as it hung on his split lower lip like a limp penis.

His injuries from the attack, for the most part, were superficial. A torn lip here, a couple bruises there, a heavy dose of homophobia everywhere.

"Seriously, yo. What bro said," Kayla told her, face twisted like someone broke out the blue Stilton wedge.

Sheree rolled her eyes at her family and they were all none the wiser. She started to skip up the stairs—*CREAK! CREAK! CREAK!*—but then decided to methodically take each step to avoid a catastrophic event like tumbling down and breaking her neck and watching the mockumentary of her life unfold before her eyes as the people who were supposed to love her unconditionally reveled in her current state of immobile being as they converted the laundry room into a space somewhat suitable for her vegetable bed. Perhaps her overactive imagination was getting the better of her. Perhaps. Then she tripped on the second to last step and barely caught herself on the rail that, mere months before, had missing posts from the last time she fell down them.

"I saw that," Kayla said, her face buried in a book but the eyes in the back of her head witnessed the whole ordeal.

"Gurrrruggh!" Sheree growled as she walked into the bathroom, slamming the door behind her.

Her clothes slipped off her body and puddled at her feet. *You can do this. You can do this,* she told herself, eyes closed and using every ounce of courage she could muster to put the stopper in the drain and begin the process of filling the bathtub. The plug was a brick that took both quivering hands to move. The faucet felt like rust had glued it permanently shut as she practically had to use her feet against the tub while turning it to the on position. Water splashed onto her arms, splattering here and there and creating tiny orbs all over her skin reflecting her face as she looked at the blobs. Steam quickly smothered the air. Heat radiated from the cast iron tub. She turned the faucet off once the bath was full, standing over it, looking at her pale distorted reflection behind the vapor veil.

Breathe.

Breathe.

You can do this.

Move your damn feet and put them in the damn tub, Sheree.

Holding her breath, she finally took the plunge.

Eyes closed.

Still holding her breath.

She waited for Death to take her, body and soul, but Death never came. Instead, warm arms wrapped themselves around her breasts. Moist lips nibbled her ears. A nimble finger tickled her stomach as it traveled lower. Sheree couldn't hold it in any longer, and violently released the breath she had been holding in. A couple small giggles escaped with it as the finger made contact with the outside of its intended target.

"Jeff," Sheree whispered.

"Shhh," he said back before his tongue tickled her ear lobe and finger slowly tunneled its way into her.

One hand pulled on his hair as he slid in and out. "Oh, baby, don't stop!" she whispered, so as to not rouse suspicion from her family.

"Technically I'm still a fetus."

"Shut up."

Another finger swirled around before joining his brother. Sheree splashed. Waves crashed, both inside and out.

"Oh, gawd!" she said louder than intending, thankful the fan was raucously whirring to drown out her ecstatic cries.

Fast.

Slow.

Fast fast.

Slow.

"Oh!" Sheree cried as her body quivered while climaxing, splashing bath water, the waves drenching her dry clothes, but in the moment not caring about anything but the feeling.

Sheree opened her eyes to find herself alone. Even though she was bathing, she felt dirty. Dirty for having sexual thoughts.

Dirty for masturbating. Dirty for being unable to control her feelings towards the unborn child in her sister's womb.

Dirty and drowning.

She stood up, kicked the stopper, and began toweling off from top to toe as the water swirled into the drain, taking with it her filthy thoughts. Or so she told herself. She swore never to think of baby Jeff again in that way. Swore it was just a fantasy that he would be full-grown straight out of her sister's vagina. Swore it could never happen once he was born.

Then she felt dirty again.

Fighting the urge to literally take a shower to cleanse herself of her figurative thoughts, Sheree wrapped the towel around her torso, picked up her dirty clothes, and walked to her bedroom where she tried to forget. Tried to forget about her sister carrying her dead boyfriend in her belly. Tried to forget about sexualizing an unborn child. But she couldn't. His jacket still hung in her closet, still faintly smelling of Obsession, reminding her of how much she still loved and lusted over him.

Vomit gurgled its way up her esophagus. Instinctually, she swallowed. The acid burned like guilt. Guilt for living; for fantasizing; for feeling like she will not be able to control herself and become one of the most terrible things on this planet: a child molester.

"Stop, Sheree. Just stop," she told herself, letting the towel fall to the floor as she slid a pair of lacy red panties on before ripping them off and opting for simple gray briefs instead.

After dressing herself in summer's finest—an oversized t-shirt, loose-fitting gym shorts, and flip-flops—she stared at the round purple pillow on her bed and fought the urge to cry. Her fight, however, lacked a skilled army, and the enemy quickly overtook her emotions. As the tears flowed, she wondered how she could apologize to Jennifer, how to make things right. What could she do? What could she say? Then she decided the only way would be to talk to her, so she picked up her pink princess phone and dialed the numbers and listened to the incessant rings and hung up after Jennifer's mother's bluntly cruel voice told her she didn't want to speak to her.

Drying her eyes with her hands, she looked at herself in the mirror and shook her head. Bloodshot eyes reminded her of the stoned girl at the Fourth of July party the other night and made her sick. A few drops of Visine cleared up her condition, and she felt confident to face the world. But would the world accept her? There was only one way to find out.

"Going for a walk!" Sheree shouted as she ran down the stairs and out the front door, not even bothering to find out if her family cared, and not daring to look anyone in the eye.

She stood at the end of the driveway and looked in either direction. Both looked daunting; cemetery to the right, road out on the left. Both made her feel dirty and guilty and shame. Both ways were equal as far as she was concerned, so she picked a direction and went.

Sheree did not intend to stop at Chad's front door, but there she was, fist inches away from it. Without much thought, her hand tapped, knocking out her usual "Shave and a Haircut" she inherited from her father.

A few seconds later after what sounded like a stampede, the door opened to Chad boisterously singing in what could only be described as the voice of Kermit and Miss Piggy's lovechild, "Two bits!" He was as horrifyingly off key as her father. "Oh, Sheree! Sorry, I thought you were Courtney."

"Well, we're both black, so I understand the confusion," Sheree responded sans any readable expression.

Chad snorted. "Did you want to come in?"

"No, I just wanted to ask how Nikki was doing?"

"Why don't you ask her yourself?"

"Because we aren't really friends. I mean, you and I aren't either, but…" *Seriously, Sheree? Try to stop being a bitch for once in your miserable fucking life!* "…I'd like to. Jennifer might complicate matters."

The smile on Chad's face melted to sadness, changing his whole demeanor. "How is she doing?"

"She won't talk to me since the incident," Sheree revealed, Mrs. Hoang's shrill voice still pounding in her ear.

"Yeah, you were a cunty whore," Chad said, lifting his eyebrows to emphasize the 'cunty whore' part.

"Chad! Language!" Ms. Walker shouted from behind him as she watched a taped episode of *All My Children*, perfectly timed by Hayley Vaughan Santos (played by the indomitable Kelly Ripa), plugging her ears and chattering nonsensical noises after walking into the afterglow of her father and mother's latest sexcapade despite their supposed impending divorce. *Soap operas are far too realistic.*

After turning towards his mother, Chad apologized, promising to keep the language squeaky clean. Better than G-rated.

Then he turned back around and whispered to Sheree, "Of course, I've seen tits in family movies before, so I don't know why hers are all in a twist."

"*Baby?*"

"*Baby.*"

They stared at each other for hours as if they were poorly operated animatronic brontosauruses waiting for the plot to move forward. Okay, twelve seconds. Then they both started talking. Then both said to go ahead. Then both started talking again. Over and over this scenario played out until Courtney showed up. Ms. Walker pressed PAUSE on the VCR, leaving an obviously disapproving Kelly Ripa to watch over the teenagers as she made her way into the kitchen, knowing full and well that she wouldn't be able to hear anything over Courtney's voice.

"Da fuck you bitches talkin' 'bout?" Courtney asked, giving Sheree the stink eye, arms crossed over a tiny blue tank top that somehow contained her sizeable breasts.

"You," Sheree and Chad said in unison, both crossing their arms in solidarity.

"Oh hell no! Now you two actin' way too the same! I ain't never no saw nothin' so Kray Kray as this shit!"

"I was asking about Nikki," Sheree said.

"I was asking about Jennifer," Chad said.

"And neither ya'll thought to ask 'em yo'self?" Courtney questioned.

"Jen won't speak to me," Sheree said.

"Nikki's mom is keeping her chained up in the dungeon," Chad said.

"Stop exaggerating, Chad!" his mother shouted from the kitchen as she filled a pint glass with ice and boxed white wine.

"Amanda, I know Nikki's mom. Chad prolly tellin' it true," Courtney said back, but if it was anyone else, the term may be considered 'shouted back' instead.

"Well," Sheree said, letting out a sigh loud enough to wake the dead, which given her recent introduction to her great-great-great-grandfather the vampire, was now a distinct possibility, before asking, "Ya'll wanna go see *X-Men* with me?"

"Oh my gawd, I'd love to!" Chad squealed like a little schoolgirl, jumping up and down.

"Me, too! I love me some Patrick Stewart, and Halle Berry makes me so moist!" Courtney squealed like a little schoolgirl, also jumping up and down.

Courtney's Ebonics, however, forgot to assert itself, causing Sheree to wonder just how exhausting it must be to play it tough all the time; to have to pretend to be from the hood, when in reality she was just from Baker Street in a small town in southwest Washington. She then tried to figure out how to apologize for her hateful words she said the other night. Tried to find a way to say she was sorry. Tried to figure out how to put the puzzle pieces back together again into a pleasant picture and pretend like the cat didn't sneak away with the part that makes it whole.

"I'll pay!" she blurted out.

"You better, bitch, after the way yo' crazy white ass talk at me three nights ago," Courtney said.

"Yeah, about that, I am really sorry. I'd blame it on the beer, but that seems like a copout story someone in one of those lame teen movies we've all decided are horrible would use," Sheree said.

"Gurrrl! It was prolly those side-lacers you squeezed yo' ass into! Those things always cramp my cootch, but they so stylin'!" Courtney said, making Sheree feel about 0.002 percent better.

"Thanks. Again, sorry."

They waved goodbye as Courtney shoved past Chad into the house. *Crap*, Sheree thought. *How am I going to pay for all of us?*

"Daddy!" Sheree squealed when she spotted him killing weeds with his bare hands and putting on a show for all the lonely neighborhood housewives as he was also doing so in nothing but running shorts and Nikes. "I need a hundred bucks by next week."

"Sounds like you need to get a job," he shot back without skipping a beat, tossing the remains of a dandelion into an orange Home Depot bucket beginning to show its age.

Sheree resembled the dead, quickly wilting dandelions in the pail. She decided her best line of defense was a good offense. Lifting her head from the ground, she assembled the most pathetic sad face her body had to offer. "Please? I want to take Chad and Courtney to see *X-Men*."

Feeling pity upon his daughter, he gave in (probably due to Chad's involvement in her planned activity) and told her, "On one condition."

"Anything, name it!" Sheree said quickly. Too quickly. This could not bode well, she figured, as her father flashed her an evil grin.

Too evil.

"You also have to take Brendon."

It was a small price to pay for free money, she decided, agreeing to his terms. But then she caught the look in his eyes. The late-night-infomercial-look that said, "But wait! There's more!" Sadly she was right.

"And all of his friends."

Her loving father had suddenly become the devil. But then Sheree realized a flaw in his evil plan to ruin her social reputation: her car.

"I can only drive five, max, and that is assuming the person in the middle backseat is a Lilliputian," she said, full of indignant superiority.

One friend. I can handle one friend.

"The station wagon can haul ten. I win," he said, displaying the same face as his daughter.

Another earth-shattering sigh escaped Sheree's body. "I agree to your terms so long as we do not exceed maximum capacity, and I can wear very large dark sunglasses and a wig and a fat-suit so nobody knows it's me driving The Beast."

The Beast was what her father had lovingly called his car, a vehicle leftover from a different era that included wood paneling and questionable paint colors. A 1973 Ford LTD Country Squire that could barely make it uphill with one person, and chugged gas like her mother chugged wine.

"You're ridiculous. You'd never wear a fat-suit," her father said, sweat glistening over his toned abs like a six-pack of beer cans and causing a nearby woman staring out her front window to faint and causing her husband to fuss over her and causing her dogs to go into a panic and her cat to be horribly disappointed she was still alive when he checked her breath.

Sheree's whole body fell into a slump. "You're right. Fine. Brendon's friends and The Beast it is."

A smug grin formed on Mr. Hollins's young-looking face as he watched his daughter slowly drag herself into the house like a slug. She was defeated. He won. Daughter: Zero. Dad: One. Ah, the life of a parent.

She grudgingly informed her brother of the plan. Brendon's shouts of glee were not far behind as he dashed past his father saying, "I'm going to invite Darryl and Kwirk and Wayne and…"

A week later, after squeezing into The Beast, Sheree, Courtney, Chad, Brendon and six of his closest friends squeezed into a long line, then squeezed into a packed theater. Sheree was relieved Brendon and his entourage chose to sit in the front row and away from her. Part of her wished Jennifer was with her. A bigger part wished Kayla had joined them so Brendon could invite one less annoying little kid. However, Jennifer was not talking to anyone as far as she knew, and Kayla felt a little out of the loop on the whole comic book movie thing due to her being, well, "away" for so long. Or so that was her excuse in front of Courtney. In confidence, she told Sheree she would have to get up to pee every ten minutes and she felt gross and fat and ugly but knew Courtney would want to kiss and touch and cuddle her to death when all she wanted was to be alone. Sheree also wished her fat-suit request had not been denied, especially after Tommy Gufflebacht showed up with another boy and sat down in the seats in front of her. They shared a popcorn. And a soda. Part of her wanted to share her fist and punch him in his little midget throat, and the other part wanted to make sure Brendon didn't turn back and see him.

As much as she hoped not to draw his attention, Sheree accidentally kicked the back of Tommy's seat. When he turned around and saw who it was, he quickly turned back around and sat very still and stiff and scared. Sheree on the other hand pretended not to notice him as she started chatting with Courtney.

"That boy in front of me is the dick who doesn't want to date Brendon," Sheree whispered.

"Not everybody gay, girl!" Courtney said so loud Sheree was sure the audiences in the other two screens of the small theater heard her.

"Courtney!" Sheree said, her face a distasteful shade of beet.

Chad full-body laughed like a silent movie.

The rest of the theater seemed immune to the outburst, including Brendon. However, the back of Tommy's neck matched the color of Sheree's face; hers red from embarrassment, his from anger.

Jesus Christ, Sheree. Stop being an asshole. "Hey, Tommy. I'm sorry. I didn't mean…"

"No, I'm sorry. I deserve it. I was kinda mean to Brendon," Tommy said, taking another sip of the soda after the boy he was with did.

"I was meaner." Sheree contemplated her next move, but unfortunately her mouth had other plans. "Who's your date?"

"Gross!" the two boys said together.

"He's my brother!" Tommy clarified.

"Listen here little shits. I be on a date with my besties and it ain't sexual, jus' a damn outing wit' friends," Courtney told the two.

Tommy looked at his brother and said, "Maybe we should find different seats. I see a couple in the front row. Ugh, my neck is going to kill me, but..."

While Tommy droned on and on about the woes of neck cramps, Sheree noticed the couple of seats he was referring to were the ones next to Brendon. Deciding that can't happen, she piped up with, "Listen guys. I promise we won't bug you anymore. Just stay where you're at, it'll be fine."

The smile on her face vanished when she turned to face Courtney whose face was anything but cuddly. One look, and Sheree knew there were going to be words spoken later. Sheree shot her a look acknowledging it, but couldn't find one in her database of facial expressions to say, "I don't want to hurt Brendon," so she whispered it softly into Courtney's ears as close as Courtney's Afro allowed. It took every fiber of her strength not to scratch her nose right after as it tickled from the curly kinky coif. Courtney half-smiled and winked back and then a loud *POP!* hit Sheree's ears and made her leak a little. She clutched her left ear, half expecting it not to be there.

Sadly, it was just the beginning of the pre-previews, and the *POP!* was just a kernel of corn popping and telling the audience to go buy overpriced movie snacks before the movie starts. Courtney, however, found this an opportune time to talk about everything her brain could think of and could not stop pulling her own Chatty Cathy cord. Chad, however, seemed immune to Courtney's continuous chatter, either through invulnerability or perhaps his hearing aids being turned off for the time being. Sheree prayed her decision not to just see the movie alone was still the correct choice as Courtney blabbered. Between Tommy in front of her, Brendon and his entire friend group way in front of her in the front row, and sitting next to Courtney and Chad, people that only a few months ago she'd never hang out with socially, and the kicker being having to drive The Beast, she found regret impossible to avoid like a fart in a crowded silent room.

The lights dimmed and the previews started and Courtney went silent as the trailer blared through the theater Kristen Dunst and Eliza Dushku as cheerleaders accused of stealing cheer routines from black people. As soon as it ended, Courtney simply could not contain herself.

"That shit's gonna be the best movie ever!"

Turned out, *X-Men* was pretty damn good as well, and the ride home was filled with everyone remarking on their favorite parts. Everyone except for Courtney, who was fuming over her favorite character that, albeit even she admitted was created solely for the cartoon, barely had a walk-on role.

"I'm tellin' ya', the industry got it out for Asians," she said bluntly.

"Fo' sho' MoFo," Brendon said from the bucket seats in the back of the station wagon.

"Umbuh!" Kwirk and Wayne said in unison.

"Oh, puhleaze! MoFo is *not* a bad word," Darryl said.

Anni, the lone girl in the equation and basically Brendon's fag hag, said, "Now mother F-U-C-K-E-R is."

"Umbuh!" Kwirk, Wayne, Brendon, Darryl, a boy Sheree never caught the name of, and a crew cut clumsy kid named Chuck said.

"It is? Goddamnmotherfuckingcocksuckingsonofabitch, yo'," Courtney said back, shaking her head but her Afro stayed in place, causing the Chad in the middle of the front seat between her and Sheree to go into hysterics with his creepy silent laughter.

The children in the backseats were horrified.

"Don't you dare 'umbuh' me, punks!" Courtney said with a closed fist waving in the air threatening pummeling action to anyone who said the word.

"Ummmmbuuuuhhh!" Brendon said quietly, failing to contain laughter.

"Oh hell no!" Courtney said to him, crawling over the front seat, her crotch stuck in Chad's horrified face as Sheree tried to regain control of the steering wheel with one of Courtney's feet honking the horn. "I gonna strangle you, boy!"

Chapter 16
Out on a Limb

Rough and viscously slobbering tongues attacked her face from either side, forcing Sheree to wake up earlier than she wanted to on a lazy summer morning. No matter how many times she shooed or flailed her arms at them, their incessant licking continued until she sat up, screaming, "Fine, assholes! I'm awake!"

Rex and Deschutes leapt from the bed, down the stairs, and scratched at the French doors leading to the backyard, no doubt leaving marks that would make her mother mad. Sheree was not amused. These dogs were not her responsibility. These dogs were Brendon's dogs. Brendon should be getting wet cheeks. Brendon should be getting up early. Brendon, however, was not in his room when she checked, about to curse him to high heavens over shirking his dog-ownership duties.

Her search continued.

Bathroom? No.

Kayla's room? Nope, just Kayla snoring loudly, causing her to cringe that she may just snore that bad as well. The covers thrashed in every direction.

Her parents's room? No. Not gonna check after that one "Very Special Episode" of *The Hollins Family* where the parents had to explain that they were not murdering each other or wrestling after intense groaning caused the children enough concern to open the door. Nope. Never again. Nah ah. Not going to happen. Instead, she braced herself as she held an ear to the door, and was relieved she heard nothing.

The scratching continued, but now included whimpering and pathetic cries, so she walked down the steps.

The dogs howled.

The clawing at the doors began chipping the wood away from the panes, leaving sawdust to settle at their feet. When she reached them, Rex was using his whole body to try pushing the door while Deschutes continued howling.

"Jesus, guys! You must really have to pee!" Sheree said as she approached the door.

She gasped when she saw what they were trying to get her attention over.

Brendon.

Tree.

Rope.

Feet dangling.

Twitching.

Face rapidly changing colors.

Fingers tangled in the noose.

"Oh my gawd! BRENDON!!!" Sheree screamed as she flung the doors open and ran towards him, Rex and Deschutes just in front of her. "Brendon!" she shouted again, climbing the tree, bark tearing at her skin while the dogs danced beneath Brendon's feet that had gone limp.

Purple face.

Blood dripping from his mouth, onto his chin, neck, down his chest where his t-shirt added it to the assortment of unidentifiable stains that have graced it over the past few years, giving it character. Sheree hated that shirt whenever he would wear it out in public. With her. Embarrassing her. Causing her to be on high alert in case a fellow Fashion Committee person saw her with him and chastised her without mercy, threatening to disavow her membership for allowing such a cataclysmic catastrophe to go unscathed. She hated it even more now that his possibly dead body was wrapped in it.

Smothering him.

Strangling him.

Crawling on the limb, Sheree refused to let tears flow. Refused to allow herself to believe what her eyes had long since processed. Refused to even let the notion cross her mind that this was not a rescue mission, it was a recovery mission. She scooted, ripping her underwear as it snagged on the fir tree's skin.

Her favorite panties.

Her only brother.

Her resolve was clear as she pulled the rope up just enough to try loosening the knot around the branch. Somehow her muscles, despite her lack of upper body strength since leaving Seattle and not making Ravenwood High's cheerleading squad, forgot how weak they were supposed to be as she undid the knot and slowly lowered her brother to the soft green grass below.

Just sleeping, she thought, brain ignoring the bloated purple head with a thick rope tightly wrapped around the neck after the body rested.

Suddenly the whole house shook violently.

"Jessica, NOOOOOOOOO!!!" she heard, only slightly muffled by the wood and plaster and insulation and glass that separated the voice from the backyard.

Kayla crashed through the slightly ajar doors and fell over Brendon, furiously undoing the rope around his neck as she chanted, rocking back and forth while her stomach thrashed about.

Rex and Deschutes dragged the rope away as if it was the culprit, a rattlesnake trying to attack their owner. They returned after killing it, taking their place a few feet behind Kayla like they were giving her space to work.

As if waking from a trance, Sheree flipped herself around, grasping the branch where her brother's body hung, and carefully held onto it before letting go. She landed just inches away from his body where her sister performed some magical nonsense that was bound to go as well as the last time she tried to resurrect the dead. She pulled herself towards Kayla, wrapping her arms around her shoulder, and tried to tell her he was already gone, but Kayla ignored her.

The dogs moved, tucking themselves into Sheree's lap, whimpering softly.

Kayla continued to work her magic.

Sheree's emotions hit her like a truck as they all came crashing towards her at once, the blow causing her to go into hysterics as she bawled into her brother's chest where Kayla's hands covered his heart. As she cried, she saw a baby's head and hands pushing until Kayla's nightshirt flipped over despite the lack of wind, exposing her bare skin.

Head.

Hands.

Nose.

Mouth.

Eyes.

"The itsy bitsy spider went up the water spout..."

This can't be happening, Sheree thought as she watched the mouth pushing against her sister's stomach move in-sync with the singing that surrounded them.

"Down came the rain and washed the spider out..."

Kayla was unfazed by the song emanating from the womb within her body.

All Sheree could do was stare.

Rex and Deschutes growled.

"Up rose my power and with it dried the rain,

"And the itsy bitsy spider has just killed again!"

Kayla screamed, shattering the kitchen window and cracking a few of the French door panes. Sheree jumped up involuntarily as her body reacted. Shivers traveling up and down her spine like dominoes. Brendon was limp. Kayla was still screaming, only Sheree could no longer hear the sound that had to be coming out of her sister's mouth as if her body was protecting itself from rupturing, cracking, shattering into a million pieces.

More shattered panes.

More broken windows.

Car alarms sang.

A crow plummeted.

Dead.

A feather rose from the crow's body, landing on Sheree's shoulder as if trying to remind her of something. It fell off before she noticed it.

"Hhhgruuuuhhhhuuuguuhhh!" Brendon sucked in, gasping for air until his lungs took over. The color suddenly changed in his bloated face back to a somewhat normal shade as his dogs whined happily while kissing him, licking off the blood from his cheeks and phlegm that had pushed its way out the back of his throat when he coughed after catching his breath; the beginnings of a cold or an upper respiratory infection that would rob him of weeks from his rapidly dwindling summer vacation.

"Brendon! You're alive! Brendon!" Kayla said, shocked she was able to actually perform considering all the decks stacked against her.

"I don't understand," Sheree said after hugging him to the point of crushing. "I thought you were Kayla's kryptonite! I thought you said she couldn't hurt you!"

"She can't," Brendon said, voice gravelly and raspy as he rubbed his throat, causing it to burn even more now that the ropes had been removed, leaving behind raw flesh.

"But..." Sheree started.

"But Jessica can," Kayla said quietly.

"Huh?" Sheree asked, her confusion as plain as her torn underwear, shreds still clinging to the tree branch above her head.

"Brendon!" Mrs. Hollins shrieked as she ran barefoot onto the lawn, followed closely by Mr. Hollins in nothing but backwards boxers.

"Mom! Dad!" he croaked, holding out his arms for them to hold him and make him feel better like good mommies and daddies are supposed to do when their children are hurting.

While comforting their son, Mrs. Hollins asked Kayla, "What happened? How?"

But Kayla's voice had broken, and all that could escape were squeaks and squawks between the tears that endlessly streamed down her face, carving canyons into her cheeks. Finally she was able to push out, "Jessica is getting stronger than I can control."

Control? What does Kayla mean by control?

"I'm calling my mother," Mrs. Hollins said, but before she could, her mother briskly walked up to them.

"I am so sorry, dears," Grandma Lowell said. "I should have known she would've gone after Brendon, especially since he…"

"Should've known?!" Mrs. Hollins cried. "Yes, you should have! Hell, you probably did and decided not to tell us because you need some goddamn prophecy fulfilled!"

"The prophecy…" Grandma Lowell started, but Mrs. Hollins refused to let her finish.

"Your cousin Leslie's prophecy is bullshit!" Mrs. Hollins shouted, standing up to put herself between her mother and child.

"I… I…" Grandma Lowell stuttered, but then looked directly at Kayla and sadly smiled.

Kayla nodded in acknowledgment of their psychic conversation, reflecting the same sad smile back to her grandmother. Grandma Lowell took one last look at her angry daughter, confused granddaughter and son-in-law, and recovering grandson before she snapped her fingers and disappeared into thin air.

"I don't ever want to see that woman again," Mrs. Hollins growled through gritted teeth.

"Mom, you don't mean that," Kayla said calmly, putting her hand on her mother's shoulder.

"I do!" Mrs. Hollins shouted, throwing Kayla's hand away.

It reminded Sheree of her own temper. Her own actions. Her own guilt.

Kayla pretended it didn't happen and said, "Your dogs will protect you from now on, Brendon."

"But, huh?" Brendon said, Mr. and Mrs. Hollins basically saying the same thing without words.

"You'll figure it out. Soon. Think about it. Use your brain," Kayla said bluntly but without being cold or demeaning.

"Let me guess, more secrets and more lies from my mother?" Mrs. Hollins said, her nails digging into the palms of her fisted hands as her face melted from tears.

"Beth," Mr. Hollins said, putting his hands on her shoulders. "Please calm down."

"No! That woman has brought nothing but pain to this family!" Mrs. Hollins yelled. "I am done with her!"

"Mom, please don't say that," Kayla urged. "You never know what could happen and you might regret saying things out of anger."

"Never! I can't have her in my life and I refuse to allow her in yours!" Mrs. Hollins shouted.

"Beth, calm down," Mr. Hollins said.

"No. Help me get Brendon to the hospital," Mrs. Hollins said, fussing over her son.

"I don't need to go to the hospital, Mom," Brendon told her.

"But your neck!" Mrs. Hollins shrieked.

"Is fine, see?" Brendon said, showing her that his neck was back to normal. That he was back to normal. That, in essence, it appeared as though the incident never took place.

"But… But…?" Mrs. Hollins asked, examining where his wounds should be as Mr. Hollins did the same, recalling all of their medical school knowledge.

Conjuring up a smile, Brendon calmly told his mother, "Grandma Lowell healed me before she left."

To make certain he was indeed all right, Mr. and Mrs. Hollins carried Brendon into the house, carefully avoiding the broken glass. He insisted on walking to prove his strength. They insisted on treating him like a baby. The parents won this round.

"I should not have come back! I should've known I'd just mess everything up again. I should've figured my presence would only make matters worse," Kayla cried after they were out of earshot, spilling tears, snot, and drool all over her nightshirt.

"You're right, but too late now," Sheree said, side hugging to avoid the assortment of bodily fluids her sister was oozing, despite the fact that she was planning on throwing the torn t-shirt in the trash.

Chapter 17
Family Dynamics

"So there's a super cute boy in front of me at Pizza Schmizza holding his little brother and kissing him on the cheek repeatedly and I'm screaming in my head, 'I'll be your little brother! Kiss me! KISS MEEEEE!!!!' And then I think about how creepy that sounds and I feel like a dirty old man," Brendon told his mother, who proceeded to spit out her coffee all over the counter, splattering Brendon's face and shirt and the tissue he was using to wipe his nose.

"Brendon! What the hell?" Mrs. Hollins said, trying to wipe coffee off her chin, but failing to catch it before it trickled down her shirt, pooling in the underside of her bra that dug into her flesh with its uncomfortably supportive wire.

As Mrs. Hollins wiped, Sheree tried desperately not to laugh at the situation, but couldn't contain herself. The house shook as her guffaws echoed and reverberated off the walls, shaking the wood-bodied-brass-winged ducks as they tried to fly away from danger but the nails in their wings bound them in place. It was enough to wake Mr. Hollins from his mid-morning nap he tended to take when a late night call from the hospital or police would rouse him in to examine a dead body and file an official report.

"Earthquake!" he cried, jumping from the den's sectional sofa, stubbing his toe on the coffee table he'd just removed his feet from, causing a string of nondescript curses to erupt out of his mouth.

"No earthquake, just Sheree," Kayla said calmly without moving the magazine she was casually perusing from her face.

"Bitch!" Sheree shouted, about to pummel her sister, but Kayla pulled the pregnancy card on her with nothing more than a finger pointing towards, uh, her pregnant belly?

Which one's Jessica? Please let me just punch Jessica in her fucking midget face? Sheree thought as she stared at her sister's stomach.

"How did this entire conversation get away from me?" Brendon asked the universe.

The universe, in all its ancient brilliancy, never responded.

Mrs. Hollins refilled her mug and calmed her soul with another sip of coffee. Mr. Hollins resumed his napping position once he realized the danger was artificially created in his own sleep-deprived mind. Kayla took another swig of pig's blood from the plastic container the butcher packaged it in, deciding to switch things up from the human stuff.

"Is it wrong that part of me gets horny at the thought of you giving birth to Jeff?" Sheree asked her sister as soon as their mother picked up a magazine frequently read by women her age.

"Yes. That is quite disturbing. He'll be your nephew," Kayla said.

That bit of truth never crossed her mind. Half the summer she spent having sex dreams about Jeff. The fact that he technically would be her nephew began stirring around her brain. But he wouldn't be biologically, would he? Her stomach indicated it might be ready to dispose of its contents.

"I hate the universe," Sheree announced.

"Don't hate the universe, hate me," Kayla said, showing no signs of sarcasm, just honest-to-God truth in her voice.

Sheree tried, but couldn't. As much as she wanted to hate Kayla for everything she had done to her over the past year, every time a bad thought entered, it left just as quickly as if by magic. Only she knew that magic had no sway over her thoughts towards Kayla after the blinds were drawn and she could see again. No, this time she couldn't hate because she knew Kayla, remembered their connection, one that could not be broken again.

"I could never hate you. Well, as long as you don't go all psycho bitch-witch-ghost again. I just can't wait to see that brown-haired blue-eyed boy," Sheree said, giggling as she put her face in Kayla's stomach, forgetting the thoughts from seconds before about wanting to sucker punch the evil one.

"You fail to take into account that he is probably, genetically speaking, all Kayla, which means genetically he is all you since you are identical twins, which means, genetically, he will be your brother," Mrs. Hollins said from the den, her eyes never leaving the page she was reading.

"Brother fucker," Sheree mumbled under her breath.

"That also means he'll probably have strawberry blond hair and teal eyes," Mrs. Hollins added.

"Thanks for ruining my sex life, Mother," Sheree said scornfully.

"You're welcome," she said back, turning a page and lighting up at the kitchen makeover spread before her eyes.

Sheree sulked in the sofa. As her mind remembered Jeff when he was alive, one of the things that first attracted her to him was his brown hair and blue eyes. Then his body. Then his mind. Then after she added all those things together she realized that the sum was basically a carbon copy of her father, and she hated herself for falling for the cliché.

The cliché, however, was not finished with her.

The phone rang, and when Mrs. Hollins answered it, Sheree prayed it was Jennifer. The color of her mother's face and the slam heard across the country, however, made her guess it was not. She did have a pretty good idea who could rile her mother up like that. Even though a week had passed since Brendon's hanging, there was simply not enough time in the universe for her mother's anger to pass. However, her insides were killing her to find out.

"What'd Grandma want?" Brendon asked, beating Sheree to the punch, to which she was eternally grateful for as he would solely bear the wrath of Beth.

Sheree's eyes widened in anticipation of the shit-show, however, disappointment soon prevailed as she watched her mother ignore Brendon's question, go straight for the corked bottle of wine on the counter she hadn't finished the night before (a rarity to say the least), and chug. After tossing the bottle into the trash, she disappeared into the basement. As Sheree settled back down into the couch, she saw a line of tears flowing from her sister's eyes.

"Mom is about to do something she will regret and there is nothing we can do to stop her," Kayla said quietly.

"I know," Sheree said, grabbing Kayla's hand and squeezing.

However, Sheree had no idea what her mother intended.

     ❦   ❦   ❦

Sitting in front of the fireplace, Mrs. Hollins tossed photographs into the flames with one hand while holding a half-full glass of merlot in the other. The fire sprites danced, reflected in the glass as they consumed. She stared at a picture of her mother taken before they moved back to Ravenwood. Before their lives were turned upside down. Before Kayla was tragically killed then tried to kill them while her soul was torn apart. It was her favorite picture of her mother; a candid shot of her at Alki Beach looking over the bay at Downtown Seattle, completely unaware her daughter had taken it.

Her face hardened.

Her merlot vanished in three large gulps.

The picture joined the rest, quickly swallowed up by the hungry orange flames that couldn't get enough. Their insatiable hunger craved more and more until they all turned to ashes.

As much as Sheree wanted to stop her mother from destroying the photos, she was powerless to do anything to prevent it. All she could do was make sure her mother didn't do something rash, like, say, throw herself into the fireplace and burn herself alive. With the sheer amount of alcohol in her system, she'd quickly combust to oblivion. Then again, she would also have to tightly pack herself into the fireplace since the opening was barely large enough to fit a couple logs into. It took every ounce of restraint to withhold the laughter begging to be released as she envisioned her mother carefully contorting herself into the tiny hearth's cave. In reality, her mother could simply step into the fireplace and sit and still have room, but for some reason Sheree saw her mother at this moment in time as larger than life. Brains are fickle creatures… from time to time.

Sheree thought her heart leapt out of her chest when her phone rang while she dreamt of Jeff in a very naughty way. Poetic justice.

"You're supposed to be my best friend," Jennifer said on the other end, words slurred from the sauce her body was filled with.

The words stung with truth.

"I know. I am. Sorry."

"You're sorry? You're sorry?!"

"Yes."

Silence.

"I'm sorry."

"Why are you apologizing?"

"No, I am. Sorry piece of shit."

"Jennifer, what the hell?"

"You haven't talked to me since the party."

"I called a million times but your mom said you didn't want to talk."

"Fucking bitch! I hate her."

A car horn honked.

"Jennifer, where are you?"

"Payphone."

"Why?"

"Looking for my dad."

No amount of alcohol could cover up the hurt in her voice. Sheree looked at her bedside clock.12:52 AM.

"I'm coming to get you," Sheree told her, slipping her feet into a pair of pink flip-flops and trying not to get tangled into the cord of her princess phone. Her purple pillow, however, had no such luck as the cord flung it onto the floor when she got up, sounding like a slamming door. She carefully placed it back onto the head of her bed as if it was a fragile seventeenth century French vase. "Jennifer?"

"Yeah?" Jennifer said, her voice mousy.

"Where are you?"

"Payphone, looking for my dad, wondering why he wants me to be perfect when he can't even stand to be near me."

Jesus Christ, Jennifer! There are dozens of payphones in town. "Which payphone? What is it near?"

"It's by the… Hey! You! Yeah, you! Have you seen my dad?"

"Uh… no?" Sheree said into the receiver, wondering if this was what it was like talking to dementia patients.

"Not you, this guy. Oh my gawd Sheree, he's really cute. Like, silver fox cute. I'm gonna have to let you…"

C-C-CLICK!

The dial tone triggered an alarm in Sheree's head, and before she knew it, she was out the door. Fumbling through her keys looking for the one for her car, she dropped them in the dark recesses of freshly watered grass. Her father insisted on twice daily waterings in the summer to keep his grass the greenest on the street, which included a midnight automatic sprinkling. Reaching for where she assumed they must've fallen based off the laws of gravity, she found nothing but the slender tendrils of Kentucky blue.

"Goddammit!" she cried, ripping a chunk from her father's perfect lawn.

The lone bald spot maddened her, so she dug and dug and kept pulling and tossing aside patches of grass that surely would cause her father to, all joking aside, actually kill her. But at the moment, she only wanted to find her keys and the grass was in the way and only a superficial superiority complex she figured her father conjured up for having nothing else to offer the world. Then the guilt set in. Guilt for tearing up the front yard; for demeaning her father; for being a klutz who couldn't even hold onto her damn keys.

Just when she was about to make a run for it, she spotted them. Not in the grass, but the driveway. Under The Beast. Mocking her like the mushroom under the dining room table quietly threatening to take over the world from the shadows.

As she reached for them, a cold hand grasped her shoulder.

Cold as death.

Well, cold as a dead person, anyway.

"Please tell me that is you, Jonathan," Sheree said, frozen with one hand reaching for the keys and the other balled into a fist in case the answer was in the negative.

"It is I," the person replied.

"Thank God," Sheree said, picking up her keys before turning around to find he was not alone.

"He runs really fast, Sheree!" Jennifer said as bubbly as soda pop while she slid off Jonathan's back before vomiting all over herself, filling in some of the lawn's bare spots with vodka and phở.

While Sheree stared at the lawn, wondering if she could push all of the blame on her drunken friend, Jonathan rubbed Jennifer's back, telling her to keep purging. Sheree had to admit that for a bloodsucking demon, her great-great-great-grandfather was a tender soul.

Once Jennifer seemed spent, Jonathan confessed, "I was in the house speaking with Kayla when your friend called. I apologize, but I must resume our conversation. Do you require assistance getting her inside?"

Part of Sheree felt violated. He was in the house and she didn't know? An intruder—a stranger but not a stranger lurking in the house? However, she didn't have time to be angry. Her friend needed help.

"No, I've got her," Sheree told him as she lifted Jennifer up and slung her arm around her waist.

A faint smile formed on Jonathan's marble face before he went into the house, up the stairs, and closed the door to Kayla's bedroom. Part of her felt uncomfortable leaving Kayla alone with Jonathan. Part of her felt like she had to protect Kayla. Part of her knew Kayla could take care of herself, but another stronger part couldn't shake that it was a mistake to trust him. *After all, the man is a vampire. Vampires are supposed to be evil. Then again, he also hated Jessica so much that he preferred death over divorce, all so he could avoid the societal taboo of the "Big D" so to speak. Of course, it was the other "Big D" that would've been the bigger scandal back in the day; Song's End's "D" that is.* Sheree cursed her tangential mind as she failed at removing the two having wild, passionate, demonical sex her brain conjured up. Then she wondered if Song's End was her great-great-great-grandfather's lover, something she instinctually knew to be true. It had to be. Which meant maybe he was evil after all. But how did she know? Did he tell her? So much information. Too much data to store and not enough memory.

Error code 00C.

Blue screen of death.

Crash dump.

Restart.

What were they talking about? What was he telling her? What was she being left out of the loop on?

"So who's the old guy?" Jennifer asked.

"I'll tell you when you sober up," Sheree told her, trying to shake the bad thoughts bouncing in her brain that insisted on lingering like the lyrics of an old The Cranberries song.

Jennifer's eyes looked so droopy Sheree was certain lead weights were pulling them down. Then she was absolutely positive Jennifer was full of lead as she struggled to get her dead weight onto the living room sofa. It was impossible for her not to feel disgusted with her own body as sweat began oozing out of places she did not realize sweat could pour from. Moist crevices. Once Jennifer was lying down, Sheree ran to the kitchen to grab the garbage can and a few hand towels in case Jennifer's puke sessions were unfinished. The gurgled gagging sound she heard while wetting a washcloth with cold water under the tap told her in no uncertain terms that they were indeed not over.

"Son of a bitch," Sheree cursed, staring at the garbage can at her feet.

Chapter 18
Things Fall Apart

"I'm afraid Kayla's pulling away from me," Courtney said quietly as she sat on Sheree's bed, eyes on the verge of welling but maintaining their invisible wall that kept the tears dammed.

"Why?" Sheree asked, though she already suspected that was the case, especially since Courtney's constant company to Kayla had diminished to practically nothing in the last few weeks. After all, she'd come over to see Kayla, but Kayla had mysteriously disappeared. However, Sheree had to admit that when she accidentally fell asleep while reading, she didn't expect to wake up and find that her entire family apparently decided to up and leave as none were home, not even Rex and Deschutes. They probably went to a goddamn movie without me. And brought the dogs?

"I don't know. I mean, I know I come off strong sometimes, but she knew that getting into this relationship."

"Yeah."

"So I thought I'd give her a little space when she started showing less interest."

"Yeah."

"Do you think it's pregnancy hormones?"

"Yeah."

Silence.

"Be honest, is it me?" Courtney asked.

Her voice was so small that Sheree barely recognized it. It was so different from the real Courtney that lied underneath the hardcore-personal-Ebonics-dialect front she put on to the rest of the world, with the exception of Chad and Nikki during moments of extreme personal connection. The hurt on Courtney's face also couldn't be disguised, even by someone so innately adept at perpetuating a false persona nearly every waking hour of her life. Sheree hesitated. Tell her the truth? Tell her a lie? Tell her anything to keep her guessing at the real reasons her sister was slowly breaking up with the girl she loved? The longer she waited to respond, the worse Courtney was bound to take the news, whatever the answer may be.

"No, it's not you, Courtney," Sheree said, hoping her wavering voice didn't set off any alarms.

A huge heave left Courtney as the breath she'd been holding released from her burning lungs, followed immediately by the tears her eyes could no longer contain. Sad tears. Angry tears. Confused tears. Sheree pulled Courtney in and let her fall apart in her arms.

"I don't know why I feel like I can talk to you about things I won't tell anyone else, and I hate to be a burden, but, you know, sometimes a girl's just gotta cry!" Courtney confessed.

Sheree brushed her hands through Courtney's hair, worried she would break it or cause some sort of irreversible damage to the magical gravity-defying Afro that was her signature style. Regrettably, she knew nothing of black hair, and didn't want to come off as racist for asking questions. "I don't know why either, but I'm glad we're on soul-bearing terms."

"Oh, girlfriend! I love you in the most platonic way possible between a lesbian and a straight girl!" Courtney cried, tears falling into her smiling mouth and seemingly replenishing themselves to no end.

This is it, Sheree. Time to share something you haven't told anyone, she thought to herself. But the problem was Jennifer knew all the dirty stuff, secret stuff, bad stuff, good stuff... all the stuff. All except for one thing. Is it worth it? Wouldn't this diminish her friendship with Jennifer, even if things were rocky and crumbling and probably never going to return back to stability because Jennifer was Humpty Dumpty and she was the mean bitch who pushed her over the ledge? Kayla knew everything as well, but only because they shared a body for a short time, and with the body came the mind, which, unfortunately for Sheree, was only a one-way street; she got nothing during their time together except what Kayla allowed her to remember during the partial possession period. Yes? No?

"Mine is petty."

"Get that shit off your chest."

"It has to do with shit."

"Shiiiiiiiiiittt..."

After slowly blowing out her fear, Sheree said, "I… love… to smell… my fingers after I wipe my ass?" Her face immediately scrunched, baring her teeth as she waited for the onslaught.

"I do the same fuckin' thing, ho," Courtney admitted quietly. "Ain't no shame, but don't be tellin' nobody 'bout that 'cuz, dayyum! That nasty!"

They laughed and cried and bonded and woke Jennifer up with a start.

"How did I get here?" Jennifer asked, but before anyone could answer she added as her face filled with horror, "Oh gawd, my breath is atrocious!"

"Sho' is, Banh Bo Nuong," Courtney told her, popping a Certs into her unexpecting mouth.

"Um, thanks?" Jennifer said, feeling both violated and grateful at the same time.

"Are you sober yet?" Sheree asked.

"Yeah, 'cuz I need chocolate in the worst way, bitch," Courtney said.

Swallowing mint-flavored saliva, Jennifer said, "Yeah. I need so much meat in my mouth it's not even funny."

"BUHWAHAHAHAHAHAHAHAHA!!!" Courtney belted out, causing Sheree to do the same. "She needs meat!" Courtney said, trying to wipe the tears as she laughed so hard her body didn't know if it'd be able to keep herself together. "In her mouth!" she continued. "One night downtown by the payphones and girl's already a pro!"

Shaking her head, Jennifer said to Courtney who probably didn't even hear due to the raucousness evading her mouth, "I really don't know why I am friends with you."

"Hey, we haven't officially reconciled our relationship yet, so can we kiss and make up?" Sheree asked Jennifer as Courtney fell off the bed, seemingly unaware she landed on the wood floor, ass first.

"A hug will suffice. Breath's still groaty," Jennifer told her as she flipped the mint with her tongue before reaching in for a hug. "Wait, who was the hot old guy?"

Sheree's eyes widened like two full moons while they embraced as laughter continued to fill the air, dancing with the dust motes. "I'll tell you later," she whispered, motioning her head slightly towards Courtney who probably wouldn't have noticed one way or the other through her over-the-top guffaws that literally shook the house, but she didn't want to risk it.

"Got it. More secrets," Jennifer said coldly.

This reconciliation was doomed from the start, and all Sheree could do was allow it to happen. Too many secrets to keep. Too many people bound to get caught up in her family's web of lies.

"Oh shit, girls, I gotta pee 'fore I wet myself!" Courtney said, springing up and out of the room and into the bathroom where the door slammed and the toilet seat slammed down with a curse about boys and their damn habits.

"We've got a few seconds, so here's the deal. That old guy is my great-great-great-grandfather and his wife is Jessica, you know that creepy woman in the painting downstairs, and he's a vampire and Song's End is his maker slash lover or at least I am like ninety-two percent certain he is, and he came back to town to help defeat Jessica once and for all after Kayla gives birth to her," Sheree blurted out.

"Holy fuck!" Jennifer shouted, quickly slapping her mouth with both hands.

"Yeah, so much fucks. Secret fucks that only family gets to know about," Sheree told her.

"I'm not family," Jennifer said quietly as her hands slowly fell into her lap where her eyes were staring.

"Yes you are," Sheree said, wrapping her arms around her.

"Yeah?"

"Always."

Courtney came busting out of the bathroom. "Bitch, you got anythang that'll fit my fat ass? Fuckin' pissed a little in my panties and shit leaked all over my shorts an' now I gotta change 'cuz yo' goddamn brotha left the seat up!"

"Um, maybe?" Sheree said as she watched a naked-from-the-waist-down-Courtney rummage through her dresser, unfolding everything her hands touched.

The search seemed endless. Anything Sheree offered that might fit, Courtney deemed unfit to wear in public. Sweatpants? Not in the middle of August. Her father's running shorts? As much as Courtney said he was a DILF, she didn't want anything his dick was free-swinging in around her va-jay-jay.

"Wait a minute, gurrrl! My effin girlfriend got some super-cute momma-to-be clothes. I'm raidin' that shit," Courtney said before leaving Sheree's room and walking to Kayla's.

Oh gawd. Please don't have a spell book just lying around, Sheree thought, pulling Jennifer by the hand.

Sure enough, there it was, sitting on Kayla's bed in plain sight. Courtney, however, had tunnel vision. She also seemed unfazed that she was prancing around the house with her junk in plain sight for the world to see; perfectly rounded ass that would make Sir-Mix-A-Lot cry and his anaconda stiff; acutely manicured pubic hair that was the antithesis of the Afro Sheree always pictured her crotch resembled. She also seemed to put a little more care into how she searched for something suitable to wear. Instead of pulling and tossing and making a huge mess like the one she left behind in Sheree's room, Kayla's clothes were given funereal respect.

"What's that say that I only fit into maternity clothes?" Courtney asked when she finally found something worthy of her body.

Sheree and Jennifer were frightened to answer, unsure how anything they could possibly say would result in a favorable outcome. After all, this was Courtney. Her fuse was shorter than that crazy uncle during election year who thinks the government is going to come knocking on his door to take away his guns.

"Well, it is Juicy Couture, so there is that," Jennifer said.

"True dat," Courtney said as she walked back to Sheree's room to look at herself in the full-length mirror.

Kayla's room was bare bones by comparison. It had a bed, a dresser, and a tiny closet with a tiny wardrobe. No pictures on the walls, mirrors, knick-knacks, or any of the random hoard-worthy stuff normal teenage girls like to surround themselves with. To be quite honest, it looked like a jail cell. The dark grey walls didn't help matters.

"Let's get our eat on. Sheree, drive," Courtney demanded as she swung her hips back and forth while walking down the stairs, exaggerating her already exaggerated ass's footprint in pink velour.

⁂

"So Courtney borrowed my clothes?" Kayla asked when she got home, watching as Sheree was busy refolding hers.

"Yep," Sheree said, stacking T-shirts into a drawer.

Kayla sighed. "Well, I guess I can't break up with her until I get them back, huh?"

"Wait, what?!" Sheree said, dropping her panties.

"I just, well, you know…" Kayla said, dancing around the answer.

"No, I don't know. Tell me," Sheree said, picking up her underwear to fold over again.

Instead of telling Sheree, Kayla burst into tears and fell to the floor, scraping her knees on the old wood planks in desperate need of resurfacing. Sheree couldn't help but notice the sheer size of her sister, especially as she sat on her heels and barely could make out the legs beneath her stomach. The twins looked as though they were ready to break out of their uterine prison any minute. Seeing how distraught it made Kayla, Sheree decided not to pursue her query.

Picking Kayla up off the floor, a thing easier said than done, Sheree said, "Let's go downstairs and pretend we like our family."

"But I do like our family," Kayla said.

"You are the worst teenager ever."

The chitchat continued as they walked down the stairs. Kayla claimed the obvious over her being a horrible teenager with the whole pregnancy scenario. Sheree claimed that was the most normal part of the teenage experience. Kayla laughed. Sheree snorted. Then they plopped down onto the living room sofa side-by-side.

"Any weird cravings lately?" Sheree asked.

"Oddly, no. Unless pickle juice counts," Kayla answered, the garlicky vinegar taste still holding her mouth hostage hours after guzzling the leftover liquid once the pickles were devoured for breakfast.

"Nope!" they heard their mother shout from the kitchen.

"Chocolate with a calamine lotion chaser?" Kayla asked, her face twisted.

"Nope," they heard their mother say much quieter. "Do you have a stupid tingle in your throat that won't go away until you take a swig of Caladryl?"

"Yep," Kayla said.

"What the hell?! Calamine lotion is not for drinking!" Sheree shouted, throwing her arms up in the air.

"It puts the lotion on the skin, or it gets the hose again," Brendon said eerily close to Buffalo Bill in Silence of the Lambs as he walked to the downstairs bathroom with his nose in a men's underwear magazine, involuntarily sneezing onto a particularly suggestive cowboy clad in boots, hat, and tiny briefs.

Mrs. Hollins hung her head in shame, opened a bottle of merlot, poured a glass, and began drinking. Rex and Deschutes licked the few drops she spilled onto the floor, a side effect of pouring too quickly. Mr. Hollins piped in with, "Caladryl has diphenhydramine, which is an antihistamine, so if your body is having a histamine reaction causing said throat tickle, I can see where that'd be soothing. My sister used to drink the stuff all the time and we all thought she was an oddball. Then one day when she was nine, she went into a coughing fit and hacked up a hard hunk of hairy phlegm and never took another drink of the stuff. She's still an oddball, don't get me wrong, but that was the nastiest shit I've ever seen in my entire life."

"Dad, that is the most disgusting story I've ever heard in my entire life," Sheree said, feeling her throat and praying to any god listening that she didn't have a hard hunk of hairy phlegm lingering. Every time she swallowed for weeks after this, she could feel the mythic creature growing, slowly cutting off her airway.

"Oh gawd, poor Aunt Tami," Kayla said.

Mrs. Hollins finished her glass and poured another. The dogs were sadly disappointed that her aim improved with drinking, so they opted to lick her feet instead.

Brendon exited the bathroom and encountered silence. "What'd I miss?" he asked, wiping his nose with his arm, the slime glistening like sunlight on glass.

"NOTHING!" Mrs. Hollins screamed, nearly spilling her wine with her violent hand gestures.

Later that night, after Brendon had gone to bed, Kayla still sat on the sofa next to Sheree, who at this point was lying down.

Rubbing her stomach, she contemplated the future for the one she hoped would survive. The closer to their birth, however, the more she doubted he would. Still, there was a tiny chance and she wanted to be prepared.

"How much do Uncle Billy and Uncle Jack know?" Kayla asked.

"In general or about family matters?" Mr. Hollins asked, pushing aside some of his wife's hair from his mouth as he spoke.

"Mostly family. Like Mom's side," Kayla said.

"Enough," Mr. Hollins said. "Why?"

Kayla scooted along the sofa, disrupting Sheree's feet that had been pushing up against her thigh for the last hour or so. "I was thinking they should raise Jeff. I mean, if they even want kids."

"Where's Jeff?" Sheree stirred at the mentioning of his name, drool trailing along the crevices of her mouth.

Mr. Hollins's left eyebrow cocked. "So you don't want to raise the babies on your own?"

"Hell no."

"Excellent…" he said, readjusting his wife whose butt was positioned in such a way that made him uncomfortably at half-mast.

The phone rang, causing Mrs. Hollins to fall to the floor and Sheree to shout, "Crap! I'm late for school!"

"School doesn't start back up for a couple more weeks, Sheree. It's just the phone at, uh, one in the morning?" Kayla assured, suddenly getting a sick pang at her side, a literal gut feeling something was wrong. "Mom. You need to answer it."

"I'm trying," Mrs. Hollins said as she crawled to the phone, pulling herself up using an invisible ladder. "What?"

"I know you don't want to talk to me, Beth, but…" Mrs. Hollins's mother said on the other end.

"Seriously, Mom? No," Mrs. Hollins said, about to hang up, but before she did, she heard her mother finish what she needed to tell her.

"Your father died."

Chapter 19
The Cure

For the next week, Mrs. Hollins feigned cordiality to help with her father's funeral. The fake smiles were beginning to take their toll by the time the memorial service rolled around, so she gave up on keeping up appearances. Gave up on pretending to be strong. Gave up on her entire family when, during the reception that followed the service and graveside burial, she watched as her sisters and aunts and cousins and grandmother and great-grandmother gathered around Kayla and her mom to discuss matters. The only thing she didn't give up on was her trusty friend, Rex Goliath Merlot.

Sheree tried to lighten matters when she caught the fire in her mother's eyes with, "Witches bein' witches."

It didn't work. Instead, Mrs. Hollins downed her wine and walked away.

"I should be over there with them, but… AH*CHOO!*" Brendon said, wiping the snot from his nose with a handful of tissues, half of which were already used for both crying and mucus collection. "This cold is literally killing me and will definitely kill the old people and I don't want to be responsible for more death while at a funeral and be accused of our life being one big ridiculous soap opera."

Watching her brother wipe his nose again, leaving behind a lint trail that looked like a bad 1980s movie featuring excessive cocaine usage, Sheree was forced to admit that, despite Brendon's childish tendencies, he was wise beyond his years. Then again, his ten were already filled with a lifetime of experiences, most of which happened in the last year alone. While she found it easier to get along with him now that he seemed more mature, a part of her mourned the childhood he was leaving behind. But at least he had a childhood. Kayla was robbed of hers, and now she was being robbed of her teenage years as she was forced to carry the fetuses of the dead while discussing with her relatives how to kill one of them once she's born.

"Do you think…?" Sheree started, but Brendon interrupted.

"Cousin Leslie is a drag queen?" His stare could not be unbroken.

"Um, no, that wasn't what I was going to say, but now that you mention it, she does resemble one. I mean, her makeup is always on point."

"Oh, then what?" Brendon sneezed again, cursing under his breath as he scraped his nostrils with tissues, digging into the tender septum wall as his fingernails cut through. "Okay, this is just stupid," he said, checking for blood he was sure would soon be flowing like a faucet as the throbbing pain stabbed him repeatedly in tune with his heartbeats.

"Yes it is," Sheree said, almost feeling sorry for her brother's face as it was puffy and red and looked undoubtedly uncomfortable. "And I was going to ask if you thought this whole notion about defeating Jessica is futile?"

"Resistance is futile."

"You're futile."

Brendon took Sheree's last jab like a punch to the gut. "I know how useless I am already! I don't need you to keep reminding me!"

As he stormed off, Sheree just watched, wondering when Brendon became such a hormonal pre-teen. However, before she had time to contemplate the inner workings of the boy, her cousin Kelly walked up to her, pulling her aside for a private conversation away from the prying ears their family was known to possess.

"What do you think they're discussing?" Kelly asked, watching the crowd of people around Kayla.

"Depends on how much you know," Sheree said, carefully cryptic in case Kelly was uninitiated into the family's best-kept secret.

The face Kelly gave could only be described as a complete and utter fulfillment of absolute disappointment. "All the witches in the family, except for Brendon for some odd reason, are congregating. Something's up, and Mom won't tell me."

Okay, so she knows things. "They are plotting to kill one of Kayla's twins."

"The evil one?"

"Yeah. Grandma Jessica."

"Shitballs."

"Shitballs?"

"Yeah. This isn't going to end well, no matter the outcome."

Sheree didn't know how to take the news. Just an hour before they were all busy saying goodbye to her grandfather after dying unexpectedly from a heart attack, and now there was already talk of killing an unborn child. She feared for the safety of the one they didn't intend on murdering.

"So I take it you're not a witch?" Kelly asked, readjusting the short red party dress she wore that, had underwear been optional, would proudly have displayed her vagina.

"Nope. You?" Sheree asked, wondering if lipstick lesbians played by different rules as she scanned the outfit her cousin deemed appropriate for a funeral.

"Nah. Oh, and don't worry about keeping my gayness secret," Kelly told Sheree with a side grin.

"Yeah?"

"Yeah. When Mom told me Kayla was back, she also mentioned she was gay and thought that was the best thing ever, so I told her I was gay and she was thrilled. I guess I always just assumed I'd be disowned or something," Kelly said, shrugging her eyebrows.

"When Brendon came out, my dad threw him a party," Sheree said, stretching the truth a bit.

"Ugh. All I got was a puppy and parents joining PFLAG," Kelly said, rolling her eyes.

Puppies and rainbows? Son of a bitch. "And no longer having to hide your girlfriend," Sheree added.

"Fucking bitch broke up with me right after I came out. Something about not really being gay? I don't know. I hate her. Cunt," Kelly said bluntly.

"Tell me how you really feel?" Sheree said, laughing.

Kelly laughed with her. Then they hugged and talked about the little things in life that didn't really matter, but are the most important part of friendship. Cousins, when boiled down to their core, really are one's first friends, and Sheree and Kelly were practically inseparable until the move to Ravenwood. Little did Sheree know that this would be the beginning of the end of their relationship.

⁂

"I can't believe summer is almost over!" Sheree cried, looking at the calendar as it mocked her with the fast-approaching first day of school circled in bright red marker over and over, creeping into the surrounding squares while listening to one of her father's CDs, *Disintegration* by The Cure.

"I don't know what your problem is. I'm looking forward to going back to school," Jennifer told her.

Why are we even friends? Sheree thought rather than said aloud this time, worried she would irreparably damage their barely mended friendship. "Ptooey."

"Speaking of ptooey, we need to talk, Sheree," Brendon said, his face uncharacteristically serious.

"And on that note, I've gotta go," Jennifer said. "Mom's taking me back-to-school shopping."

"So you two are okay?" Sheree asked, hopeful her best friend was healing from her hurt.

"I don't know. But I figure I should give her another chance since she offered to do something parental. And buy me stuff," Jennifer told her. "See ya' tomorrow for cheer practice!"

The air in Sheree's balloon let out. "Craaaaaaap. Why did I want to be a cheerleader so bad?"

"Because you love me!" Jennifer said before rustling Brendon's hair and leaving. "Oh my gawd! Get a room!" they heard her yell at Chad and Nikki while they made out in front of his house. She used her hands to block the scene as she walked by.

"I need an iced coffee. Want one?" Sheree asked, about to prepare the espresso machine.

"No, I'm good. Too much caffeine and I get the jitters," Brendon said, twitching on the last word like an addict needing his next fix.

"Cool. What'd you want to talk about?" Sheree asked, scooping ground coffee into the filter basket, forcefully tamping it down and adding more until it was at full capacity.

Brendon watched. "It can wait until you're done."

"Nonsense! Time is already slipping away faster than I can handle!" Sheree said, only slightly dramatic.

They stared at each other for an inordinate amount of time.

"I think I know how to save your life."

"Oh gawd, um, well, okay, so, about that whole gays for Jesus youth group thing you've been going to…"

"Oh! No! I don't mean… it's not… I'm not pandering to your eternal soul like a freakazoid. I meant how to protect you from evil so you don't, you know, die?" Brendon clarified.

"Oh," Sheree responded, waiting for the carafe to start filling with the life-sustaining drink of the gods.

"Please don't get grossed out," Brendon said, face serious as Death about to go down on the devil's dick.

"Oh gawd, what do I have to do?" Sheree asked, cringing as she awaited whatever horrific idea she was likely to regret but knew she didn't have a choice about considering. After all, this was a life and death situation, and unless she decided to choose death, she knew she would have to go along for the ride her brother was about to take her on, especially since he was driving and she was just Miss Daisy.

The espresso finally started to slowly drip into the carafe, foamy and thick. *Maybe I tamped too much?* she thought as viscous brown blobs puddled into the bottom of the glass container.

"You're not going to like it."

"Of this I have no doubt."

"You need to swallow my snot."

A little vomit bubbled up into the back of Sheree's throat before she instinctually swallowed. "Too late. Grossed out."

"I am being completely serious."

"I know. Still grossed out."

"My snot in your body will protect you from Jessica. Not just now, but forever. If we can't kill her, at least you will be immune to her power."

"What?!"

"My phlegm is like witch antidote. Means you can't be swayed by magic."

Was she hearing her brother right? An antidote to magic?

"Why now?"

"I didn't know about it until I tried to make my last tissue disappear and it wouldn't."

"Oh my gawd, Brendon! Your scientific basis is not being able to magically dispose of mucus-filled Kleenex?" Sheree yelled, her eyes wild and wide.

"Yes."

Well, shit, Sheree thought. "How do you know it will work?"

"Because I tested it a dozen times, and anything my snot touched could not be magicked!"

"You're disgusting."

"True, but disgusting in the name of science!"

Science. So now witchy magical shit is science. Fantastic.

"What the hell," she said, giving in.

And with that, Brendon scraped his sinuses, violently sucking in air through his nostrils. A few throat clearing hacks gathered more of his phlegm. His cure.

Sheree closed her eyes, opened her mouth, and waited for the grossest thing she had ever agreed to take from another human being. She had to fight hard to not resist the slime as it drizzled into her oral portal, and harder still not to fight the urge to purge when she knew she had to swallow. But swallow she did. She felt dirty. Unclean. Incestuous. Something about swallowing her brother's bodily fluids made her sick to her stomach.

A violent scream shattered the quiet just as the "Lullaby" track started.

"I hate my life!" Sheree cried as steam splattered espresso out of the overflowing carafe while the phlegm monster cuddled with its newfound friend.

Chapter 20
Bang

"Mom, Dad, I love you," Kayla said quietly.

"Kayla, I hear a but," Mrs. Hollins said, setting down her morning coffee.

"I don't like buts. I mean, I like butts, just not the but you've got dangling from your tongue," Mr. Hollins said before hanging his head in shame. "I'm just going to stop talking now."

Kayla smiled sadly.

"Oh great, Kayla's hormones are out of whack again," Sheree said, rolling her eyes as she rolled the marshmallows in her Lucky Charms.

"Ha ha, whore. How's your throat?" Kayla asked, looking deep into Sheree's soul and spotting the blemish.

"Ew." Sheree's face turned clover green. Suddenly she was no longer hungry, like her stomach went from a raging ravenous pig to an I-just-had-a-bean-for-lunch-and-now-I'm-like-totally-stuffed gastro-bypass patient who only had the surgery to go from a size ZERO into the negatives. She slid the bowl forward and walked away.

Watching her family be lazy on this lazy Sunday morning of Labor Day weekend that, in a typical Pacific Northwest family, would include camping and s'mores and blissfully moist memories from the usual wet weather, Kayla could only feel sadness. Soon the babies will be born. Soon the battle will begin. Soon it would all be over. Soon she would be dead. Again. Or at least that was what she kept telling herself until her water broke, gushing all over the kitchen floor.

"Gross! Kayla's peeing!" Brendon said, covering his eyes.

Mr. and Mrs. Hollins bombarded Kayla with questions. "Are you in labor? Do you feel any contractions? On a scale of one to ten, how much pain are you in? Considering supernatural involvement, are they full term? How many licks does it take to get to the Tootsie Roll center of a Tootsie Pop?"

"Seriously? You still use the Tootsie Pop commercial during your medical interrogations?" Kayla asked, causing Sheree to wonder if she indeed heard her parents right after being pushed off the stairs a year ago, landing practically in the same spot she was standing, staring at the puddle her sister's feet were drowning in.

"Yes, have to make sure you're listening," Mr. Hollins said.

"Can't be too careful," Mrs. Hollins said.

They were both far too calm, especially considering evil would soon conquer good. Perhaps they were merely keeping up appearances as they were quite adept at it. Perhaps they were feigning ignorance. Perhaps their calmness was the only coping mechanism they knew, considering freaking out hasn't worked out so well in the past.

Rolling her eyes, Kayla responded with, "No contractions, no pain, and pretty sure by the looks of my overly expansive belly, these bastards are ready to bust out."

"Well…" Mrs. Hollins started, shaking her head. "Maybe you can just, you know, move them out using your magical finger thing you do?"

"Won't work," Kayla said.

"How do you know?" Mrs. Hollins asked, head tilting like an inquisitive dog.

"Already tried to remove Jessica and all I got was a migraine and paralyzing spinal pain," Kayla said, completely unaware of what was going on beneath her.

Sheree watched in disgust as Rex and Deschutes happily lapped up the amniotic fluid at Kayla's feet. Apparently Q and A's were more important than cleaning up the mess. Brendon, on the other hand, was horrified and appeared to be in shock.

"Brendon? Brendon? Are you okay?" Mr. Hollins asked, shaking his shoulders for a response.

But Brendon remained a statue.

"Brendon!" Mrs. Hollins screamed as she watched her unresponsive son.

So still.

Unmoving.

Unblinking.

Something's wrong. Something's very wrong, Sheree thought, then she caught Kayla's eyes that basically looked like they were saying goodbye and suddenly her fear felt justified.

"Take my hand, Kayla! We have to go!" Brendon said frantically.

"Wait, what the hell…?" Mrs. Hollins started, but before she could fully grasp what was going on, Brendon and Kayla had vanished.

"Well, shit," Sheree said, staring at the empty space where her brother and sister once stood. Okay, so mostly empty. The puddle hadn't been completely devoured by the dogs yet, so there was still that.

"Where'd they go?!" Mrs. Hollins screamed, her body twisting as she seemed to look around with it instead of her eyes, contorting like one of those miniature filbert trees Sheree saw once in a Japanese garden.

Putting an arm around his wife, Mr. Hollins said calmly, "We will figure it out."

"No we won't, Frank!" Mrs. Hollins shouted, spit flying into her husband's face.

"Mom, please. Dad's right," Sheree said, trying to maintain the calm demeanor she thought her mother required as she watched her father slowly wipe his face with his hand.

Instead, calmness now had the opposite effect. Mrs. Hollins became enraged, thrashing about, unable to comprehend how they could be so composed during this time. Why they weren't out looking. Searching. Trying to find Kayla and Brendon. Bring them home to safety. The madness took control and she rampaged out the front door, leaving it wide open for Rex and Deschutes to chase after her as she darted down the street barefoot.

Sheree was about to go after her, but her father held her down. "Let her go."

"But…"

A tear fell from Mr. Hollins face, wetting the area he'd just dried. "Let her go, please."

Knowing that there really was nothing she could do to make the situation better, she pulled at her father, pushing herself in for a hug, and allowed him to fall apart, letting loose a torrent of tears watering her strawberry blond field of hair. Time stood still. Stopped. Defying every theory it could defy. Not unlike Courtney's Afro.

"It won't be that difficult to figure out where they went," Sheree said, her voice muffled into her father's strong biceps that smelled faintly of Old Spice and perspiration.

"They're at the cliff," Mr. Hollins said.

The news caused Sheree to jerk back, nearly hitting the phone on the wall behind her. "How do you know that?"

"Just a hunch," Mr. Hollins said, a grin threatening to break through as if he was a toddler getting away with lying about eating the cookie and unable to keep in the thrill.

"Liar." Sheree's eyes shot her father in the heart.

After recovering, Mr. Hollins said, "Brendon and Kayla told me."

"Then why didn't you tell Mom?" Sheree asked, her stomach churning as the Lucky Charms got their revenge, knees buckling.

The smile faded into oblivion. "Because… your mother…" Tears threatened their escape once again from the orb jailers trying their damnedest to keep them in.

Sheree waited impatiently for her father to tell her, failing just like the toddler getting away with lying to keep in a smile. She felt the same way when a stutterer got stuck in a rut: irrationally angry. Then she would feel guilty about getting angry with stutterers, and the guilt would keep stacking like bricks until she collapsed and fell and cursed herself for being a horrible human being.

"Your mother can't be there. It will kill her," Mr. Hollins finally managed, deflating.

As much as Sheree wanted to believe he was exaggerating, the soft pleading in his eyes told her otherwise. Now she was the one being shot in the heart.

Bang bang.

Dead.

She also realized for the first time that she was no longer bulletproof. That those point blank gunshots should have killed her, but swerved to avoid her. Eve. Lilith. Another spell. Another lie. Goddamn you, Kayla, Sheree cursed in her head, not fully understanding how she knew the protection spell had been lifted, or when. Then the guilt bricks piled higher and higher as the senseless victims who paid the price to keep her alive flashed before her.

So many hurt.

So many dead.

All so she could live.

"We have to go!" a breathless voice said as her hands hit the open door.

"Jennifer!" Sheree said, rushing to her friend before she collapsed.

Mr. Hollins was at her side in the flap of a butterfly's wing. "Where? How?"

"Sorry, I should have called you to pick me up," Jennifer said, breathing heavily. "My legs are Jell-O now. Complete crapola. Courtney's gonna kill me."

"I don't understand, where do we have to go?" Sheree asked, trying to hold her friend who had practically become a waterlogged sandbag.

"To the cliff, fool!" Jennifer said loudly.

"Wait, Jennifer. How do you know that?" Mr. Hollins asked.

"Kayla told me. Well, she used the Psychic Friends Network to tell me I had to get over here and make sure you two got the memo," Jennifer said, seemingly unfazed at her mind being invaded by a witch. Again.

"We already know to go to the cliff. Brendon and Kayla told Dad," Sheree told her, helping her get up.

"I'm a failsafe. You know, in case the trauma of Kayla's water breaking and sudden disappearance caused him to get all cuckoo for Coco Puffs," Jennifer said, her smile eerily unwelcome.

"Thank you, but I didn't," Mr. Hollins said.

"But Mrs. Hollins did, right?" Jennifer asked. "That's part of the plan."

"The plan?" Sheree asked, her confusion so obvious a blind man could see it.

"Yeah, she's out running around with the dogs," Mr. Hollins told Jennifer, realizing the flaw in their plan. "The dogs."

"Crap," Jennifer said, coming to the same conclusion.

"Do not worry about Brendon's canines. They know to throw her off their trail," a voice said seemingly right in front of them, but nobody could figure out where.

Nobody except for Sheree. "How do you know that, Jonathan?" she asked.

Jennifer and Mr. Hollins now wore confusion like last year's Versace.

"They cannot see me," Jonathan revealed.

"But how?" Sheree asked.

"Yeah, why can't we see the creepy voice that sounds an awful lot like the hot old dude who gave me a piggyback ride a few weeks ago?" Jennifer asked.

"Huh?" Mr. Hollins barely spilled out like his penis was trying to do as the polyester shorts he was wearing left nothing to the imagination.

"Sunlight makes vampires, in a sense, quite invisible to the human eye," Jonathan said.

"So why can I see you?" Sheree asked, fist at the ready in case she didn't like the answer. He was, after all, potentially evil.

"Magic," Jonathan told her. "Or more specifically, the lack of magic."

"Brendon's snot!" Sheree shouted, channeling William Shatner, eyes bulging to the point they almost fell out of their sockets.

Jennifer turned green. "Ew."

Mr. Hollins said, "Huh?" once again like a broken record.

"I swallowed Brendon's phlegm and now magic has no power over me," Sheree said, mostly to Jennifer as the mentioning of the deed caused her to divert her eyes from her father over the perceived incestuous act.

"Precisely, my dear," Jonathan said.

"Groaty!" Jennifer spewed.

Mr. Hollins picked himself up, brushed himself off of the thought of his daughter swallowing his son's diseased bodily castoffs. "We should get going if we are going to make it before Kayla goes into labor."

"Just because her water broke, doesn't mean she's going to go into labor soon," Sheree informed her father, smug smile firmly planted.

"Gush equals labor or labor will follow soon," Mr. Hollins informed his daughter. "You forget that I'm a doctor."

"Doctor for the dead," Sheree shot back.

"I am dead," Jonathan said, winking at Mr. Hollins.

"Yeah, but super sexy dead!" Jennifer said to Jonathan, or at least in the general vicinity she saw Sheree speak to him. "So, I know there's probably, like, a thousand year age difference and all, but we should totally go out."

"Gross!" Sheree said. "What the hell, Jen?"

Jonathan laughed. "I apologize, young lady. However, I am in a relationship with another."

"And he's gay!" Sheree told Jennifer, jabbing her finger into her upper arm for emphasis.

"Figures," Jennifer said, slumping over herself. "I always fall for the gay ones."

"And on that note, we need to go before Beth gets home," Mr. Hollins told the crowd, including the invisible member.

"I need to change!" Sheree yelled, running up the stairs.

"Seriously?" Mr. Hollins asked.

"You should probably put some pants on," Jennifer said. "Oh my Buddha, I can't believe I just said that."

Mr. Hollins looked down at his running shorts and agreed.

"I see what my great-great-granddaughter sees in that man," Jonathan said, eyes following Mr. Hollins as he ran to change into societally acceptable outerwear. "He is a beautiful specimen."

"You say that like he's just a piece of meat," Jennifer said to the air, practically in the opposite direction of Jonathan.

"My dear, I am a vampire. I eat humans for a living," Jonathan said bluntly, yet with an effortlessly seductive undertone.

Scrunching her face in a most unsexy way, Jennifer said, "Well, when you put it that way, he really is just a piece of meat. Sweet DILFy meat. Drool."

"Stop talking about my dad like that, pervert!" Sheree shouted as she ran down the stairs, forgetting she was supposed to be afraid of them.

"Stop having superhuman hearing!" Jennifer shouted, sticking out her lower lip as it frowned.

Mr. Hollins jogged down the stairs and met them at the door. "Okay, so there's only one way I know to get to the cliff, and that's through the forest from the park."

"Yeah, that's the only one I know," Sheree said.

"Me, too," Jennifer said.

"There is another," Jonathan said.

Sheree sighed. "Then by all means, Yoda. Tell us."

"It would be easier to show," Jonathan said.

"Yeah, it would be easier to show, but seeing as you're all invisible and stuff until the sun goes down, I really don't know how that is going to help, especially since we've gotta get going pronto!" Jennifer said impatiently, hating herself for her lack of gaydar.

Jonathan smiled, but only Sheree could see it. "Take my hand and I will take you there."

"Ooh! Another piggyback ride?" Jennifer squealed like a schoolgirl.

"Not exactly," Jonathan said, holding out his hands.

Since her father and friend could not see the person they were all talking to, Sheree guided their hands to his. After making sure everyone was holding hands and pretending to be in a kumbaya circle, she said, "Okay, Jonathan. Let's go."

"You all. Need to step away. From that guy," someone said from the other side of the door where they all stood.

"It's fine, Anna," Sheree said. "He's my great-great-great-grandpa." She couldn't help but wonder if people thought she was merely stuttering as she said this again for the hundredth time.

"Step away. Now. He's not the man. He says he is." Anna's eyes were black, face cold as stone.

As Anna spoke, Jonathan's grip tightened, nearly crushing the bones in Sheree's hand. She winced off the pain. "It's fine. I know he's a vampire. I know he's a witch. I know all about him," Sheree said.

"You can't trust him. He's lying," Anna said, unmoving.

"Anna, I get that you see dead people and think we can't trust them, but he really only wants to help," Sheree said before turning to Jonathan. "Okay, let's go."

And with that, Jonathan, Jennifer, and Mr. Hollins disappeared. Sheree stared at the open space. Her empty hands. Her father was gone. Her best friend was gone. The man she was told to trust was gone, taking them somewhere she could only guess. "Well, shit."

"Shit is right, bitch," Anna said. "That man. He's a bad man."

"I know he's a vampire witch and he drinks human blood, but that doesn't make him a bad man," Sheree said, still not believing that she was left behind like a poorly written book series.

Logic, however, was failing her like a cheap bra.

Fear set in.

Father.

Mother.

Sister.

Brother.

Friend.

Gone.

Taken.

Where?

It was impossible for Sheree not to feel like her family abandoned her. Even the long dead and presumed murdered one. Maybe Anna was right not to trust Jonathan. Maybe she should have listened to her warning. Maybe there was another explanation, but at the time, she was clueless what it could be. Motives aside, she couldn't help but wonder if she just sent her father and best friend to their deaths. Everyone always remarked about how delicious her father was, so perhaps Jonathan being a bloodthirsty vampire wanted to suck him off as well.

Anna just stared.

Anna knew, Sheree thought. Anna knew and you didn't listen and now they're all going to die because you wanted to trust someone who told you they wanted the one person or ghost or witch or unborn fetus dead and out of your life for good. As usual, you took the easy road and now everyone else has to pay the price.

"Calm down. It is not. Your fault," Anna said, remaining in place on her possibly dead father's lawn still bearing her recent acts of violence against it.

Hot tears streamed down her face, causing her to laugh-cry as Linda Ronstadt's version of "Tracks of My Tears" firmly played itself on repeat in the forefront of her internal dialogue. Suddenly her brain flooded with memories of listening to that album on family road trips. Happy memories; long car rides that seemed endless but could be easily tracked by how many times they listened to her father's cassettes. Two equaled camping. All five equaled Grandma and Grandpa Lowell's here in Ravenwood. All five repeated five times equaled Disneyland. Her childhood could be tracked by song tracks, including "Tracks of My Tears" which was playing sporadically from random parts of the song that Sheree thought the tape would break any second, causing a tangled mess in her head no pencil could fix.

Trying to ward off a catastrophe, Sheree started singing the lyrics from the beginning. Anna was not impressed. In fact, she looked rather annoyed.

"Ugh Sheree. I hate Linda Ronstadt. You know her. Greatest Hits album? They were all. Other band's hits first. Stupid whore," Anna said. "Sorry about losing. Your family."

Sheree missed the usual smiles between breaths Anna was lacking. Missed the devious twinkle in her eyes that said she knew more than she was letting on. Missed the oftentimes-inappropriate fun-loving girl that, despite their obvious differences, reminded her of Sky before Sky's life fell to shit and ended itself.

With a bang, Sheree fell to the floor.

"Oh my gawd. I need to go. Now. I can't worry about Dad or Jennifer. I have to make sure Kayla survives," Sheree said, struggling to pick herself up off the floor. It felt like she was in quicksand; the more she struggled, the more it pulled her in.

"I may have. Underestimated. The vampire witch," Anna said.

"What? No! You were right not to trust the bastard! He took my dad! He took my pillow… I mean Jennifer!"

"Yeah he did. But…"

"No buts!" Sheree was frantic. Without control, she became the one person she never wanted to become in her entire life: her mother. Wildly thrashing about, threatening to run without destination or direction, she was about to crawl through the door on hand and knee when a calm voice spoke.

"My dear, I truly do not know how I could have forgotten so soon that magic does not work on you," Jonathan said, quiet laughter following.

Sheree put her arms around the man as her body forgot it was drowning and stood up on the water like the blond blue-eyed Jesus the church replaced the original one with in her childhood Bible. There was an eerie chilling from his living deadness as she held onto him. She could have hugged him forever had her mind allowed it, but there were pressing matters that required attention, and this time it wasn't poop pushing on her sphincter, but shitty nonetheless. Her family needed her by their side. She had to make sure that, at the very least, Jeff was born. Jessica on the other hand…

"I suppose a piggyback ride, as your oriental friend says, is in order?" Jonathan said.

"Offensive much!" Sheree shouted.

"She's Vietnamese. Asian. Oriental is a rug. Or spices. I may be a retard. But even I know that," Anna added before storming off towards her car. "Be careful. I still don't. Trust him."

Sheree smiled. "I don't have a choice."

"Watch your back. Okay?" Anna said.

"Always," Sheree told her.

With a swish, they were off. As the wind whipped her hair back and forth, she hated herself for not putting it into a ponytail like she often strangled her mane with. The houses whirred past her like a cheap previously filmed television car scene background playing, bouncing and turning out of sync with the action. As they entered the park, Sheree wondered if this was what fleas felt like as they clung to a sprinting dog for dear life. Jonathan was the dog and she was the flea; a role reversal considering he was a bloodsucker and she usually played the part of the prey. Nearing the forest, the place she felt the most vulnerable—getting lost; losing precious jewelry; being chased; getting gang-raped—she counted how long she could hold her breath with her eyes closed.

Twenty-two. Twenty-three. Twenty-four. Twenty…

The first branch that hit her face, followed swiftly by Jonathan saying, "Sorry, my love. That one caught me by surprise," punched out her breath and forced her to open her eyes for the remainder of the trip, unable to check for blood, but knowing it left a mark. She also was forced to admit that at the speed they were traveling, it was harder to feel afraid of the dense trees trying to pull her into their trap. No longer a weak housefly unable to free itself from the spider's web, she was now a bird in flight, a phoenix about to catch fire to the world.

The world slowed down as they entered the great basalt plateau. Kayla greeted Sheree first after she slid off Jonathan with the gracefulness of a salted slug. Definitely not the Super Samurai variety Brendon loved so much.

"Don't hate me for continuing to lie to you about stuff!" Kayla said, her eyes wetter than a prostitute's vagina after a long night, heart burdened more than a loaded ass.

"Goddammit, Kayla!" Sheree shouted into her sister's ear as they hugged, their golden hair becoming one. "You have got to stop protecting me!"

"I can't help it! I put you through so much!" Kayla said, tears tickling Sheree's ears.

"That doesn't mean you need to keep paying for your mistakes, dumbass!"

"Yes I do."

"No, you really don't."

"You don't understand how important you are."

"I'm not more important than everyone who died!"

A cold hand pulled Sheree off of Kayla. "Actually, my dear. You are."

Was she hearing Jonathan right? Others had to die so she could live? Jeff? Sky's boyfriend, Chad? Kylie, Monique, the West Seattle Rapists, Adam, Eve, Mr. Riley? Who else had to die? Who else would become the next brick in her house of guilt?

"You are the only person who can kill Jessica," Kayla confessed.

Chapter 21
Labor Day

As Kayla's contractions started getting longer and closer together, Sheree was still swimming in a sea of shock over the recent revelation. Her task. Her job. Her reason for living. For lack of a better argument, her sole purpose for existence was to be an assassin. Had the universe really been preparing her? Was this all part of God's plan? Her questions were endless. Her resolve built on sand.

"You're doing great," Mr. Hollins told Kayla after her latest contraction receded.

Sweat matted Kayla's hair to her sad, angry, fearful face. "Dad, I don't know if I can do this."

"Yes you can, sweetie," he said, brushing her hair behind her ears, but it clung to his fingertips like wet toilet paper as he pulled away.

"Daddy, I'm scared," Kayla said, voice small and childlike and almost reminiscent of when she would sing through the air vents and scare Sheree half to death.

Mr. Hollins stared at his daughter and faked a smile, knowing there was nothing he could do to take away the thing lurking in the dark that frightened her, no matter how much he wanted to. Desperately trying to think of something to pretend that everything was going to be okay, normal, he had to admit defeat.

Failure.

The sky was uneasy; swirling, twisting and turning, whipping the nearby forest into a frenzy as Kayla tried to steady her breathing. Mr. Hollins encouraged her as best he could, but kept laughing as images of Bill Cosby flashed before his eyes performing The Breathing Cosbys from his 1983 classic *Himself* well before he became known as a serial sexual assaulter. Jonathan and Jennifer tried comforting Sheree on the reality of her situation and what the world would soon be asking her to do to prevent total and utter chaos from reigning supreme. Brendon sat around, feeling as useless as two left socks.

"We should have brought snacks," Brendon said to his stomach. It growled back its agreement, punching him with pangs as if it held a grudge.

"Yes, you should have," a voice said from the shadows which, had the moon not been smothered by clouds, would have perfectly illuminated the speaker. However, things being as they are in the small town of Ravenwood, cloud cover was simply inevitable.

"Mom?" Sheree asked, squinting at the silhouette as it approached.

Everyone waited for a response. The summer night air began to freeze as the wind picked up pace. It was Mrs. Hollins, wasn't it? As unlikely as it was, it sounded so uncannily like her voice. However, the figure kept walking towards them silently.

"Grandma?" Sheree asked, wondering if maybe her ears were mistaken.

"Jesus, Sheree! I'm not a grandma yet!" Mrs. Hollins said, dropping the bags she carried on either side of her.

"Sorry, Mom," Sheree said, getting up to hug her. "I… I…"

"It's okay. After I calmed down, and scolded the dogs for leading me down the wrong trail," Mrs. Hollins said, causing Rex and Deschutes to rush towards the useless left socks, "I went home to an empty house and was about to go into conniptions again, but that Down Syndrome girl? Anna? She told me where you were. She also said I didn't want to be here, but obviously I ignored that poor advice."

Kayla started bawling as she lay on the cold stone ground. "Mom, you really shouldn't be here!"

"Nonsense!" Mrs. Hollins told her, releasing Sheree's hands to grab one of Kayla's. "I'm not missing out on the end of the world because you think I can't handle it."

"But…" Mr. Hollins started, but the knot in his throat caught the rest of his words, tugging at them until the rope retracted into the coiler.

"Frank, I am not going back home," Mrs. Hollins said sternly. "I talked to Cousin Leslie, and she confirmed what

Anna said. I even made her swear on her Smashbox Photo Finish Foundation Primer that she wasn't lying."

Jennifer quietly said to Sheree, "Your mom's pretty smart. Just sayin'."

"Brie, bread, and bubbly?!" Mrs. Hollins asked, popping the cork off a bottle of champagne as she became Martha Stewart. After all, who else would bring a wine and cheese spread to a birth slash death event in the middle of nowhere?

"Oh my gawd, Mom, you're my hero!" Kayla said, forgetting the pain.

Mrs. Hollins laughed. "Not for you, hon. You get ice."

The glare Kayla gave caused a car wreck two counties away. In Oregon.

"Sometimes I wonder about your sanity, Mother," Sheree said with a side-grin and furrowed brows.

"I don't!" Brendon declared, grabbing a Brie wedge and hunk of baguette. "You're the best!"

As Brendon stuffed face, Jennifer did the same. Sheree and Mr. Hollins joined them. Mrs. Hollins poured the champagne into red Solo cups because there was only so far she was willing to take the fancy picnic idea she read about in one of those magazines older women and gay men read. Brendon, Sheree, and Jennifer all reached for one of the two cups, but Mrs. Hollins shooed them off.

"Sparkling cider for you kids. I won't be responsible for you becoming alcoholics," Mrs. Hollins said, immediately regretting her choice in words as Jennifer's demeanor faded into flatness.

"It's for the best," Jennifer said, faking a smile. "Besides, champagne gives me a headache. I mean… uh, er… I've heard it can?"

Patting Jennifer's back, Sheree said, "There there, Jen. You should stop before you dig yourself into a hole so deep you'll never crawl out of it."

Unfortunately some holes become a lifetime battle.

"FUUUUUUUUCCCKKK!!!" Kayla screamed, ripping another crack into the cliff and sending a few rocks on the edge to their death.

Mr. Hollins dropped his cheese.

"It's time," he said, seeing one of the babies start to push its way out.

"Honey, squeeze my hand and push," Mrs. Hollins said calmly.

The fear in Kayla's eyes could not be avoided. It was as if they were pleading for help, real help, not the handholding type. Of course, she knew the sacrifice she would have to make, be forced to make as part of her plea bargain to get a sliver of a chance at living once again in the real world. Little did the rest of her family know what that would entail. Instead of let them in, Kayla squeezed. Pushing, however, would never happen.

"Shit," Mr. Hollins said.

"What? What's wrong?" Mrs. Hollins asked.

But Kayla knew. Sheree and Jennifer both saw the problem as well. Jonathan and Brendon steered clear because, ew, girl parts.

The tiny hands began clawing their way out of Kayla's vagina.

Ripping her open wider and wider.

Growing.

Growing into adult hands.

Clawing the ground.

Pulling.

Singing as her face inched its way out.

"The itsy bitsy spider went up the water spout!"

The body continued to grow at an alarming rate as the newborn made her way into the world.

Kayla screamed so loud it knocked over a few nearby Douglas firs. Mrs. Hollins feared her hand was going to be crushed by Kayla's strength, but kept hold despite the pain.

"Down came the rain and washed the spider out!"

The child's hair got longer and longer as more and more of her slid out.

"Up rose your sister, pregnant from the grave."

Over half way out of Kayla's body, the girl became a woman. A woman ripping an adult sized hole between Kayla's legs.

Blood.

So much blood.

Blood gushing as Kayla became paler and paler.

"And soon I will rule this lowly world again!"

Jessica stood up, turned around, and looked at the girl. Her mother. Her great-great-great-granddaughter. Then she said to Kayla, "I could not have done it without you," as she watched the life in Kayla's eyes fade to black.

Kayla's hand went limp.

Mrs. Hollins said, "No! No no no no no no no!" as she patted the hand, checked for a pulse, checked her nostrils and mouth for breath.

But there was nothing.

Dead.

Again.

Chapter 22
It's the End of the World As We Know It

"Nighty night, mother," Jessica said before laughing.

Evil laughter.

Laughter that froze the air.

As Jessica walked away, completely ignoring the rest of the people around her like they were nothing more than ants surrounding a piece of rotting fruit, her blood drenched naked body began clothing itself as thousand upon thousands of spiders covered her flesh, giving their lives to be transformed into a dress. Closing her eyes, she breathed in the cold night air, drinking in the moon as it begged to shine through the clouds, letting it out slowly as she tiptoed away from the grieving family.

Brendon was visibly shaking. His sister was gone. Then Jessica turned around and stared right through to his soul and said with disgust, "You."

This was all Brendon needed. His anger shook off his fear like a deer sheds its antlers, leaving nothing for it to cling to should it try to come back. He balled his hands into fists. Eyes became fiery red. Suddenly he fully realized his power. This woman, this evil woman who had tormented him so many times, would finally feel his wrath.

"Ha ha ha ha! You really think you can do anything to me? You are nothing more than an abomination. A blemish on the face of this earth that has to be wiped out," Jessica told the boy, laughing once again as if, for no other reason, to emphasize how unafraid she was.

Brendon stared at Jessica, unfazed by the threat. He's faced worse. He's been through worse. Then, just as Jessica looked like she was about to unleash, Brendon looked straight up into the night sky, took in a deep breath like it was helium and rose up. As he hovered, Jessica waited. Sheree had no idea what he was trying to do. Had no idea he could even float, but there he was, levitating in front of her and her family. Then let out a roar so ear piercing, a dozen bats fell, landing at Jessica's feet, splattering as they hit the hard ground like water balloons.

With his arms stretched to either side of him, Brendon turned himself into a human shield, protecting everyone behind him, flanked on either side by Rex and Deschutes. The fire in his eyes stayed firmly lit. Mr. and Mrs. Hollins held each other. Sheree held Jennifer's hand as long as she could until the spell took full effect. Jonathan hid behind them all.

Wasn't this the part where Jonathan was supposed to attack Jessica? Wasn't it his turn to act? To do his part of the plan? Sheree turned around and caught the tortured terror in his eyes and knew she had to assure him that when the time came, she would also have to make a sacrifice. As she looked into his frightened eyes, she recalled the conversation they had months ago on the Fourth of July while she flicked a stolen lighter over and over as fireworks punctuated the air, leaving behind a burning sulfurous cloud in their wake...

"Jessica is a toxic person," Jonathan said.

"I get that your ex-wife is all evil, but..." Sheree said.

"No, I mean, what I have to do might, no, will, kill me," Jonathan said. His expression was stone.

"Why would you sacrifice yourself?" Sheree asked, the bench suddenly freezing her butt.

Jonathan's cold eyes shimmered like a placid mountain lake. "Sometimes one must give up everything for the good of the world."

His words hit her like granite. Would she have to make a similar sacrifice? Would she also have to die so others could live?

"I don't understand why you have to do what you have to do? If she is so powerful, why bother?" Sheree asked.

"Because, my dear, her blood is the base of her power. Nothing can touch her so long as she is at full strength..."

"But if you drink..."

"Precisely."

"Jonathan, you know what has to be done," Sheree said, clutching the BIC lighter like a good luck charm, taking everything she had to stay calm after watching Kayla die once again; letting shock do what it does best: feign ignorance.

"I know." Jonathan's alabaster face melted.

"If I could…" Sheree started.

"I know," Jonathan said, letting his melted face smile for no other reason than it would be one of the last times he would be able to feel it.

Sheree faked one of her own, unable to shake the fact that she was sending a family member on a suicide mission. But she had to keep reminding herself that this wasn't just her war. It wasn't just her family's war. This was bigger than her. Bigger than Jonathan. Bigger than Ravenwood. Jessica was evil incarnate, and she had to be stopped once and for all.

"It's time for you all to die!" Jessica shouted, wind whirling around her, building up her tornado of hate.

Closing his eyes for a second before plastering on bright, happy, fake versions, Jonathan began to walk away. "My Jessica, I knew you would return to me," he said as he walked out from behind Brendon's protection bubble towards the woman he once called wife.

Jessica was caught off guard, or so it appeared. "My Jonathan! I do not understand how, but what I know not matters not!" she said, walking towards the man she once called husband.

Their hands grasped each other once they were within reach. His ice, hers fire. Both powerful. Both remembering the other like it was only yesterday they parted.

"Song's End," Jonathan whispered into her ear.

"Song's End?" Jessica whispered back.

The air became eerily calm.

The storm would be coming soon.

Then he told her everything.

Jessica stared at her husband in disbelief as he told her of Song's End's deception, eyes growing wild and eerily resembling Kayla's last Christmas in the same spot she now stood, mouth snarling like a wild dog. "I'll kill you," she growled, teeth clenched so tight they started to chip.

"Darling, I am already dead," he told her with a smirk. "And soon you will be, too."

"Grrraaawwww!" she screamed, lunging herself towards him.

He flung himself around her, holding her tightly as he shouted, "Now!"

Fangs pushed themselves out before Jonathan forcefully gashed Jessica's neck, her blood dribbling down her chest and his chin. She dug her nails into his flesh, but found his stone-like skin difficult to penetrate, the nails bending. Breaking. Shattering like glass.

"I have dreamt of the day my parents would be reunited once again," an older voice said from the darkness, causing Jessica to pause while her husband drained her of the one thing she needed to survive.

"Julia?" Jessica asked, feeling herself weakening.

Mrs. Hollins saw as her great-grandmother slowly walked towards Jessica and Jonathan. Julia was the eldest member of her family, outliving two husbands and eight of her own children. She hadn't seen Julia walk for years, but there she was, unaccompanied by her usual wheelchair, making her way towards the woman she once called mother. The woman who stole Kayla's life from her. Twice.

"Yes, Mother. It is I," Julia said, her fragile voice about to break.

"Oh, Daughter! I need your help," Jessica pleaded, unable to free herself from Jonathan as he continued to drink in her poison.

He was also showing signs of failing strength as the poison began eating away at his living dead body. But it was too late to back out now. He had to finish what he started. He had to make sure Jessica was weak.

"No, Mother," Julia said, a faint laugh escaping her mouth.

"No?" Jessica asked. "How dare you speak to your mother in that tone!"

"How dare I?"

"Yes, how dare you!"

Jessica could feel Jonathan beginning to fail, but just as she was about to try prying him off of her, Julia struck her with a spell that nearly knocked her off her feet. She was unable to comprehend how her own daughter could turn against her. Unable to understand why she would attack her.

With a full on sprint, Julia ran towards Jessica like a firestorm, building up her energy as she ran. Jessica pushed Jonathan off of her as Julia came at her. Before Jonathan fell to the ground, a figure sped past Sheree and picked him up and carried him off in a blur.

"That had to be Song's End," Sheree said out loud.

"Really?" Jennifer said. "I missed the only semi-living legend Ravenwood has?"

"Well, he was fast, so…"

Before Sheree could finish, she watched as Julia launched herself off the ground towards Jessica, releasing all the pent up energy she had at her. For some reason, Sheree half expected that to be it. That the nightmare would be over. But instead, she watched as her great-great-grandmother's flesh burned away to ashes, leaving behind nothing but a scattering of broken bones at Jessica's feet.

"Ha HA! Was that your plan to kill me?" Jessica yelled to the air, staring right at Brendon.

"Yes," Brendon told her before plastering on a smile as big as his face would let him as the dogs did the same. "Part of it."

Just then, other family members came out of the woods. Older members. All witches.

"This is heresy!" Jessica cried as they surrounded her from all sides, trapping her like a spider before squishing it.

Sheree looked down at her mother and father as they continued to hold each other over their dead daughter. Her twin sister. The one person she thought she could never live without, but somehow forgot about after she died the first time, then wanted to forget about after she began haunting her, then wanted to swap places so she could live in her place. Kayla's face looked so peaceful, a disturbing departure from her broken body.

Then one by one she watched in horror as her family all suffered the same fate as Julia. No matter how many perished, it didn't seem to weaken Jessica, each adding to the pile. Sheree counted four skulls on the solid basalt cliff base, and wondered how many it would take before Jessica could be killed? How many before she would have to step in and do the same?

Die.

Five.

Six.

Seven.

The sky ripped open, revealing not the moon or stars, but blackness swirling overhead. A tear in space? A black hole? Sheree didn't have time to question the phenomenon. Soon she would have to take the stage. Soon she would have to do her part of the plan. Soon she would have to kill. Soon she would have to die.

"Jessica, there is no way you can win this!" Cousin Leslie shouted, her makeup, as usual, completely spot on and immaculate.

"And you have no idea who you are dealing with!" Jessica shouted back, her voice gravelly, cracked, and dry.

As Sheree watched Leslie's flesh fly off her body like someone throwing flour, the ashes wrapped themselves around Jessica's body and burst into a rainbow flame. Mesmerized by the horrifically beautiful scene, she didn't notice there was still one person standing. One more person about to make the ultimate sacrifice.

"It's too late, Jessica," the person said, her voice calm, cool, collected.

"Mom?" Mrs. Hollins asked, wiping the tears from her face as she got up.

Grandma Lowell turned to face Mrs. Hollins and Sheree, a sad smile in her eyes before she gathered up a storm of her own around herself.

"Mom!" Mrs. Hollins cried, about to run out of Brendon's bubble, the one that Sheree was just outside of because nothing could protect her any longer.

Jennifer caught Mrs. Hollins first, barely holding her long enough before Mr. Hollins could keep her behind it. Sheree wished she could have stopped her mother herself, but then she would risk Jessica killing her and that was unacceptable. Too many people had already died for the plan not to work.

Locking eyes, Sheree saw her Grandma Lowell give her a nod telling her that it was almost time for her part in this final act of a tragic play. Sheree mouthed, "I love you," hoping to get actual words out, but an invisible force strangled her throat. Then in a flash, her grandmother leapt straight up into the air and sped down towards Jessica, disintegrating into a million tiny pieces.

Now, Sheree. Don't chickenshit on me, Sheree thought to herself, fighting back the urge to cry as her mother's wailing began anew just as a crow feather caught her eye. She picked it up, closed her eyes, breathed in deeply, then tossed the feather aside.

Running at full force, Sheree bolted.

Running towards Jessica.

Running towards her as she lay on the ground in a pile of her relatives's bones and ashes.

"No!" Mrs. Hollins cried as she watched Sheree run further and further away, about to chase after her but Mr. Hollins and Jennifer kept their hold.

Sheree stopped at Jessica's feet and stared down at the woman she was so afraid of. Here she was, weak and helpless. Almost dead.

Or so she thought.

A low laugh fell from her mouth. "Oh, Sheree. It really was a scream!" Jessica said, picking herself up and throwing a teal fire bolt towards Sheree.

As the flames sped towards her face, time slowed down. Sheree said goodbye to her family. Goodbye to her friends. Goodbye to the world. She closed her eyes and waited for the fire to consume her.

But it didn't.

Instead, the blue-green fire that burned with the heat of a thousand glaciers dissipated before hitting her. Magic. Or, as Sheree finally understood for the first time, magic's inability to affect her any longer.

"What is this?" Jessica asked, staring in shock as her spell fell apart before her eyes.

"This is how you die, bitch!" Sheree told her, flicking the cigarette lighter in her hand, locking the flame in place.

Brendon watched as Sheree seemed to be taking her time, staring at the flame. "Now, Sheree! Do it!" he said through clenched teeth.

But Sheree couldn't hear him. She couldn't hear anything except the fire burning in her hands, sucking the life out of the air all around it. She couldn't hear Jessica screaming curses, bombarding her with useless spells, weakening with every one.

"What is she waiting for?" Jennifer asked Brendon as he started showing signs that he couldn't hold up the bubble much longer.

Rex and Deschutes looked like they were about to pass out just outside the bubble.

"I don't know," Brendon told her, sweat pouring down his face.

Then Jessica caught Sheree's eyes and froze as fear took hold of her.

"Ah, Jessica, my old friend, do you know the Klingon proverb that tells us 'Revenge is a dish that is best served cold?' It is very cold… in space."

Sheree threw the lighter towards Jessica and watched as her eyes filled with terror. So many years Jessica spent planning her return, planning her rise back to power, and now it was all about to go up in flames. No matter how many spells Jessica tossed towards the fire to put it out, it quickly overtook her. Surrounded her. Smothered her. Her cries drowned out as the flames gobbled up her breath.

The fire went nova, knocking everyone but Sheree off their feet. The bones of her family turned to ash. The flames jumped towards the tear in the sky, slowly healing the rip. As the fires burned, Brendon walked towards it. He gave Sheree a mischievous grin as he pulled from behind him the large painting of Jessica, her eyes wild as ever as he threw it into the flames.

And then it was over.

The flames disappeared.

The ashes floated away into the cliff before falling to their final resting place at the bottom.

The sky went back to its usual cloudy self, choking out the dying moon in the moments before the sun stole all the glory. They walked back, hand in hand, knowing that evil was finally free from their lives. However, the price they paid was far too high.

While Mr. Hollins tried consoling his wife over the loss of so many family members all at once, Sheree, Brendon, and Jennifer couldn't help but notice Kayla's lifeless eyes staring into the abyss. Her motionless body some artist's cruel joke of a statue.

Dead.

"Mom, Dad! We need to get Jeff out of her!" Sheree cried as this realization smacked her in the face, not knowing where to even start making a corpse give birth.

Sheree half expected her parents to be useless lumps of flesh in the aftermath, but E.R. mode kicked in and they stoically began working on Kayla. Mrs. Hollins felt around her stomach while Mr. Hollins checked to make sure she was still dilated after Jessica clawed her way out. Sure enough, the hole was plenty large enough to simply reach in and retrieve the unborn child.

The hole.

Their daughter's torn body.

Their grandson still inside her.

Brendon chanted, his hands on Kayla's forehead. Jennifer cradled her head in her hands like the pillow she was. Sheree watched it all like it was nothing more than a spectator sport and she was a pathetic fan for the opposing team. After all, she had nothing to add. She would be in the way if she tried to help. She only had one good play and already spent her token.

Then her father's hands disappeared into Kayla's vagina, and all Sheree could think about was how different this scenario played out when her body was violated. She wondered why some touches were sexual and others were lifesaving, even though they were essentially the same. Did he think about what he was doing? Did he think about the consequences of performing this action? Sheree cursed herself for thinking about her father using his hands to molest her sister's cadaver when all he was doing was saving Kayla's unborn child. Assuming, of course, that he was still alive after everything that happened.

Soon, her father took one hand out and slowly pulled his other to reveal a tiny bluish-purple face with a shock of matted brown hair. Then he pulled a little and gently cradled the back of the baby until its legs limply fell out of the hole in her sister's body. It didn't move as her father pulled it closer to his chest. Death had taken yet another on this bloody day.

Brendon stopped chanting.

Mrs. Hollins broke down in tears over Kayla's body once again.

Mr. Hollins tried his best to hold the lifeless child and his wife at the same time.

Jennifer couldn't bring herself to stop holding Kayla's head even though her hands were tingling with numbness.

Sheree just watched in shock for what seemed like eternity until a low guttural growl escaped Kayla's mouth, crescendo-ing into one that shook the surrounding forest and woke the dead and made a motorcycle on Main Street overturn, pinning the rider against a tree.

Both Kayla and the baby sucked in air quickly, releasing it back out in loud cries. As Kayla breathed in, she felt the burden of every soul she killed lifted. Floating away. They were no longer trapped in her purgatory. They were free to move on. Only one soul remained: hers.

"Kayla!" Mrs. Hollins blubbered, petting her hair and kissing her cheeks.

"Dad! Dad! Is Jeff okay?" Kayla asked as she looked at the lizard-like baby in his arms.

"Yes!" he told her, placing the tiny human chameleon into Kayla's awaiting arms as he was still tethered by the umbilical cord that disappeared into her quickly healing body.

Brendon hugged Sheree, crying into her, then said as he let go, "You seriously had to make a Star Trek reference before offing Jessica?"

Epilogue

The following day, Sheree begged her parents to let her stay home. "I'm in mourning!" she cried.

"Really? You're going to pull that one on me?" Mrs. Hollins said, holding baby Jeff in her arms.

The hurt in her mother's eyes could fill Jupiter into a solid. Sheree took one look at Jeff and melted as his blue eyes met her teal ones. "He's not going to grow as fast as She Who Shall Not Be Named, is he?"

"Nope. Doesn't look like it," Kayla said as she trotted down the steps.

"Where do you think you're going, young lady?" Mr. Hollins asked, stopping her as she walked into the kitchen.

"Uh, school?" she said.

"But you died yesterday!" Mrs. Hollins said loudly, forgetting she was holding a baby.

"And gave birth, but I'm fine now," Kayla said, shaking her head.

It was true. Kayla looked better than ever. Practically a mirror image to Sheree again. Normal. Her weights lifted and she felt lighter than air.

"Do you think fifth grade boys will be better than fourth grade boys?" Brendon asked his dad to distract him long enough to let Kayla into the kitchen.

"What?" Mr. Hollins asked.

Kayla poured herself a bowl of Lucky Charms. "Boys are stupid, Bren. Doesn't matter what grade they're in."

"Says the lesbian!" Sheree shouted.

Kayla looked into her bowl and screamed, dropping it onto the floor and watching in horror as it shattered at her feet.

"Oh gawd, Kayla! What is it?" Sheree asked, looking at her sister for an answer and the splattered mess of milk and marshmallows beneath her.

"Spider!" Kayla squealed.

Sheree choked on her own spit. "Really? A spider?"

"Kill it! Kill it!" Kayla cried.

"You're a witch. You are a witch who used to sing a song about a spider to scare the living shit out of me and now you are crying like a little bitch over one?" Sheree said, laughing in between her mocking.

"This is ridiculous!" Kayla said.

Sheree spotted the black spider. As she approached it, it turned to face her. Putting her hands into the milk, the spider crawled inside her palm. She swore it smiled at her as she walked towards the dining room's French doors. Rex and Deschutes were already lapping up the remnants, undiscriminating between food and shards of ceramic.

"Be free, little guy," Sheree said as she put the spider down outside.

It scampered away into the grass.

"Okay, well, that was weird," Brendon said, stating the obvious.

"Yep," Mr. Hollins said before adding, "When's my brother coming? I was hoping to see him before heading in to work?"

There was a knock at the door before it opened. Billy walked in. "I hear you have a baby for me?" he said.

"Uncle Billy!" Brendon squealed, rushing towards one of his two favorite uncles. "Where's Uncle Jack?"

"Right here, Bren," Jack said as he walked through the doorway, rustling up Brendon's hair before putting it back into place.

"Oh thank God!" Kayla said, ripping Jeff from her mother's arms. "Here, take this."

Mrs. Hollins was about to scold her daughter, but she recognized the pain in Kayla's eyes and knew that what she had to do was tearing her apart. Even if she wanted to raise Jeff, she was ill prepared to be a parent. Even if Mr. and Mrs. Hollins wanted to help, it would be a constant reminder of her own failure. Instead, Mrs. Hollins took the opportunity to get up out of the chair she was sitting in and say hello to her brother-in-law and his husband, even if 'husband' was only in the respectful sense as marriage rights were still years away from taking effect for the gays. She also knew what a blessing being a parent was, even if so much of it was filled with heartache. Even if the choices parents made alienated their children.

Even after they're gone.

A few minutes later, Billy and Jack put Jeff into a car seat in the back of their car. Their hearts overwhelmed with love at first sight, and their tears of joy made it almost impossible to buckle the baby in. Mr. Hollins told his brother and brother-in-law that it never gets easier, but it's all worth it.

Sheree watched at a distance, Kayla at her side. For a moment, Jeff turned his head and locked eyes with Sheree. *I'm not going anywhere this time*, he told her in her head. *I know*, she told him in his head.

"Are you going to be okay?" Jennifer asked as she came up from behind Sheree and Kayla.

With all the morning's commotion, Sheree had almost forgotten she was there.

"I'll be okay," Sheree said, squeezing Kayla's hand and taking Jennifer's with her other. "I can wait for happiness."

"Yeah?" Kayla asked.

"Yeah," Sheree told her. "As long as I know there is a light at the end of the tunnel waiting for me, I can hold out hope. I just need to have a little patience."

The End

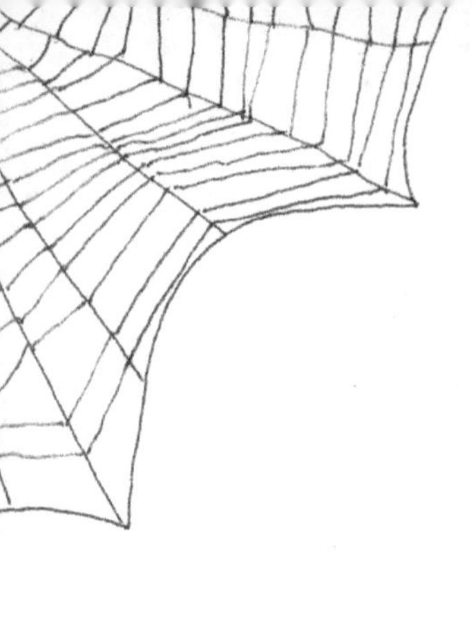

Author Bio

Cory Blystone lives in Vancouver, Washington with his husband Greg, their dogs Chuck and Sunny, cat Dexter, and their flock of chickens named after *Buffy the Vampire Slayer* characters. When not in school and doing homework, he enjoys writing, drawing, painting, reading, quilting, gardening, making absurd videos for YouTube, reading, rapping, cooking, baking, oh, and reading. He also was the Managing Editor for Clark College's award winning art and literature magazine, *Phoenix*, for the 2015 edition where his hand can be seen on nearly every page. Literally. He drew or wrote every title, and wrote all of the writer's statements for the literary works by hand to give the magazine a personal journal feel. You can check it out at ClarkPhoenix.com.

Deadly Rhymes

Deadly Rhymes Trilogy Book 1

Deadlier Rhymes

Deadly Rhymes Trilogy Book 2